THE COYOTE HUNTER OF AQUIDNECK ISLAND

THE COYOTE HUNTER OF AQUIDNECK ISLAND

JAMES
CONROY

The Permanent Press
Sag Harbor, NY 11963

For information, address:
The Permanent Press
4170 Noyac Road
Sag Harbor, NY 11963
www.thepermanentpress.com

Library of Congress Cataloging-in-Publication Data

Conroy, James, author.
The coyote hunter of Aquidneck Island / James Conroy.
Sag Harbor, NY : The Permanent Press, 2017.
ISBN 978-1-57962-493-4
1. Coyote—Control—Fiction. 2. Man-woman relationships—Fiction. 3. Hunting—Rhode Island—Rhode Island (Island)—Fiction.

PS3603.O55767 C69 2017
813'.6—dc23 2016053619

Printed in the United States of America

To my wife, Helen.
You always make the good possibilities happen.
All my love, all my life.

&

To my late brother, Tom "Don Tomas" Conroy.
We walked many paths together and I miss that every day.
Your side of the trail ended way too soon.
Duerme bien, mi amigo.

ACKNOWLEDGMENTS

I would like to thank several people. Some made a difference in this book. Most made a difference in my life.

Jo and Coach Tony Grimaldi for your never-wavering faith and encouragement that I write.

Judith and Marty Shepard for giving me this opportunity.

My incomparable editor, Barbara Anderson. I learned more about writing from you than I've learned in the last forty years.

My two dearest friends, M. and L., who continue to insist on anonymity. You've always been an inspiration.

Sincerest appreciation to you all.

PROLOGUE

i.

"*canis latrans*"

The Coyote's nocturnal serenades—a chorus of howls, barks, and wails—epitomize the American West. But Coyotes have drastically extended their range and now commonly occur in the northeastern states. They adapt well to the presence of man (even to the extent of raiding garbage cans) and have moved into areas extensively cleared for farming. Frequently condemned as livestock killers, they are primarily predators on rodents, rabbits, and other small animals. Occasionally several adults cooperate in hunting large prey such as deer. Coyotes belong to the dog family. They resemble German shepherds and have been known to mate with domestic dogs.

—Susan J. Wernert, *Editor*
Reader's Digest
North American Wildlife
New York, 1982

ii.

The Island of Aquidneck is comprised of 37.8 square miles and is home to three townships (pop. 56,396): Portsmouth, Middletown, and Newport. The charters of these towns predate the American Revolution by more than a century.

Access to Aquidneck is by three bridges, boat, or aircraft. The bridges point west, north, and east. South is the Atlantic Ocean.

iii.

"*Coyote Morning*"

Old men
and old coyote dogs
boil their dreams in the sun
served steaming within a bowl
filled with shadows
rolling sticks onto the ground
and making wild songs
while they smack their lips
and spit out the dust
blown in by the winds
nameless
and place-less
but hard to ignore.

—Jicarilla Apache Poem

CHAPTER ONE

The meeting was contentious from the first gavel strike. Mayor Mary Boyd was not one for skirting issues. Her opening remarks were well prepared.

She did not get far.

"It's a wild animal," someone yelled.

He was answered by someone else, female, just as loud.

"So's a jackrabbit, you moron."

A free-for-all ensued.

"I'm afraid for my dog."

"We're the wild beasts."

"There's a school bus stop nearby."

As more people spoke out at will and in competition, there was a shuffling of chairs until the room was virtually divided into two opposing camps. Council members from the dais among them.

Having no opinion yet on the matter, Micah LaVeck remained where he was. His usual spot for town meetings. By the exit, leaning on his cane, and pretty much in the middle. Micah was not on the council. Never sought elected office. But was a concerned citizen and attended Middletown Town Council meetings regularly.

The fevered discussion waged on.

Micah was watching Mayor Boyd, but out of the corner of his eye detected Laurie Catlett drifting along the sidewall behind the pro-animal, live-and-let-live contingent, then turning in his direction.

Laurie Catlett was Boyd's fixer and closer in the guise of chief of staff. Nothing much got done in Middletown government that did not have Catlett's manicured hand in it. She was a pragmatic, foul-mouthed, smart woman under the coif and couture, camera-ready exterior. Had seen Boyd through reelection twice. Micah knew her well. Years before, a short, definitely no-problem series of assignations between them. She was next to Micah shortly and he feigned noticing her for the first time with a nod before returning his attention to the mayor on the dais as Boyd insisted on order above the melee.

"She's bringing in a professional hunter," Catlett stage-whispered. "It's cleared with the state conservation people. Reduce the coyote population by 50 percent. That's the goal."

"The mayor hasn't said that yet."

"She will, when everybody shuts the hell up and listens to her."

"You're telling me now because . . ." Micah said.

"There are several land issues and then there's the hunter. We want to keep this as low-key as possible."

"Who's the hunter?"

"A native," Catlett said.

"From Middletown or just Aquidneck Island?"

"Native American, Narragansett Indian. Was a sniper in the army."

"He can shoot, can he hunt?"

"I said a fucking Indian, Micah."

"That's racist."

Catlett grinned. "Bite me."

"What do you want from me?"

Catlett drummed her fingers on the leather portfolio she always carried.

"There's going to be lots of press coverage. Not only local. Shit, Mary's getting e-mails from Arizona and Colorado and the goddamn *National Geographic*. All kinds of animal rights people. Then there're the hunters. There must have been a blurb in an NRA magazine or blog. About sixty gun-crazed volunteers want to come here and shoot coyotes. Even the local gun club wants to start some kind of hunting posse. Don't give a damn about Middletown, only want to shoot something. That's why we want this professional and quiet. So far Police Chief Harry Reismann has been keeping the locals in check, warning they not let a gun club openly hunt on private property as a matter of public safety. They are not town-sponsored and are not insured for accidents. It's worked, but now the mayor has to act, and she is."

Micah turned to Catlett, but did not pose his question a second time. Catlett's fingers stopped rapping the leather.

"We don't want to put the hunter up in a motel where the press can camp out. He's got an RV. You've got that spit of land out back on Green End Pond. We're hoping you'll accommodate him for the duration. It's private property and we can contain things better."

It sounded practical. Micah thought of only one objection.

"I can run an extension cord for power and hose for water, but what about waste? Black water?"

Catlett was prepared as always. "This is a town project. If we have to, we'll get a Parks Department truck to pump out his shit."

"When's he coming?"

"I'll e-mail you. Thanks, Micah. I'm speaking for Mary when I say it's much appreciated."

Micah turned his attention back to the dais. Order had been somewhat restored and the council members were back in their places. Mayor Boyd was calling for the vote on a matter that Micah just heard from Catlett was already decided.

"All those members in favor of having a professional hunter, humanely as possible, reduce the coyote population of Middletown, raise your hand."

THE FOG came and settled on Green End Pond. Micah looked from his window over the desk. Spring and fall brought morning fog, but different kinds. The fog in fall was slate gray, thick and even over the water and shoreline. Spring fog was wispier and its gray was cloud-like with tinges of greens and blues. It was March and an early spring fog had descended.

Micah had heard the coyotes, long before he learned that was their sound. Starting at Green End Pond, the Kempenaar Valley divided this part of Middletown north to East Main Road. Houses on High Street and the rear of Valley Road businesses edged the valley's flanks. Micah had not seen a coyote himself but neighbors, especially those whose property rimmed the valley, said they had. For years the animals were dismissed as stray dogs. Sightings prompted calls to animal control. Many responses, no captures. Then someone that actually knew said no, definitely coyotes, and the trouble started.

He closed a document on his computer and gazed back out the window. The first rays of sunlight appeared in the fog.

There was an old chicken coop in the yard he could see from the window. Micah did not raise chickens; the previous owner of the house had. When Micah bought the place the owner was dead and the chickens gone. The contractor who did Micah's landscaping offered to tear it down. Micah said no, leave it, for no particular reason. The man shrugged and never asked again. That was ten years ago. Each year a piece or two of rotted wood fell from the henhouse with the weight of ice and snow or ripped away with late summer storms.

Eventually the fog evaporated completely. The spit of ground that jutted obliquely into the pond became visible. Laurie Catlett was right. It appeared suitable for a decent-sized camper or RV.

To the west of the spit, exactly at the property line with Micah's neighbor and the town line between Middletown and Newport, was a sign on a post. One of many identical signs every 200 yards or so around Green End Pond.

City of Newport
Drinking Water Supply
No littering, fishing, boating, swimming, hunting, ice skating, bicycles, horses or motorized vehicles allowed.
Thank You
Newport Water Division

He went online to check for e-mails. He was expecting a hunter with an RV. Despite what the sign said.

There was no e-mail from Catlett that day or the next. The only word about hunters and coyotes was in the newspapers, on the Internet, or in the stores and bars on East and West Main Roads. Mayor Boyd carried the vote but the issue was far from resolved. According to the *Providence Journal*, there was a flurry of legal maneuvering to procure an injunction against the hunt. The *Newport Daily News*, Aquidneck Island's sole daily newspaper, published three times as many Letters to the Editor as usual arguing both sides of the plan.

Micah's mind was still not made up. He could muster no malice for the coyotes. Yet, when he reflected impartially, he did not have a pet scampering around his property as easy prey, no children waiting at a bus stop in the gray dawn, livestock, or even a lone chicken. Only an empty coop.

"SEEN ANY?" Melvin Sturgis asked. Sturgis owned the Aquidneck Wine and Spirit Shop.

"No," Micah said. He put money on the counter for his four bottles of wine. "I've heard them, usually after dark. Not every night, once in a while."

"How many it sound like?"

"Hard to tell, definitely two or more."

Sturgis rang the sale. He slid the bottles into plastic sleeves so Micah could stow them in his backpack without their clinking against each other.

"Gretchen Miller says a coyote snatched her kitty cat right off her porch," Sturgis said.

"She saw it?"

"I can't say for sure. Gretchen's a bit odd. We deliver a case of red zinfandel to her every week. Each time she reorders she tells me one or two of the bottles tasted funny. Or the label was different. Never stuck the cork back in and brought it in to show me. So, who's to say? She told the cops it was a coyote and they filed a report."

"Where does Mrs. Miller live?"

"Over on Paradise, near the windmill."

Micah wedged his walking stick against the counter while he shouldered his pack. "Paradise Avenue, that's a ways from the Kempenaar Valley."

"They're all over. Albro Woods, the bird sanctuary, the reservoir." Sturgis pointed at Micah's cane. "I've always admired that stick. Keep meaning to ask you, where'd you get it?"

"I made it from a stout piece of privet hedge. Peeled it, sanded and shellacked it."

"Pretty handy. Bet you could sell them."

Micah shook his head. "Took me a year to finish this one."

"How long you had a bum leg, Micah?"

"Since before I knew I had one."

"Know what you mean."

"Take care, Melvin."

Sturgis nodded. "Next time. Watch out for them coyotes."

The journals were old, leather-bound, and the pages dull, creamy vellum, half color, half age. The exteriors had no markings. To sort them chronologically Micah needed to consult the first page of each for the date span of its contents. There was a smell to them, Micah detected, more an aroma, and more than mere musty papers and dry leather. It made him think of tobacco and whiskey with a trace of something else. The odor prompted images, Micah's own creations, of the author long dead. A small room with table and chair, lit candle, pen and inkwell, perhaps a vintage rifle racked on the wall (*was gunpowder that smell?*) and a seated old man with pipe jutting from jaw and brandy within reach.

The professional Micah LaVeck undertook such projects. Before the Internet it was a newspaper ad, which he still ran occasionally. More recently it was craigslist and other sites.

Paper or cyberspace, it amounted to only thirty-three words aside from his contact information:

> **Professional writer and published author turns your personal or loved one's diaries and journals into publishable memoirs. Complete rewrite, editing and formatting suitable for submission to publishers and printers. Free evaluation and estimate.**

His first client had been a surgeon who worked for Doctors Without Borders in Serbia and wanted to publish his journals. That led to a Savannah, Georgia, family in possession of an ancestor Confederate general's war diary. Then a teacher whose pupils were part of a traveling circus. A dozen came quickly after and he often worked on two simultaneously.

Of course the finished product, if indeed it did get published, usually privately, never bore Micah's name except sometimes a mention in the acknowledgments.

The price paid for the money made.

There was another cost as well. Author Micah LaVeck had not written anything original of his own since this business succeeded.

But he was not thinking of that as he stuck Post-it notes on the journals to sort them by date. The family had even proposed a "working" title:

The Life and Times of Icobar Ohlm

The spelling of Icobar was correct and not to be mistaken for the Ichabod of Washington Irving fame. As if the Ohlm family cared. It was the "Ohlm" that mattered since no one of descending lineage was named after Icobar anyway. Fact was, as Micah learned during his free evaluation, no living Ohlm ever read the journals. The last soul to peruse the pages was the present issue's great-grandmother. That Ohlm matriarch extracted a solemn promise from her progeny that the books be preserved.

The volumes were old, well preserved, and indeed intact. They must be worth something. To the present generation of Ohlms' dismay, they weren't. Yet they persisted in trying to sell them.

Then an antique book dealer, who read a few snippets of the journals, suggested they have the volumes transcribed for easier accessibility. For family posterity, not profit, he clarified. However, as he intimated, if they happen to contain a reference to some famous scandal, perhaps with a fresh insight, or personal account of a major calamity, or even an unsolved murder, then they might conceivably be worth something after all. All of which required someone actually read and edit them in their entirety. A few Googled prompts turned up Micah LaVeck repeatedly. There followed evaluation, estimate, and negotiated finder's fee for the dealer. Micah left with the journals.

It was late when the Post-its were all in place. Micah went to the kitchen and opened a bottle of wine. He almost spilled it when a sudden chorus of coyotes seemed to rise right out of Green End Pond itself.

LAURIE CATLETT did not e-mail. She showed up on Green End Avenue, unannounced, and knocked on Micah's door around nine thirty A.M.

"Figured I'd stop by as I made my rounds for Mary. We want a tight lid on this, Micah. The hunter's due tomorrow. I don't know what time."

"What about the injunction?" he said.

"Fuck 'em."

It had been a brief affair, three years earlier. All of three months. A Town Hall meeting. A group going for drinks afterward. The group thinning out to the singles with no babysat children at home. Finally just Micah LaVeck and Laurie Catlett. Two middle-aged, intelligent, unattached—not looking for anything special, wouldn't pass up something casual—consenting adults. He liked her profane, gruff to-the-point manner, and dry wit. She was intrigued he was a writer and thought his cane made him look distinguished. The chickens Micah didn't have didn't need to be fed in the morning.

"Mary's got lawyers of her own, damn good ones. I should know, I vetted every one."

"So, Her Honor's position is . . ." Micah said and stopped. It was a personal game they had played—her finishing his sentences. He a writer, yet she a master of instant phrases for her boss.

Catlett smiled at the familiar ploy. "Respect the laws of the State of Rhode Island and Commonwealth Plantations. In the Township of Middletown, County of Newport, and the whole goddamn state, it is not illegal to kill varmints on your own property. Or pay someone else to do it for you. Kind of like an exterminator for really big bugs."

Micah scoffed. "But a professional hunter?"

"Long as the gun is licensed."

As Micah was aware, much of Middletown's acreage was comprised of privately owned farms. There were even two wineries with fields of grapes. Catlett explained that the local farmers knew about the coyotes long before the general, suburbanized public. Rumor was a few coyotes had even been shot by local growers. In New England fashion, they simply hadn't bragged about it.

"Besides the accommodation," Micah said, "is there anything else you need me to do? About the hunter, I mean."

Catlett thought a moment, then produced the portfolio. She scribbled a note. "Give me a heads-up if anybody comes nosing around. Somebody you're not expecting."

"I'm not expecting anybody. This is a quiet part of town."

"Regardless, it might be the newspapers or council people or their flunkies. Keep a lookout."

Closing her portfolio, something written caught her eye.

"Almost forgot. There will be one person. A ranger from the Conservation Department. The department wants to be kept in the loop since they're not fighting the mayor on the hunt. Mary's agreed to full disclosure with them. They will also take possession of the carcasses of any coyotes killed. Some kind of study they want to do. It's okay with us. In fact, we welcome it. Puts a better spin on this whole affair, like it's for science."

Micah stifled a smirk. "Right, Laurie, science. Not campaign contributions from the farmers and vintners."

He took his stick and walked her to the door. There was a cane holder in a corner by the door with Micah's other walking sticks.

"By the way," Catlett said, noting it, "how's the leg?"

"Comes and goes on its own schedule."

She smiled, almost fondly, which never came easily. "I remember."

CHAPTER TWO

The next morning, no fog to be seen. Instead, heavy rain fell on Aquidneck Island, coming off the ocean and seemingly stalled overhead. Micah heard it at two A.M., rose to shut the window in his study, check the windows in the rest of the house, and retire again. It was still raining when he awoke the second time at four thirty.

The house was a one-floor cottage, originally built in the 1880s and extended in the 1950s when the owner converted the existing structure into a year-round residence. The transformation was a frugal one. Number 18 Green End Avenue was pleasant to behold, two acres of waterfront property adjacent to the pristine and spacious Green End Pond. The inside was less appealing. Haphazardly cordoned-off rooms, little closet space in the master and spare bedrooms, drafty and ill-insulated, outmoded kitchen and bath, and temperamental electricity and heat. Realtors had labeled it a fixer-upper. Hence the comparatively modest price for the area.

Micah was no fixer-upper despite crafting his own walking stick on impulse. He loved the hardwood floors, three fireplaces, two bedrooms, and den, half the realtors calling it a study, overlooking the pond. The rest was function and when it didn't function he paid a local contractor.

Satisfied his home was as secure as possible, Micah repaired to his study to immerse himself in Volume One of Icobar Ohlm's journals . . . awaiting his itinerant guest, at least Micah surmised itinerant based on the RV.

Icobar Ohlm had been a feisty fellow, not the contemplative scribe Micah had envisioned with brief analysis. He didn't like his family and didn't trust his neighbors. And it pleased him to commit these dislikes to his journal. Volume One commenced a year shy of the Civil War. Icobar was an apprentice printer in his uncle's shop in Portsmouth. The first entries, all dated, were criticism of the uncle's business acumen. He should charge more and buy cheaper paper and inks. The shop could be thriving instead of merely providing a modest living for the master printer's family and nephew Icobar.

Sandwiched between two caustic entries on the same day was a brief sentence on another matter. Miss Cecilia Morris had, yet again, declined an invitation to accompany Icobar to the Sunday afternoon social after church service.

It was still raining midmorning when someone knocked on his front door. Though the house had a functioning doorbell, Micah learned early in his residency that locals preferred to knock instead. He grabbed his cane and went to the door.

Rain, rain, and extra fat droplets dripped from the eaves of the front porch roof. A figure in rain slicker with hood shedding water stood a pace back from the door.

"Can I help you?"

The figure looked up. A woman's face, young. "Mr. LaVeck?" The voice deeper than the face intimated.

"Yes, Micah LaVeck. What can I do for you?"

The woman gestured with one hand over her shoulder. With the movement Micah noticed the slicker was the mottled brown of camouflage.

"I've got a trailer out on the road," she said. "They told me I could park here while I'm in town."

"You're with the hunter?"

"I'm the hunter." She turned her hands palms up and peered at Micah from under the rim of her hood. "Did you notice it's raining?"

"Of course, I'm sorry. Please come in."

He stepped back. The woman shook herself like a wet dog, drew back the hood, and stepped inside. She had onyx-black hair pulled severely straight back. Light brown skin with tinges of red and orange that made Micah think of the color of terra cotta though its texture was incredibly smooth.

Micah closed the door. "Let me have your coat."

It was really a poncho and when she drew it over her head and away he saw the tight hair tied off in back forming a long ponytail down between her shoulder blades. She held the dripping poncho out and Micah took it and hung it on the back of the door beside his own mac.

"Would you like coffee?"

"That would be nice, thanks."

"Follow me . . ."

"Kodi."

"Kodi," Micah repeated. When he turned, she hadn't moved and was looking at her feet.

"I'll drag mud all over. Can I leave my boots here?"

"Sure, I'll get a chair for you to take them off."

"Don't bother."

Kodi squatted and untied each bootlace. High, black military-style boots. She rose, slipped off the boots, no socks, her bare feet on the wood plank floor. Above that, stonewashed jeans and black sweatshirt. She picked up the boots and deposited them beside the cane stand.

Micah led Kodi into the kitchen. Even with his limp, he felt she was lagging farther and farther behind. Stopped to see. She was looking about the room, the parlor off the front door, as if taking in every detail. No expression, merely observation. Then she looked at Micah. No embarrassment, no apology. Micah started again for the kitchen.

"The floor's a bit cold, it's an old house. Would you like a pair of clean wool socks?"

"No, thanks."

In the kitchen he gestured to a chair at the table. As she sat, he prepared the coffeemaker.

"You took me by surprise. Laurie didn't say it was a woman hunter."

"Who's Laurie?"

"Laurie Catlett, the mayor's chief of staff."

"Don't know her."

"Then who was it that hired you?"

"Boyd-something, through someone I know at the Department of Environmental Management."

"That would be Mary Boyd, mayor of Middletown."

"Okay, like I said it was through a friend."

Micah sat down across from her at the table. The rain could still be heard on the roof. He looked Kodi in the face. Definitely young, late twenties, perhaps thirty, at most. Eyes as black as her hair with pinpoints of light in the centers. Smallish nose over a cleanly cut, blunt jaw.

"I heard you were in the army."

"Eight years," Kodi said.

"And a sniper."

"Check, was that."

Long moment of silence. Coffee almost done, but not yet.

"Kodi. Interesting name."

"I like it, my father didn't."

"Then why did he name you that?"

Slight roll of Kodi's shoulders, not quite a shrug, more like a chill. "It wasn't his place to name me. Parents in my tribe go to our chief, or sachem as we say, for a name. My father was old-fashioned that way."

"What does it mean?"

"Depends on the dialect. Some say it means helpful."

"What else do they say it means?"

"Cold."

The coffee was ready.

Kodi took her coffee with one-third milk and three sugars. When she thanked him and again called him Mr. LaVeck he insisted she use Micah.

"How'd you get involved in this?" Kodi asked.

"The mayor and I have a mutual friend, the Laurie I mentioned. She asked, I said yes."

"Heard there's a big squawk about it. You in favor of this hunt?"

He wanted to answer honestly and not appear like an idiot at the same time. Decided the latter wasn't his call anyway. "I don't know."

"Me either."

Micah hadn't expected that from her. "But you're the hunter."

"That's a job. Whether it's the right solution or not to your town's problem is not up to me. I'm here to do what I'm paid to do."

Cold, thought Micah, *like your name.* He did not want to pursue that line any further. "What's the best way to hunt coyotes?"

"In fresh snow, like most animals."

From Micah, a half laugh. "You're too late, snow's over. Hear that rain?" He nodded toward the window. "Won't be any snow now for seven or eight months."

"No hurry."

"Mayor Boyd's not a patient woman, trust me."

"She pays me for blood; I'll give her all she wants."

Cold.

"If you don't mind my asking," Micah said, "how's this all work? Is it a bounty, paid by the kill?"

"There's that, plus expenses. And a flat daily rate starting tomorrow. Room, board, the usual."

"What room? You're in a trailer on my property free of charge."

"Sucks for them. They agreed before they knew. What isn't spent is mine."

"Nice piece of negotiating," Micah said.

For the first time Micah saw Kodi smile. Not an amused smile. More one of modest satisfaction. Micah collected the empty mugs and brought them to the sink. He staggered a bit without his cane and felt Kodi watching him.

To his back she said, "I'll move the trailer off the street and set up."

Micah almost suggested she wait for the rain to stop but decided against it. "Need some help?"

"Nope, I got it."

Over the sink Micah pointed out the window. "Despite the rain, you can make out the spit for the trailer. It's to the right, between the big red maple and the pond sign. If you . . ."

"I already checked it out. Was around back before I knocked. Have to back it through all the way. It's gonna rut-up some turf. You mind?"

Micah shook his head while still studying the rain through the window. He heard Kodi get up and put the chair back in place.

"Thanks for the coffee."

Micah turned from the sink. "There's a pot every morning. Help yourself, but it usually goes on about four thirty. If there's none left, make your own. The back door's unlocked."

Kodi didn't respond to that, instead, "I was told you had power and water for me."

Micah said there was a garden hose attached to the house with enough length to reach the spit. Also an outdoor electric jack. He had fifty feet of extension cord somewhere around.

"Got my own," Kodi said.

Micah folded his arms across his chest. Kodi left the kitchen. He heard her pull on her boots with a shallow huff and grunt.

Bare feet, wet boots. Tough lady. He called after her. "Was it merely good negotiating or do you seriously hunt well?"

From the next room, "I'm Indian, remember?"

It sounded completely different than when Laurie Catlett made that same point. Micah heard a gust of wind from outside and then the front door close.

KODI DIDN'T want his help. *So be it,* Micah thought. *Maybe it's the cane. Hey, your choice.* Back to his desk and the journal.

Icobar made some comments here and there between his gripes about the inevitable war to come. All simple observations with no political point of view. Never mentioned slavery. Next came a two-page rant, the longest entry thus far. It was announced that date at church that Cecilia Morris was betrothed to Benjamin Wakefield. Wakefield, a local fishmonger, according to Icobar, was far more undeserving of Miss Morris's affections than himself.

Gravaroom!

Micah dropped the journal with a start.

Gravaroom . . . again and again.

He looked out the window. The rain had lessened from a downpour to a shower. Coming into view at the side of the house was the rear third of the trailer, its hind wheels plowing furrows in the muddy yard. Then half the trailer, front, hitch, and tow bar. Dead stop. Gravaroom! Nothing, wheels spinning. Silence, wheels still.

Kodi, clad in poncho with hood up, inspected the impediment. Around both sides, down on one knee in the mud to view the undercarriage. Up again, hands on hips. A frustrated glance skyward followed by a long look around the yard. Finding something, she went across the yard passing below and six feet distant from where Micah sat behind his window completely unnoticed.

Beside the chicken coop she assumed the same akimbo pose until she decided. In one steady motion Kodi ripped a plank free from the coop and strutted back to the mired trailer. With determined effort she wedged the board under the right rear tire creating an inclined plane out of the mud, then walked along the side of the trailer and out of sight beside the house.

Gravaroom . . . the plank bent, cracked, but held.

Ten minutes later the trailer was perfectly situated on the spit jutting into the pond and Kodi was unhitching the pickup.

MICAH DID not see Kodi the rest of the day. In the evening, as he washed his supper dishes, he saw a light in the trailer's lone window. It flickered continually and he concluded it was some type of camp lamp with a flame.

That trailer must be as drafty as this house.

The light held his attention for a long moment only to be disrupted when he noticed the rain had finally stopped. Another light, behind and farther away. Moonlight on the pond.

CHAPTER THREE

When Micah rose at four thirty the next morning the pickup was gone. He went to his study to work but found it hard to concentrate on Icobar's ramblings and soon merely gazed out his window. Not at the idyllic pond scene, but at Kodi's trailer. Adjacent to his desk was a LaCrosse weather station atop a file cabinet, its all-weather sensor affixed outside beside the window. It read fifty-five degrees with a sun icon blinking in forecast of a beautiful day. By six A.M. Kodi had not returned and enough was enough.

He went to the kitchen and pulled on a pair of rubber boots kept for snow and mud. After yesterday's deluge, the yard would still be its own pond of mud. He also donned a peacoat kept there for fetching firewood from his pile.

Outside the air smelled wonderful. Crisp and fresh with prespring aromas. Off the back steps, Micah sank an inch into soggy turf. He didn't have a lawn to speak of; that's not what his landscapers did. They were contracted to keep the natural growth of this rural shore from overrunning the place.

Heavy, sucking steps to the trailer. Where Micah sank an inch, the cane tip drove two. He hoped nobody was watching his pathetic progress across the yard. Had to step over the water hose and not trip on the electric cord. Those and the deep ruts left from moving the trailer reminded him to keep his ears pricked for Kodi's truck. How would he explain his curiosity?

Slowly and unobserved, he made it.

What confronted him was its own class of fixer-upper. Up close the trailer appeared to be a hybrid of blunt-ended, vintage dirigible and dilapidated Pullman railroad car. Metals of various colors joined at crudely welded seams. The presentation was one of homemade from an eclectic collection of non-trailer, though quasi-suitable, parts. No continuously smooth surface anywhere.

With slow progress, Micah made his way around the whole trailer. It occupied most of the spit with only four feet of earth on either side before the shore of his tiny peninsula. The window that faced his house was the only one. The opposite sidewall was bumpy aluminum, sheet metal, wood, and whatever the hell else contributed to its fabrication.

Another slog around the rear of the beast. Rhode Island license plate and to Micah's disbelief a valid-looking, current registration tag that meant someone had inspected this vehicle and approved it roadworthy. A sanction that astounded Micah.

Around front, the window had a yellow shade pulled down to the sill. No opportunity to observe the interior. A foot farther, the door. More a hatch, roughly cut as everything else, and imbedded in a wood jamb.

Without thinking, Micah tried the handle. It was unlocked. He willed his hand to let go and stepped back. He would not allow himself to become that rude. *Must be the New Englander in me.* He'd said she could stay but it gave him no rights other than Kodi not abusing his hospitality.

Micah worked his way off the spit and stood awhile on the shoreline. Waiting for his breath to come naturally again, he watched a heron glide in to land on the water. Then another. Saw them start to fish, necks extended, feathers smoothed back.

When he'd rested enough, he felt up to the trek back to the house.

An hour later he saw the pickup pull up to the trailer. Kodi got out pulling a backpack and slung it from one shoulder. She walked to the pond edge and stood gazing out over the water. Micah kept watching her in profile from his window. Saw her squat down and dip one hand into the water and swirl it around. When the hand came out she put it to her face and dampened her forehead and cheeks. Next she cupped her hand, put it back in the water and lifted a handful to drink. Micah felt strangely moved by the scene. A vague appreciation of the innocence, and then a tremor of guilt for having observed uninvited. Then he remembered.

This is a professional hunter, not a Disney movie. She's here to kill some of the wildlife out there.

The two opposing sensations unsettled him and he looked away. When he looked back, Kodi was entering the trailer, and closed the door behind her. Micah watched only long enough for the shade on the window to rise.

Back to work. Icobar had begun recording his finances in detail: what he earned, what he spent, what he managed to save. He did not live with the uncle and the family but had a room in a boarding house. The room and board ate up most of his pay. His savings were meager.

Odd, thought Micah. He felt the paper of the page. Took a magnifying glass to the ink and penmanship. Definitely not cheap paper or ink. The script indicated a decent nib for the period. Micah had reviewed many old manuscripts. He recalled the war journal he had worked with for the family in Savannah, which was roughly of the same time period. The binding, which Micah also inspected through his glass, had certainly come later. All was in conflict with Icobar's claim of near poverty.

Hah! You're a thief. Stole this paper from your uncle's shop. Probably the pen and ink too. No wonder Cecilia Morris didn't marry you. Better an honest fishmonger than a thieving printer's apprentice.

There was a bonus clause in his contract with the Ohlm Family if his effort was taken by a publisher. Micah was convinced there would be no bonus. *Who would want to read this? Let alone pay for it.* Micah was tiring of it himself and had to force himself to turn the next page. One word was scrawled across the whole page. Repeatedly thickened with extra pen strokes: WAR.

Three knocks. It took a few seconds for Micah to realize the difference in sound. No one had ever knocked before on his back door. It definitely sounded different from the New England summons to the front. Three more. Micah went to see what she wanted.

"You don't have to knock. I told you the door is always unlocked."

Kodi wore a hooded sweatshirt, hood off, blue with "Army" stenciled in gold across the chest. Black jeans this time and the same boots.

"Didn't want to surprise you," Kodi said.

Micah couldn't resist. "Isn't that what you do?"

Puzzled face. She didn't get it.

"Sorry," he said, "never mind. What's up?"

From the sweatshirt pouch Kodi produced a compact digital camera. "Do you have a printer for photographs? I have a computer but no printer. And no photo paper."

"Sure, come on in." Micah stepped back.

As she stepped over the threshold she said, "I'll pay you for it. I know that paper's not cheap. I have expense money, but I'll need a receipt."

"Don't worry about it. Consider it a donation to the cause."

In the study he loaded the photo paper and changed the printer settings. "You can . . ."

"I know how it works. You mind?" Kodi asked.

"Not at all, have at it." He shifted his cane and moved out of her way.

Kodi slid into his chair, popped the disc from the camera, and inserted it in the computer.

"I'll be in the kitchen," Micah said, and left her to her work.

Kodi came into the kitchen, sat across from Micah at the table, and placed a stack of photo prints in front of her.

Micah pointed at the photos. "How'd they come out? You get what you wanted?"

Kodi nodded.

"May I see them?" he asked.

Kodi slid the prints across the table.

"It was a recon," she said. "You people definitely got coyotes."

There were eighteen prints. Micah examined each one before moving it aside for the next. He didn't recognize the location specifically. With so much open land on Aquidneck Island, they could have been taken in a hundred different places. Every one captured a coyote. In more than half, the animal stared directly at the camera. Even if the body was turned, the head was cocked back as if to pose. One, clearly oblivious to the camera, had its head round 180 degrees, snout to back fur as if dislodging an insect or preening the spot. Some had tawny brown and orangey coats. Others were silverish and gray.

Micah was impressed. "These are beautiful. As good as *National Geographic*."

"Think I can sell them?"

Micah neatened the stack. "I don't know." He looked up from the photos. "Maybe the local paper or island magazines would be interested. I couldn't say."

"Know anybody to ask?"

"Not off the top of my head. Want me to check around?"

A shake of her head. "Don't bother, but if you hear something."

Micah slid the prints back. He was still impressed with what he'd seen. It must have been the earliest of dawn light. The proximity was amazing for surely Kodi's tiny compact camera had limited range for such clarity.

"Where'd you take them?" he asked.

Kodi pushed back from the table and took a folded map from her sweatshirt pouch. Micah recognized the cover. An Aquidneck Island map common to tourist centers, real estate offices, and convenience stores. The kind with local merchants advertising around the borders and free of charge.

She unfolded the map on the table. "Pretty much anywhere I found open land and critters about for prey." She pointed a finger at spots and said their names. "Aquidneck Vineyards and Winery, Albro Woods, Paradise Windmill,

Sweet Cherry Farm, Tyler's Farm, Hanging Rock, Sachuest Point."

"Wait," Micah interrupted. "Sachuest Point is a nature preserve. You can't hunt there. So's the Norman Bird Sanctuary next door, behind Hanging Rock."

Kodi lifted her head, face defiant. When she met Micah's eyes it softened into amusement.

"I wasn't hunting. Not gonna hunt protected areas. Told you it was recon. Recon and tracking. Coyotes don't read road signs and don't give a crap about postings and fences. They come, they go, and I have to learn where."

"No offense," Micah said. "Wanted to make sure you knew."

Kodi rose with a start. "What's that?" she snapped.

"What?"

"That sound." She darted for the kitchen window, leaned over the sink, and looked about the yard. "Damn. Somebody's messing with my trailer."

Kodi was about to make for the door but Micah had stood and was in her way.

"Let me check," he said. "It's my property out there too."

He clasped his cane and was at the door ahead of her only because she didn't push him out of her way. Micah flung open the door and yelled, "Hey, this is private property!"

The figure at the trailer turned.

"Bite me," Laurie Catlett called back.

The three of them sat at the kitchen table after introductions.

"What do you mean you don't have a cell phone?" Catlett demanded.

Kodi made a dumb face. "Indigenous savage no trust white man voice magic."

"Bullshit," Catlett said. "I'm not driving down here or calling Micah every time I need to reach you. You've got expense money. Go to Walmart and buy a throwaway."

Kodi didn't answer, met Catlett's stare. Catlett flinched first.

"Next, I need a copy of your license and permits, serial numbers on the guns and," Catlett consulted a list in her portfolio, "make and model of ammunition." Looked up. "The mayor promised it to the chief of police."

"Why?" Kodi said.

Now Catlett made the dumb face. "Christ, like maybe you shoot something that ain't a coyote. Some bird-watcher or fisherman out early and you wing him, or worse." Serious face. "It's not up for discussion."

Mutual stare down again.

Kodi first. "It's in the trailer, I'll get it." Rose to go.

"My fax machine works as a copier," Micah said.

Both women looked at him as if he'd only instantly appeared in his chair. Another stare at each other and Kodi left.

"Why didn't you tell me it's a goddamn woman?" Catlett said to Micah.

"Why didn't you tell me first?"

"Cause I didn't know either. Conservation people said 'Cody' so I thought Buffalo Bill Cody. Like a friggin' cowboy."

"It's K-O-D-I. It means helpful in Indian."

"Aw, Christ, no way. The press is gonna love shoving that up my ass."

WHILE MICAH made the photocopies and then faxed the documents to the Middletown Police Station, he overheard the women in his kitchen iron out the rest of the details.

Two local farmers and one of the wineries had given permission for the hunts to proceed on their properties. The aggregate was over 500 acres of fields and woodlands. Catlett had brought topographical maps of the precise areas. When Micah entered the kitchen she was defining boundaries for Kodi with a red marker.

"I wasn't kidding about shooting the wrong thing," Catlett was saying. "The town's full of nature lovers. Not to mention the joggers out on the back roads. We're taking for granted you're not gonna shoot in the direction of public roads or private residences. Right?"

"Check," Kodi said. "And could we not forget I'm a highly trained marksman."

"Yeah," Catlett said grudgingly, "that too. When are you starting?"

Kodi said she would make one more recon that evening and the following morning. She had already scoped out the vineyard but neither of these two farms. If all went well, her first hunt tomorrow evening or the next morning.

"Make it go well," Catlett said. "And get that damn phone. I'll tell the mayor your schedule and alert the property owners. Any change, call me." She put her business card on the table. "I'm reachable twenty-four-seven."

"Check."

Micah cleared his throat. "The faxes went through."

CHAPTER FOUR

Catlett left and Kodi went to purchase a cell phone. Micah returned to Icobar in the study. Perhaps, he hoped, the outbreak of war between North and South would provide something interesting to read in the journals instead of the author's incessant carping.

For a while, it did.

Icobar Ohlm decided to enlist in the Union Army. His uncle and the family did everything to dissuade him. Icobar stated he felt it was his duty, both as an American and a man. In the end they wished him well and conceded they were proud of him. He accepted their respect more graciously than was his nature.

Only in his journal did Icobar confide the truth. After his failed pursuit of and subsequent embarrassment by Miss Cecilia Morris's betrothal choice; the uncle's deaf ear to his business suggestions; and the stagnant state of his finances, Icobar had had enough and welcomed any opportunity to leave and seek his fortune elsewhere. At least enlistment made the departure seem honorable.

Over the next week Icobar stowed his scant possessions in a cupboard at the print shop and squared his debt with the boarding house matron. He hadn't been to church since the announcement of the marriage banns, but was prevailed upon to go one last time by the family. Word of his decision had spread through the town and the congregation was kindly, wishing him God's protection in the perils ahead of him. Benjamin Wakefield shook his hand and made a farewell present of a knife for Icobar to carry.

"Instead of fish guts, I'll bring it back christened with Johnny Reb blood."

Micah had a fair idea Icobar never actually said that to Wakefield, but imagined he enjoyed recording it as though he had.

Kodi returned from her evening reconnaissance around seven P.M. Micah heard the pickup, then saw the light in the trailer window. He put on his peacoat, crossed the yard, and knocked. Kodi opened the door only enough to frame her face. Micah still could not see around the interior.

"How'd it go?" he said.

"Good, I'm ready."

"For tomorrow? You're starting tomorrow?"

"No, your friend left a few things out. Or, she doesn't know them. Gave her my cell number and she gave it to the police. I don't know, for some kind of emergency, I suppose. So there I am hunkered down in a swale tracking a coyote and the damn thing starts beeping. Forgot to turn it off. Coyotes, they got good ears."

Micah was amused. "What did they want?"

"Rules of engagement."

"Huh? It's a coyote."

"Not tactics, timing. I'm barred from hunting Friday nights through late Sunday afternoons. They fear too many locals may be about. Weekend stuff. So only Sunday night through Friday morning." She stuck her head out and looked up at the sky. Without looking down she said, "It's Friday night. If they want to pay me to cool my heels, roger that."

Micah nodded as if he understood the idiosyncrasies of municipal logic. *Kill for the public good, but not too publicly.*

"You hungry?" he said. "I made a pot of stew."

Kodi seemed a bit taken aback and didn't answer.

"There's plenty. If you only make enough for one, it never comes out right. So there's way more than I can eat."

Kodi considered it. "Got any beer?"

"Only wine. But I can run to the store."

"It's your party, wine works for me."

"It's not a party . . ."

"I know, you said stew."

Micah felt a sudden rub of irritation. He stepped back a pace forcing Kodi to widen the door to keep him in view.

"I have a friend," he said, "who likes to finish my sentences. I used to think that was cute. I don't anymore."

Kodi's shoulders, now visible in the doorway, drooped a little. "Sorry. I'll watch that from now on."

The peevishness left Micah. "Stew's ready anytime you want." He pivoted with his cane and walked back to the house.

Kodi called after him. "A couple of minutes, I'll be right over."

Micah waved over his head without turning around.

KODI ENTERED without knocking. Not surprised, Micah pointed her to the chair. At the stove, Micah stirred his stew. The table was set and Kodi put her napkin in her lap. He noticed her hair was down for the first time. Parted in the middle, rolling down the shoulders of the wool gray-green sweater she wore and falling over the backrest of the chair.

"What's in this famous stew of yours?" she asked.

Micah continued to stir. "Famous, but only in my family. My mother told me it goes back generations to Alsace-Lorraine."

"Smells great."

Micah filled two large bowls and brought them to the table. Then retrieved a baguette poking out from the bakery bag on top of the refrigerator. He spread a napkin in the center of the table and put the bread on it.

"Tradition requires we don't slice the bread, simply tear off a hunk when you want some." He was about to sit. "Almost forgot the wine."

Micah fetched two glasses and poured from the open bottle on the counter. As he sat down, Kodi ripped the crusty end off the baguette.

"That's right," Micah said, "dig in."

Kodi helped Micah clean up afterward.

"What's the first rule of being a good hunter?" he asked.

"Same as being a sniper, patience. Eventually you'll get your opportunity, but you must be ready when it comes."

Micah tilted his head in thought. "That can be applied to many endeavors. Business, sports, love, even life itself."

"Those don't have rule number two."

His head tilted forward and his eyes widened to pose the question without words.

"Stay downwind," Kodi said, "and don't let yourself be skylined."

When Micah asked what skylined meant, Kodi explained the necessity not to stand out against a backdrop of sky or flat terrain. Dense, diverse background was favored.

Micah nodded, then became confused. "Isn't that what camouflage is for?"

"Rocks and trees don't move on their own. Animals know that as well as people. The camo is to blend and be still."

"I get it," he said.

"Were you ever in the service?" Kodi asked.

"No, well . . ." long pause, "not really, but kinda."

Now Kodi tilted her head. "Kinda how?"

"I worked for the Department of Defense for twenty years. Twenty and done, as they say, full pension."

"If I can ask, doing what?"

She's military and thinking classified. "Field work, observation, then wrote reports, guidelines, pamphlets."

A slight impression she was impressed. *Don't be,* he thought.

Kodi asked, "You mean for military intelligence?"

"Hah," Micah laughed involuntarily. "Not even my own. Stuff about field hygiene, signs of substance abuse in the ranks, cultural sensitivity in foreign lands, sexual harassment from superiors, sunburn and blisters, even venereal disease."

Kodi's turn to laugh. "You wrote that one?"

"Don't look at me that way. I didn't do the graphics, only the verbiage. After research, I wrote the texts for all of them. Remember *Gambling Doesn't End with Your Hitch. If You've Got a Problem, Deal with It Now*?"

She nodded. "Why'd you get out?"

Micah lifted his cane. "This was coming on and I'd really had enough." He wedged the stick beside the table and continued before she could ask. "I wrote the kind of stuff you people on the front lines laughed at and threw away. Got a crazy idea I should go off somewhere and write something of my own that was worthwhile. Hell, Uncle Sam paid me to be a writer for two decades, why not give it a real shot?"

Kodi took it all in, then asked, "What happened?"

"Not much, I don't do it anymore."

"Why not?"

"I just don't."

They had eaten late and now it was very late. The last of the wine was in their glasses.

"Thanks for the stew and wine. Both were great."

Kodi got up and rinsed her glass in the sink and put it on the drain board.

"Another recon in the morning?" Micah asked.

"No. If the whole town is out and about on the weekend, I'd best keep a low profile. I've got some errands to run, but nothing here on Aquidneck Island."

"Need some help?" He was going to say: Want some company? but knew it wouldn't come out of his mouth.

"I've got it," she said. "You've been nice and a big help already. A place for me to squat with the trailer, hot coffee, the printer, good food, wine. I gotta run some things down and then get in my *nuhsh-ahta* for Sunday night." She moved to the door. "Thanks, Micah, good night."

"Night."

And Kodi was gone.

Nuhsh-ahta*, what's that?* he thought. *Tracking mode, hunting psyche-up. Zone. Killing zone. That's it, isn't it? You poor kid. Kid*, he reminded himself again.

Kodi was gone all day Saturday. Micah had a different visitor instead.

"So where's Pocahontas? She left me a message she can't hunt until tomorrow night."

Micah bristled at the cheap caricature, but decided not to get into it with Catlett.

"No idea," he said. "She works for you not me."

He stepped back to let Catlett enter.

"What time is it?" he asked.

Catlett checked her watch. "Two fifteen. What's the matter? Were you working?"

"Unlike you town officials, we self-employed tend to do that, even on weekends."

"Fuck you." She smiled, a trace wickedly. "I could use a drink with an old friend."

Catlett took off her coat and hung it on the peg herself. She went to the sofa in the parlor, kicked off her shoes, and sat back, folding her legs up on the sofa beside her. Micah went to the kitchen and opened a bottle of wine, returning with two glasses, but leaving the open bottle behind. He gave her one glass and sat at the other end of the sofa. Catlett wore jeans and a pullover sweater. Middletown was casual, even in its business, but not so Laurie Catlett. She only dressed casual when she was truly casual. Micah baited her.

"Here on official business?"

"The town has an investment here. And she's already been paid a decent advance," Catlett added. "Who's to say she wouldn't hitch up and leave town with what she's got."

"You don't believe that for a minute." It occurred to him in an instant. "Right, you didn't vet her. She was a conservation package directly through Boyd. Now, how did you let that happen?"

It was clear Catlett did not like his tone. She seemed to want to say something, didn't, and smiled. The smile Micah knew was not amusement. It was the tight smile Catlett used to buy time and form a strategy in an unexpected confrontation. A second later, Micah knew she came up with a tactic.

Catlett stretched both arms above her head while rotating her neck as if releasing tension and settled back.

"You guys seemed cozy yesterday when I stopped by. Did I interrupt something?"

"Laurie, don't be an ass."

She pretended not to hear that. "When was it, three years ago? And since then it was, let me think." She paused. "I remember. First you dated that librarian for a little over a year. Then a lull before the English professor. After that, another sabbatical in the monastery before the hostess at the Chart House." Catlett shook her head. "I wish you hadn't done that one, Micah. It ruined that restaurant for me and I miss it."

Watching her from his end of the couch, Micah reflected in flashes as to why it ended between him and Catlett. She had a cruel streak, and his nonresponsiveness irked her.

"Oh, God, Micah, please tell me you didn't make her your mother's stew."

"Fuck you," he said softly with a forced smile. "You and I used to have . . ."

"Ground rules," Catlett said. "I know."

"I was going to say, manners."

The little they said after that didn't matter and both knew it. Catlett finished her wine and left.

CHAPTER FIVE

At this point in Icobar's journals Micah got the impression the entries were written later than the cited dates. He couldn't put his finger on it, but they seemed somehow edited, not as raw as those written on a daily basis previously. There were frequent and longer gaps between dates, sometimes as much as three weeks. Perhaps Icobar scribbled notes somewhere when he could and made formal entries at a later date.

After the war? Very possible. The preceding journals were what he stashed at the shop before leaving.

Whatever way, the chronological flow was maintained.

Icobar Ohlm left his hometown and made his way to Providence on foot, hitchhiking wagon rides with tradesmen and farmers going to markets. Saying he was headed to enlist for the Union always brought extended generosity and accommodation. A few miles out of the driver's way or a free meal. Without yet donning a uniform, Icobar already was enjoying a new status in life.

Providence proved less accommodating. Icobar was only one among hundreds, maybe a thousand lads, who heard the call of duty. The cheaper inns and hostels were overcrowded and many, Icobar among them, wound up sleeping in barns or public places with minimum shelter.

After an ill night's sleep he followed the crowd to the enlistment area in a public park. Three newly formed regiments were seeking recruits: one each of cavalry, artillery, and infantry.

Icobar got on line, the longest of the three, for the cavalry. Though not boasting a horseman of any distinction, he reasoned it better than marching all day in the infantry or doing mule work hauling and positioning a heavy cannon or a caisson of cannonballs.

Five hours of waiting and ten men away from the registration table, an officer announced the regiment's quota filled. There followed a scramble to join artillery. Only the infantry continued recruiting until sundown. It was nearly then that Icobar committed his name to the roll and pledged himself on his word of honor.

Not so bad after all. He received a hot meal, a half cup of whiskey, and a clean cot and blanket in a huge tent.

As Micah closed the journal, a ragged piece of brown paper the size of an index card slipped out from between pages further on and fell to his desk blotter. Micah picked it up and examined it with his magnifier. It was a dated note fragment written in pencil. The journals were all in ink.

I was right. He kept this part of the journal in pieces to write later.

The penciled words were: In the army now. Infantry only option. Start training tomorrow.

It was Sunday, just after sunset. Micah had not seen Kodi all weekend. He had checked for the pickup several times. Done with Icobar Ohlm for the day, he went to the kitchen. Made a ham and cheese sandwich and poured a glass of wine. Rinsing his mustard knife, a light out the kitchen window caught his eye.

Kodi was sitting on the trailer steps. A droplight was above her head affixed to the trailer door. Across her lap was a rifle, in her right hand a cloth. She wasn't polishing, more like stroking, barrel to butt, slowly, again and again.

Micah's sandwich went in the refrigerator, but he drank the wine to the bottom of the glass.

"Getting ready?"

Kodi did not look up. "Already ready. Patience, remember?"

"Tonight?" Micah asked.

"Closer to dawn." Kodi looked up. Not at Micah, at the sky. With the light overhead there was no way she saw the stars. "0300, thereabouts." Head back down to her work.

"If they let you hunt at night, why wait?" Micah didn't know why he asked except that he didn't want to walk away.

Kodi folded the cloth and put it beside her on the step. Put the butt of the rifle on the ground and leaned the barrel against the trailer. Then she finally answered.

"Don't like to hunt at night. Can only see the eyes and gotta sight on the head. Can't be sure how the animal's positioned. Takes a head shot."

"I thought you were a sniper."

"Didn't say I couldn't hit one, meant I don't like to kill that way, animals at least."

He took a closer look at the rifle. It was smaller than he expected. Certainly not the kind of sniper rifle he'd seen in Defense Department manuals or in movies. This appeared small and compact.

"Whatcha shooting?"

"Winchester 70 Light, 22-250." She said it crisply, as if answering an officer.

"Good gun for coyotes?"

She looked from the Winchester to Micah. "Best there is, unless you're some kind of sicko. Clean shot, clean kill. Anything heavier is butchering it. I didn't take this job to be a butcher. Do what I have to do, the way it should be done."

Micah was going to ask about the scope atop the rifle. Knew nothing about scopes, so didn't.

Kodi stood up, picked up the rifle, and walked to her pickup. She put the Winchester behind the seats in the cab and locked the truck. Micah stayed by the trailer steps.

As Kodi put the keys in her pocket she called out. "Yank the plug on that light."

Micah saw the coil of electric cord, seized the plug, and pulled.

Darkness. Neither one of them made a sound. Micah's eyes adjusted slowly. He turned, almost lost his balance, jabbed his cane down firmly, and leaned. The only light now was coming from his distant kitchen window, more a glow, so it was still pretty dark. Micah saw her still beside the truck. Kodi was looking skyward again.

"Nice night," she said.

From his weather station Micah knew it was in the low forties and would get colder before midnight. He looked up too.

"Bit cool, but yeah, crystal clear."

When he looked at her she was casually pointing across the yard.

"If it's too cool for you, you know that old chicken coop would make a nice bonfire."

"I knew there was a reason I didn't tear it down. Sometime, maybe I will."

"Tear it down or burn it?"

"I like your idea better."

Kodi started walking toward him. "I'm gonna Z for a while and then gear up."

Micah started walking the other way. They passed each other.

"Good night, Kodi."

"You too, Micah."

"Wake me when you get back in the morning."

"Would, won't have to."

"I guess not. Good luck."

"Don't need luck."

Micah stopped still. "I think I was trying to say . . ." He didn't finish.

Kodi didn't finish for him.

They went their separate ways.

DESPITE THE occasional reminder of his affliction, a cramp or sudden awkward jerk and painful turn, Micah LaVeck normally slept well. Not so that Sunday night. He seemed to only grasp chunks of sleep of ever decreasing duration, always awakened with a start. Without any tangible lingering evidence, his mind supplied possible circumstances. It was coyotes howling up in the Kempenaar Valley. It was Kodi's truck grinding gears in the yard. It was Gretchen Miller's cat screeching in final agony. Or a rifle shot, not too far but not too close. Then another.

Useless. At two thirty any hope was abandoned and Micah rose, showered because he felt sweaty, and dressed. He made coffee and while getting his milk, noticed the uneaten sandwich on the fridge shelf.

I don't usually miss a meal. Might as well be breakfast.

He took the plate to the study and powered up his computer, then did a double take on the origin of an e-mail. Mayor Mary Boyd. Micah knew Boyd quite well. Occasionally had dinner with her socially, always with other guests, even after it ended with Catlett. Was yearly invited to the Christmas party at her home. Not the one for politicos and contributors, the smaller one for friends and neighbors. Even so, the mayor had never e-mailed before this.

Double click:

> Micah,
>
> Spoke with Laurie this evening. I owe you an apology as it seems we've taken advantage of your good and civic-minded nature. Forgive me if I say it plain as an old friend: I know you're not entirely well and get about as best you can. So if the hunter's presence on your property is any inconvenience or hardship whatsoever, please don't hesitate to say so and we'll make alternative arrangements. Your comfort is my primary concern here, as always.
>
> Wait to hear from you.
>
> Sincerely,
>
> Mary.

Followed by the Middletown official seal and the standard confidentiality claim.

Micah hit RESPOND and started typing:

> Tell Catlett to go fuck herself.

Backspace delete, delete until it was gone.

Typing again:

> Not at all. Hardly know she's here. But thanks for asking. See you at the next council meeting.

SEND.

He looked at the pile of journals on the credenza.

Fuck you too, Icobar.

He looked at his weather station. Thirty-nine degrees. The clock at the top: three thirty.

Have to bundle up good. Gonna find a new stick to work on. Maybe go into business after all.

THE SUN wasn't up, only dusky light and Micah had his flashlight. He made a close inspection of the red maple at the edge of the spit. Every storm season, like the chicken coop, that maple lost a branch or two. Three times around the thick trunk, searching above and below, and no prospects.

The firs and the elm behind the coop also disappointed him. Micah walked around the side of the house to examine his privet hedge, the source of his original stick. A few stalks seemed perfect but posed a problem. Thickest, they were near the base and supported offshoots above. To cut one out would leave an unsightly gap in his hedge. He turned and walked back to the pond.

A quiet morning as usual, he heard the occasional car on Valley Road on the other side of the pond. Once in a while a headlight flashed between the trees. He turned off his own light.

Thought he saw something else, swept his sight along the shore on the far side. Found it. A doe by the water. She too was watching. Maybe saw Micah or didn't. Stretched her neck and then dipped to drink. Micah made not a hair's move to disturb her. The earliest birds started calling. All was peaceful.

Suddenly, she flinched convulsively. Stared at a spot midway around the arc of the shore between her and Micah. Crouched, turned in one motion, and sprang between the trees into the brush and was gone.

Micah approximated her sightline and stared into the thick brush at the north end of Green End Pond. A pair of golden-yellow eyes met his and held. Slowly the head rose. Without breaking contact, a few sniffs of air. Then the coyote turned and headed through the thickets back up toward the Kempenaar Valley.

First time, first one Micah had ever seen.

The sun came peeking over the hills behind Aquidneck Avenue to the east. Micah wasn't sure how he felt. Part pleasure and amazement, or maybe privilege. The coyote hadn't looked fierce, despite having spooked the doe. Quite the opposite. As natural as the deer he'd seen, and many others before her, that bolted at the slightest sound. It was their nature. And just as beautiful to observe. Indeed, a privilege.

Micah savored the moment until interrupted by what sounded like a truck out front on Green End Avenue. A heavy truck, not Kodi's pickup.

The truck was a green box, common size for commercial deliveries, with a blue/white/-gold/green shield on the cab door and on the box panel.

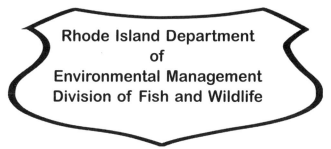

Rhode Island Department
of
Environmental Management
Division of Fish and Wildlife

Micah heard the cab door slam on the street side. The engine was left running. Presently, an F and W ranger came around the front of the truck.

"Mr. LaVeck, is it?"

The ranger was a woman. Near Micah's age, grayish hair pulled up under a Smokey the Bear hat but still visible on the sides. She wore a green parka with the same insignia as the truck.

Micah told her who he was and they shook hands. She had a firm grip and shook like a hatchet chop.

"Ranger Flavia Ferzoco. This is my district."

"What can I do for you, Ranger?"

"I'm here to meet with Kodi, the hunter."

Micah realized no one ever used a last name for Kodi. Not Kodi, not Catlett, and now the ranger.

"She's not back yet. Is she expecting you?"

Ferzoco removed the hat and smoothed her hair, which wasn't out of place, a large knot of a bun in the back near the top to fit under the hat. She held the hat at her side.

"She called me," Ferzoco said. "She's on her way back with two kills. I'm here for the remains. I must have beaten her home."

Two kills.

"You always up this early?" Ferzoco asked.

"Pretty much."

"Me too. Comes with the job, but I like it."

They stood in silence, then Micah remembered his manners.

"The truck's okay where it is if you shut it off. Come on inside."

The hat went firmly back in place. "Appreciate it."

Micah felt as if his motions were completely mechanical. What he really felt was only one thing:

One night, two kills.

Something Kodi said came back to him and made him pause a moment.

"She pays me for blood; I'll give her all she wants."

Micah knew she was serious at the time. Like a kid about to play in the high school championship. It was only . . . well, it was at that time. Now it was something different.

Two kills.

CHAPTER SIX

They were inside only moments when Micah heard the pickup pull into the yard.

"She's here," he said, and led the way out the rear door.

There was a tarp over the bed of the pickup. Kodi was sitting in the cab staring out the windshield at Green End Pond. Micah approached and tapped on the driver's side window. Without a start, Kodi turned her head. It was Micah that had the start. Her face was covered in camo face paint: streaks and blotches of green, brown, and black. Blackest around her eyes, and with her black irises, the whites of her eyes became pronounced. The window cranked down.

"Hey, Micah." Softly, not like a greeting.

"You okay?"

"Of course, only tired."

"There's a ranger here."

"I saw the truck."

Micah backed up and Kodi opened the door. As she came out, Micah saw the camo brimless cap on her head, and then a thick trail in black as the rest of her hair slid down between the collar of her jacket and the nape of her neck to disappear from view.

Ferzoco came forward. "Long night, eh, Kodi?"

Kodi only said, "Hey, Ferzie."

Ferzie, right. Kodi got this job through a friend in conservation. I guess I've met her now, thought Micah.

Kodi and Ferzoco shook hands. Ferzoco's other hand went to Kodi's shoulder and applied a quick squeeze. They broke off and started talking but Micah was no longer listening. He had noticed Kodi's pants and was staring, despite himself. Down her camo-clad thighs were slashing stains of red, actually more maroon. It was, Micah assumed, blood. He stopped staring the instant he realized it wasn't hers.

The women were still talking. Micah could hear again.

"The larger," Kodi was saying, "I'd say he's about fifty to fifty-five pounds. Took him at the vineyard. Not where the grapes are, in a fallow field down by the creek."

"And the other?" said Ferzoco, taking down notes in a notebook.

"At Gabby's Farm, near the compost heap. He's forty to forty-five. With what I smelled in that pile, and all the varmint running over it, he'd a been a lot fatter by summer."

Ferzoco closed the notebook. "Let's take a look."

They went to the side of the bay, Micah behind them. Kodi untied the rope lashing and drew back the tarp. The two coyotes lay side by side. Both of the reddish, rather than the gray, variety. Taller than both women, Micah had a good view.

To him, they hardly seemed dead, more like asleep. One with its head on its front paws, the other curled with its snout tucked between forelegs. All eyes closed, no tongues hanging out, and no sign of blood. It seemed so natural, or arranged to be so.

"I'll get the tags," Ferzoco said. She turned to Micah and asked if she could back her truck up this far or should they drive the pickup out to the front.

Mindful of Catlett's concern about keeping this quiet, but more concerned about not wanting to make Kodi go through all the maneuvering, he told the ranger pulling back here was fine with him. She went to do it.

Micah and Kodi were alone with the dead coyotes.

"Want anything?" Micah said.

Deep sigh from Kodi. "I'm good. Let's get this done and I'm gonna crash for a few hours."

They said nothing else until Ferzoco returned with the backed-up truck and lifted open the rear door.

Ferzoco wrote out tags with ties and secured these to the forelegs of each animal. They were ready to be transferred. Micah volunteered to help. Ferzoco said the two of them could manage it. Both women drew on gloves.

As they lifted the larger one, Micah saw the wound in the center chest and the blood trail down its fur in a single, centered, thick line. Exactly the color of the stain on Kodi's pants.

The move from the pickup to the truck was—all Micah could think of—gentle. The smaller coyote had an identical gunshot. When finished, they lay side by side in Ferzoco's truck as neat and peaceful as they'd been before in the pickup.

"I'm gonna need a receipt," Kodi said to Ferzoco.

The ranger brought a clipboard from the cab. Filled out two forms and handed the detachable copies to Kodi. Kodi thanked her, folded them into a pocket, and went to her trailer without another word.

As the trailer door closed, Ferzoco said to Micah, "Headquarters is anxious to see this through the first time so I best be going. See you next time." She got in her truck.

Next time. A melancholy thought.

Micah went inside. If he'd had any whiskey, he would have poured himself a stiff one. Wine wasn't going to cut it so he didn't bother.

As he hung up his peacoat he shook his head. The first official coyote hunt on Aquidneck Island was over. He looked across the kitchen at the hallway to his study. Looked at the kitchen clock. Minutes shy of eight A.M.

What the hell am I supposed to do now?

At the Aquidneck Wine and Spirit Shop, Micah selected his bottles of wine and placed them on the counter, one at a time after each selection, so his right hand could still grip his cane. Melvin Sturgis knew the routine and never rang any up until Micah said he was done.

"One more thing, Melvin," Micah said after the last bottle, "what kind of beer do the younger folks drink these days?"

Sturgis scratched his chin. "It depends. If they got their noses in the air and a payday wallet, some like those darn microbrews." He pointed to the cooler along the wall. Shelves filled with ornately rendered six-pack cartons. Then he pointed to the far back wall at another cooler. "The regulars usually grab Bud or Coors. Why you ask?"

Micah felt embarrassed. "I haven't had a beer in twenty years. Even then, I was no connoisseur." He thought a minute and wasn't embarrassed anymore. "I've got some company coming and heard one of them likes beer. Gotta be a good host."

"If you don't know, don't gamble. Stick to basics. Most of those micros taste like crap anyway. I mean, who really wants a turnip in their beer? Bud or Coors. But get a light one; they're the big thing with the kids."

"Thanks." Micah walked to the back and returned with a six-pack of Coors Light. He put it on the counter next to his wine.

"Silver Bullets," Sturgis said. "That's what the young folks call Coors Lights, Silver Bullets. On account of that silvery can."

Macabre, thought Micah, *silver bullets for a hunter.*

"That be it?" Sturgis asked. Micah nodded. "Can you handle all this or you want my delivery guy to bring it? No extra charge for you."

Micah wasn't offended, but it did seem lately everyone was concerned, or declined his help at anything physical.

"I'll manage, thanks all the same."

Sturgis took the bar-code reader and started scanning. "How come you stopped drinking beer yourself?"

"I kinda lost the taste for it and I was peeing every five minutes."

"You'll be back," Sturgis said.

"Why's that?"

"You're a young'un yourself compared to me. Get to my age, my friend, you'll do anything to take a nice long, easy pee."

"Sounds like it beats the hell out of pills."

"Amen."

AFTER THE wine shop, Micah went home, dropped his purchases, and headed back out for the butcher shop. He bought two Angus steaks and a wheel of sausage. By the time he was home again it was past noon. His legs were tired and left hip sore, but walking always made him feel good, at least in spirit if not the flesh. The discomfort would pass. Exercise was essential, his doctor had said, provided he was careful about his balance. Micah's problem wasn't propulsion so much as equilibrium.

It was still a Monday and, his government pension notwithstanding, Micah did work for a living. So it was into the study and back to the journals.

Icobar was training to march, shoot, and thrust a bayonet.

"Excuse me, Micah."

He had not heard her come in. Swung his chair around to see her in the doorway. The face paint was gone, hair loose over shoulders. Kodi wore the gray-green sweater again, black jeans, and the first pair of sneakers Micah had ever seen on her. Off her shoulder was slung an army-green duffel bag.

"Could you tell me where's the nearest laundromat?"

Laundry. The thought made Micah smile. The professional hunter and veteran United States warrior had dirty clothes and wanted them clean. He'd once written a manual on the proper way to do laundry in extenuating circumstances. *Hygiene is always a priority*. Then he remembered the blood on her camo pants. Only for a second. He refused to let his smile slip away.

"Hope you got your quarters, because you've found it," he said.

She gave him the same puzzled look he got from all his other lame attempts at humor.

"I have a washer and dryer. I'll show you and you can help yourself."

He went to rise but, in moving his chair, the stick was out of reach. Kodi sensed it immediately. For a second Micah thought she was going to extend her hand to help him. She did, but changed her mind, stepped with hand extended for the cane and passed it to him. He came to his feet and changed the unspoken subject back to the practical matter at hand.

"It's that closed door in the kitchen," he said. "Half-pantry, half-laundry room. I keep the door closed because there's barely any heat in there, as you're about to find out."

Kodi followed him back to the kitchen where Micah opened the pantry door. A small room with the only linoleum floor in the house. The left sidewall was shelving, stocked with dry goods and household supplies. On the right were a washer and dryer. It was noticeably cooler than the rest of the house. Micah ushered Kodi in and she set the duffel on the floor.

"You do your own laundry?" she asked.

"Ever since the elves went on strike."

Another stupid joke. Kodi laughed anyway.

Micah pointed to the shelf. "Anything you need should be there; soap, bleach, softener. You know how to work the machines?"

"I don't have elves either."

Micah moved past her and returned to the kitchen. Wasn't entirely sure what to do with himself. From the pantry he heard the water start to fill the washer. Kodi appeared.

"How long you figure?" she said.

"Forty-five minutes."

"Then I'll get out of your way and come back."

"You're not in my way."

They stared at each other a minute until Kodi gave a little shrug and slid into a chair.

Micah figured now was as good a time as any.

"If you don't have plans, I bought a couple of steaks and thought I'd grill them for dinner. How about you join me?" He hesitated, then added, "Only if I'm not messing up your schedule."

"No schedule," Kodi said. "Won't be hunting tonight or in the morning."

Micah wasn't sure if he was surprised or not, so asked why.

"They only gave me three areas," Kodi said, "the vineyard and two farms. Gabby's Farm borders the Kellwood Farm so the same family of coyotes covers both. Eastern coyotes rarely belong to large packs. So they won't be out tonight. Not at the vineyard either."

"How come?"

"For two families, their daddies didn't come home this morning. The mothers, who may be with pups this time of year, won't leave the dens until their hunger makes them. You can be sure it won't be tonight."

The whole concept was foreign to Micah. "Are they really like that?" he asked. "Families, I mean."

Kodi said most mature coyote males were monogamous in mating. Couples built their own dens, sometimes renovated from badger holes, the females had pups, the males hunted and protected.

Another silence until Micah shook it off and said, "So you'll have dinner."

"You're inviting and got the steaks, hell yeah. Can't remember the last time I had steak."

Micah saved the best for last. "I've even got beer."

They sat at the kitchen table, placid as neighbors exchanging local news and the washing machine whirred in the background.

So if he wasn't writing for himself, she asked, what did Micah do with most of his time? Not the slightest insulted, he answered honestly—told Kodi about the surgeon, the circus tutor, the general, and finally his current project, a common man from the Civil War era.

"Will it make a good book?" she asked.

"Not a chance. Dreadful stuff. Though, to be fair, I'm not even a quarter of the way through it all, so I suppose there's hope."

"Is that a motto of yours," she asked, "that there's always hope?"

"Not especially, but I'm not the fatalist that implies. I do like to be firmly rooted in reality."

It simply came out of her. "So what's with the leg? You have an accident or something?"

Micah shook his head. "No accident. There's a long medical name for it that I've forgotten how to pronounce but the concept is simple."

Kodi leaned forward to listen.

Micah was saying, "Sometime ago, my brain and my leg had a disagreement. They never patched it up. So now when they talk to each other at all, they argue. The brain says, 'Move.' My leg says, 'I'll move when I wanna move, any way I wanna move.' And the feud continues."

"What do the doctors say?" Kodi asked.

"The feud is spreading. Little by little the other appendages—right leg, arms, and hands—are siding with my left leg and not following orders from my brain."

"Can they cure it?"

"I don't know if anyone is even trying, it's pretty rare. There's no medication and it's irreversible." He picked up his stick and leaned an elbow on it. "Only adjustments to be made to compensate. That means: do whatever you have to for getting around. It progresses through walkers to wheelchairs and other aids. But when you think about it, I'm lucky."

Kodi was incredulous. "Lucky how?"

Micah was earnest. "It's not cancer or a tumor, and I got it late enough in life that by the time it gets too bad, I'll be dead from something else anyway. Hopefully, old age."

"I hope so too," she said. "I mean, you know what I mean."

Micah sincerely believed her. The time passed with talk about Middletown and the rest of Aquidneck Island. The washing and drying were done. Kodi folded everything back into her duffel.

"What time should I come back for dinner?" she asked.

"This isn't the army; you don't have to be rigid. All right, make it six."

"1800, roger that." Duffel on shoulder, like a sailor on a gangplank, Kodi went out the back door.

Micah went to the parlor and prepared a fire in the huge hearth of the original cottage. It still had a drop-down grate for cooking and an iron hook to hang a kettle or cauldron. He wanted the fire just right for grilling, which meant glowing embers, not flames, but the flames had to come first.

As he lit the match he thought: *A white lie, if that. After all, what does it matter?*

The inexorable deterioration of his cerebellum was not really as slow as he implied to Kodi. And the argument included more than only his appendages; organs would follow. Yet, he still had his dignity and his choices.

Pity's not on the menu.

The kindling took and the flame spread.

CHAPTER SEVEN

Kodi had her beer, Micah his wine, and the steaks were grilled perfectly.

"What's the Aquidneck Land Trust?" Kodi asked.

"A not-for-profit on the island that manages natural areas and saves them from being flipped for commercial or residential use. Very successful at it too. Why?"

"Laurie Catlett called before, while I was in my trailer. She said they have endorsed the hunt."

Micah wasn't sure which surprised him more, the direct call from Catlett or the trust's decision. Then he thought: *Of course she'd call direct, that's her job. I'm only the innkeeper. Or trailer keeper.* As for the trust, they were dedicated conservationists so maybe the coyotes were a legitimate threat after all.

When he didn't say anything, Kodi went on: "Know what I call her?"

"Who?" Micah said, even though he was sure whom she meant.

"Catlett, I've given her an Indian name, like my people usually do. I call her '*Wawotam Kokac.*' It means 'Cunning Crow.' And as we often do too, there's a shortened slang form: '*Wawokak.*' "

Micah repeated it. "Wawokak. I like it, and very insightful on your part. It fits at every level," though he did not elaborate.

"She once your woman?"

That came as a surprise and again Micah said nothing.

"It's a scent she gives off," Kodi said.

"Scent? She was here? I thought you said she phoned."

"She did, only I hate the word vibes, so I use scent. For a sniper, it's pretty much the same thing. All the senses running at full power, they tend to blend into one instinct."

Micah could understand perfectly. Not from any hunting experience, from his disease. Everything had to work together to carry on for the parts that didn't work. Otherwise, he fell on his ass.

"Got an Indian name for me?"

If it's possible for a reddish-skin-toned American Indian to blush, Kodi did exactly that.

"Yes," she hesitated, "but it was kind of before we got to know each other."

"Let's have it."

" '*Pumsha Pokasu*,' shortened to '*Pumpok*.' "

Micah raised his eyebrows for the translation.

"Walks Tilted."

Micah lifted his wineglass in toast. "Helluva lot better than Cunning Crow."

When Kodi left later that evening, Micah still had not confirmed nor denied a relationship with Catlett. It really didn't matter. They enjoyed the dying fire in the hearth and never came back to the subject. As the last embers faded into smoke, Micah had gone to his computer, found the Aquidneck Land Trust website, and printed out a list of properties they managed within Middletown. He had given the list to Kodi.

Notable among the names were the Kempenaar Valley and Albro Woods, two locations with confirmed coyote sightings.

Like not mentioning an affair with Catlett, Micah also never shared the coyote he'd seen from his own yard on the northern shore of Green End Pond. He wondered why. Kodi would know soon enough. Across the road from that spot started the Kempenaar Valley.

Kodi came back in the morning. It was nice for Micah, having her around. Never a parent himself, he compared it to having a niece visiting from college for a holiday visit. Plenty of space between them, but the shared times somewhat special. The difference in their ages, and many other factors, precluded anything else. That made it, happily, very simple and somehow, he searched for the word in his mind as an uncle might: *precious.*

She didn't seem in any particular hurry. It had only turned five o'clock.

"I did Albro Woods on my first recon here," Kodi said. "Took some of the photos you liked there. But I missed the Kempenaar Valley so I'll have to do that today. How do I find it?"

"You can throw a rock from your trailer to where it starts," Micah said. "But this end is all boulders and thicket and barely passable on foot, even for someone who doesn't walk tilted."

Kodi laughed at that. Micah continued.

"There's also some private property at this end that could limit your access."

He went on to say she could take her truck up High Street and park in the Aquidneck Shopping Center by CVS, then double back on foot to the north end of the valley. From that end she'd have a view of the whole thing. See the clusters of trees and brush at various spots along Bailey Creek that ran down the center. The rest was mainly open grassland maintained by the trust.

Kodi took out her tourist map, folded it open on the table, and Micah traced the area with his finger.

"We can download a better map from their website," he suggested.

"That would help," Kodi said.

They went to the study. Micah had the site bookmarked and they printed a better map in a few minutes. Kodi studied it.

"Forty-five and a half acres," she said. "Close quarters for a coyote. Must be a small family."

"And lucky," Micah said. "That valley is teeming with small animals. Until now," he stopped for a moment realizing what he was about to say, "it's been protected land, so I guess the coyotes had their pick."

Kodi was reading a second page that printed with the map. "And birds too. Coyotes love birds."

"I remember that from a town meeting," said Micah. "The local Audubon was all upset with the coyotes because the Kempenaar Valley hosts a rare species, the white-throated sparrow."

Kodi handed the papers to Micah. "I think we've established that our coyote brothers are politically incorrect."

"That depends on your politics."

Kodi grew serious, almost melancholy. "I don't have any politics, Micah. I'm here to do a job and get my money."

He handed the map back. "Then you'll need this to find your way."

Kodi took it, folded it, and tucked it in her pocket. She looked around the study, eyes finally settling on the stacks of Icobar Ohlm's journals.

"Of course," she said, "if I'm not keeping you from work and you wanna come with me, that would be a big help. Not the hunt, I only mean the recon."

Micah felt himself nodding before the answer ever came to his lips.

THEY PARKED in the shopping center lot and walked back up High Street, past the tiny colonial cemetery, to the rim of the valley. Micah was aware Kodi's stride was purposefully slower so she wouldn't get ahead of him. Micah appreciated it though neither one said anything. Though a warm day, Micah had on his mackintosh, Kodi only a windbreaker over her hoodie.

From the ridge, the valley opened up below them. Micah had brought his own binoculars, uncased them, and handed the pair to Kodi. She stood up tall, squared her shoulders, brought them to her eyes, made a focus adjustment, and began scanning the valley. Micah watched her, not the terrain. Short, smooth movements as Kodi seemed to study the area precisely as if by coordinates in her head. Methodical, no jerks or sweeps; it was easily ten minutes before she lowered the glasses.

She pointed with her right hand. "What's that smokestack near the far end?"

"Kempenaar Clambake Club. During the summer they cater private parties or corporate events. A real New England clambake with a real fire. Never done it myself, but I hear it's good. Doesn't open again until May."

No comment. Kodi swung the glasses up to her face and sighted due east. "What's that over there? Got the out buildings like a farm."

Micah said it was a Christmas tree farm. Part of the valley, but private property and not managed by the land trust.

"I think it's off-limits," he added.

"Good place for a den. Might have to talk to Wawokak about it. See if they'll give me access."

"I don't think she'll have a problem getting permission. If the owner ever needs a favor from Middletown government, he'd be out of luck if he refuses."

Kodi lowered the glasses and grimaced. "Politics, again."

"It does seem to turn the wheels."

Kodi handed the binoculars back to Micah. "Are you up for a little hike? I'd like to recon that creek. Look for tracks and fresh kills from this morning."

"No problem, I walk everywhere I go in this town: food shopping, wine shop, the bank, and post office. Lead the way."

Kodi smiled, half in encouragement, half in appreciation, and off they went down the side of the valley toward Bailey Creek. She watched the ground constantly, scanning left and right. Many times she stopped to bend over and examine a rock, or feather, or run her hand lightly over the top of the grass. Occasionally she picked something up, passed it from hand to hand, sniffed it and tossed it behind them. Might have been a rock or an animal turd for all Micah knew. And there were plenty of birds, all kinds. Sometimes the birds sprang up out of the grass right in front of them and shot skyward with much noise and flurry to end in lazy loops overhead. Micah looked carefully, but was almost certain none were white-throated sparrows.

They arrived at the creek. Kodi crouched and stuck in her hand. It reminded Micah of the scene at the pond he had observed. This time, she didn't wet her face or drink.

Still squatting, something farther downstream caught Kodi's eye. She rose, beckoned Micah, and led him to it. It was what remained of a bird carcass on the shore of the creek.

From the feathers and length of neck, Micah recognized it as a Canadian goose. Common this time of year. Their presence, not their deaths.

"Somebody had a good breakfast," Kodi said.

"Was it a coyote or something else?"

Kodi picked up a stick and poked around the remains. "Bite's too big for a fisher cat. Definitely full-grown coyote." She dropped the stick and turned completely around pausing at each point of the compass: north, east, south, and west. Her eyes moved up and down, sizing up the terrain.

"Lot of open ground," she said aloud, but Micah felt she was talking to herself. She pointed around absently, as if now including him. "These clumps of trees aren't much help. Coyote probably knows every inch of them."

She said coyote like it was someone's name. Someone she knew, or intended to meet.

"You were right," Kodi said. "Coyote's got a nice home here. Plenty of food and fresh water. Sparse coverage, but enough for Coyote and good for his style of hunting. But not enough for me to get that close. In the morning, it's gonna take a very distant shot."

She did her circular survey again. Micah did it too and asked, "From where?"

"Won't know that until I read the wind. Low, open valley, wind right now out of the north, Coyote probably smelled us when we got out of the truck. So I'll make that call in the morning."

"Check," Micah said, and couldn't believe he had said that like a soldier.

Kodi was done. She and Micah left the creek and headed back out of the valley. Halfway up the slope, a man was coming down with two Irish setters on long leads. He wore boots, open leather jacket, emblem sweater beneath, and gave Micah the impression of a country squire. As the proximity closed between them, the man shortened the leads until the dogs were to each side of him.

Micah said, "Morning, lovely day."

The man nodded. "Yes, very fine." He bent to one knee and stroked one of the dogs. "I saw you as I drove up High Street. Got a strange idea, so I stopped my car and thought I'd add in a little romp for Kelly and Liam." The setters' heads came up at the sound of their names and the man switched to petting the other one.

"Strange idea?" Micah said.

The man unclipped both dogs and after he waved his arms they bounded past Kodi and Micah down into the valley. The man straightened up again.

"Maybe not an idea so much as a hunch," he said. "My name is Bill Mackey and I pass this valley every day, let the pups loose three or four times a week. The birds and jackrabbits give them a workout."

"I'm Micah, this is my friend, Kodi." Micah didn't use his last name because he didn't know Kodi's.

Mackey shook both their hands and Kodi had yet to say a word. Releasing Kodi's hand, Mackey looked back at Micah.

"I hope you won't mind telling me, Micah, if you are by any chance the coyote hunter the town's hired. Haven't seen you in this valley before and, well, it's common knowledge there's coyotes around down there." He pointed in the general direction of Bailey Creek.

Micah laughed for two reasons. One, he was using his cane and negotiating the climb with difficulty as Mackey must have observed. Two, in his arrogance, Mackey didn't even consider that the young woman at Micah's side might be the hunter.

"Not me," said Micah. "Merely an amateur bird-watcher." He patted the binocular case for emphasis. "Been meaning to get up this way for sometime, maybe catch a glimpse of the white-throated sparrow." He glanced over his shoulder at the valley. "No such luck today, only a couple of whimbrels. Why do you want to meet him," emphasis on him, "the hunter, I mean?"

"It's front page of the *Newport Daily News*," Mackey said. "Bagged two his first time out. Real sportsmanlike kills too." He took a wallet from his pocket and produced a business card. "I'm president of the Middletown Rod and Gun Club and we'd like to offer him a free, honorary membership." He handed the card to Micah. "If you encounter him in your bird-watching, would you pass my card and invitation on to him? We'd be obliged."

Micah scanned the card. It was "Dr. William Mackey" under a crossed shotgun and fly rod, with an address and phone number for the club.

"Like I said, Bill, I'm strictly amateur," Micah told him. "Maybe two times a month and," he nodded at Kodi, "if my companion, the real bird expert, can spare me some time, but if I ever do meet up with him, I'll pass it along."

Mackey said, "Thanks, and so I'll say good morning again and be after my dogs." He looked at Kodi and touched his forehead in some kind of absurd salute and said, "Young lady."

As Mackey walked past Kodi and Micah he whistled for his dogs barking up a storm somewhere down in the valley.

Out of earshot, Micah handed the card to Kodi. "You've got a fan club."

A shrug. “I don’t join clubs anymore, this is my business.”
“His dogs safe down there in coyote territory?”
“This time of day, sure. But he already knows that.”
“Okay by me. Let’s go home.”

CHAPTER EIGHT

When they pulled into Micah's driveway, Micah saw his home-delivered copy of the *Newport Daily News* on his porch.

"Want to read your reviews?" he said to Kodi.

"I'm not much for newspapers, I'll pass."

"Lunch?"

"Pass again. I got things to do before tonight."

Micah remembered: *Nuhsh-ahta.*

He said, "You know where to find me if you need anything." He opened the truck door.

"Listen," Kodi said. "Thanks for coming along and not giving me up to that Rod and Gun guy."

"This is New England; we help our neighbors and respect their privacy."

Micah got out of the truck and closed the door. A small wave from Kodi before she pulled the truck around back to her trailer.

The *Newport Daily News:*

"COYOTE HUNT UNDERWAY IN MIDDLETOWN WITH INITIAL SUCCESS"

Middletown, RI—The identity of Middletown's professional coyote hunter is the best-kept secret at Town Hall since a long previous

> administration aided the FBI to flush out German spies in 1943. What is known is that he is obviously very skilled at what he does. In the wee hours of Monday morning two coyotes were killed at separate locations. Per an agreement between Mayor Mary Boyd and the Department of Environmental Management, the carcasses were turned over to the Fish and Wildlife Division for analysis. Neither the township nor the DEM will disclose the areas of the successful hunts and no reports of gunfire were made to the Middletown Police Department.
>
> Monday afternoon, necropsies were performed on the two adult, male coyotes. A source within Fish and Wildlife who attended the procedures, and insisted on anonymity, stated each was shot with a single bullet through the heart. A veterinarian consulted claimed their deaths would have been near instantaneous. Mayor Boyd promised the public this campaign would be conducted as humanely as possible. Town council members are satisfied she is keeping her word.
>
> In the meantime, according to Town Hall, and with broadening public approval, the hunt continues and similar results are anticipated.

Micah had an e-mail from Roger Ohlm, the family signatory on his contract, requesting an update on his work with the journals. It was barely two weeks into a project Micah advised could take from six to eight months. There was no obligation in his contract for status reports.

Nevertheless, he drafted a response that the reading was progressing, but transcription was at least a month away, that alone requiring an additional month or more, before rewriting and editing could begin. Respectfully, etc., etc.

You won't like it when it's done anyway, he thought, but didn't add to the draft. *Icobar was a selfish, conniving malcontent. Makes for a great family hero and a captivating read. Aw, shit.*

Then Micah relented and inserted in the e-mail draft that if a significant entry presented itself, defined as one of family importance or historical appeal, Micah would promptly advise such. Cut and paste: Respectfully, etc.

SEND.

Micah looked over at the journals.

Come on, Icobar, give me something. If not for me, for your family. All right, screw the family, for me and you. You get famous, I get a bonus. I'd split the bonus with you but you're dead. So it's only fame for you. Whatya say?

Icobar did not respond.

After weeks of training, Icobar's regiment boarded a troop train for Washington, DC. He noted it was the farthest he'd ever been from home. Army life was tedious but he felt in the best physical shape of his young years.

From scuttlebutt acquired during the train ride, most regiments from New England were being deployed in and around the capital. When the amassing was accomplished in a display of Northern power, the Confederates, according to gossip, would realize the futility of their quest and surrender. Or be invaded and subdued by superior force. In short order, according to most speculation.

Nice thought, but not to happen, Micah knew from history.

Formed into brigades in Washington, Icobar's regiment was told President Lincoln advocated a full-out drive on Richmond for a swift, decisive victory if the rebellion was not called off. A few soldiers around the campfires warned that the will of the Southerners was strong, regardless of what officers, the newspapers, or the gossip implied.

Marching on foot now, hour after dusty hour, Private Icobar Ohlm entered Virginia with his regiment. Their destination: a strategic railroad center named Manassas Junction. On the third day, he found himself dug in along a creek called Bull Run. The enemy was in sight on the other side.

At least in his journal, Icobar still refused to pray. Indeed, was cocky. This was simply another hurdle on his road to personal independence and, hopefully, fortune.

He wrote: *July 20, 1861—Tomorrow the battle will come. I am ready.*

It was almost seven p.m. when Micah finished the volume that ended on the eve of battle. He sat back in his chair and felt a tinge of shame. He had been judging Icobar Ohlm since the earliest pages. True, Micah didn't like Icobar, would have avoided his acquaintance had they been contemporaries. But now there was that last entry.

"Tomorrow the battle will come. I am ready."

This, from a boy no more than eighteen or nineteen, far from home, briefly trained in lethal effectiveness, and yet, according to his journals, never before confronted with his own mortality.

"I am ready."

Naïveté, innocence, or bravado? In any case, there's courage in it.

This was a side of Icobar Micah had not encountered before, and was not sure how to weigh it against his previous contempt for the author's pettiness.

Micah had met many soldiers in his years at the Defense Department. Many were combat veterans. To a man, they didn't tell war stories, at least not to a civilian.

Micah got up, reached for the next journal, stopped. *Tomorrow*, he told himself. *Tomorrow*.

He was about to sit back down, glanced at the time on his weather station clock, and realized he hadn't eaten all day. Not like him. A missed breakfast was no big deal, but he usually paused for something in the afternoon.

Odd. Am I hungry? I don't know.

He went to the kitchen anyway. There was the sausage he'd bought with the steaks. He sliced it up and started frying it on the stove. Out the kitchen window, the last rays of sunset streaked Green End Pond. When it completely faded, the sausage aroma convinced him he was hungry after all.

A hoot and a shriek outside, rustling of tree branches. He looked out again. Birds taking flight from the bushes and trees on the shore, quickly swallowed by the deepening darkness out on the pond. It happened like that sometimes, if he walked out in the early morning, inadvertently flushing them. But there was no one out there now.

He looked toward the chicken coop, an outline within shadows, here and there some white paint on a few boards that hadn't been completely weather-stripped.

Micah squinted, not sure he'd actually seen anything. Did see it, was sure now.

On the single step up to the coop sat a silver-gray coyote, placid as a retriever waiting for its master. Shoulders erect, head slightly forward. Turning now, only its head, toward Micah, golden rings around the black eyes, ears back.

Bigger than the one he'd seen on Monday morning and more silvery with black highlights.

Micah's landscaper had warned the coop might attract varmint. The scent of rotten eggs and chicken crap, though undetectable to Micah, would hold forever, the contractor said. But aside from the occasional raccoon it hadn't seemed much of a lure during Micah's years on the property.

What do you want? Micah felt himself mouth the words.

Nothing. The coyote straightened its head and looked forward, its profile fading into the shadows.

Micah looked where it looked.

Kodi was sitting in the darkness on the steps of her trailer. Micah could make out the camo pattern of her clothes, though her face was unpainted. The rifle was not in sight.

The coyote and Kodi contemplated each other for a moment. Ending when Kodi nodded once and then bobbed her head toward the north.

An agreement, a primal signal?

The coyote stood leisurely, made a circle on the dirt at the foot of the coop, and drew one more glance at Kodi. Walked a half-dozen strides toward the pond, veered sharply, and bolted up in the valley's direction.

When Micah looked back for Kodi, she was walking toward the shore. She squatted, as he'd seen her do before, and began doing something with her bare hands in the dirt.

Micah shut off the stove, his meal burnt beyond salvage. Put the frying pan in the sink to cool before disposing of its contents. Looked back out the window. Saw only the first rays of moonlight. No Kodi, no birds, only shore and water, the water still as glass.

Micah didn't bother attempting another supper. Cleaned up the mess in the sink and read for a while, then went to bed to continue reading. When Micah last looked at the clock on his nightstand it was eleven forty-five. He wasn't exactly tired but his eyes felt strained so he shut the book and turned off his lamp.

He tried to blame it on not eating, because for the second time in less than a week, deep sleep was elusive. Could have made a sandwich or had a glass of milk, but didn't, so continued to drift in and out.

The clock showed three A.M. when he distinctly heard Kodi start her pickup and back out to the street. Micah thought about her encounter with the coyote. More precisely, his own encounter also for he and the animal had stared at each other before he realized Kodi was in the yard as well.

A triangle, he thought. *Coyote, Kodi, me. But not completely. Kodi and I never looked at each other. At least not at the same time. Maybe she did notice me in the window.*

At four-thirty Micah got up and dressed. He donned his peacoat and found his flashlight. This time, he wasn't pretending to hunt for a new walking stick.

It was two hours to sunrise. He went first to the chicken coop. The coyote's paw prints were still in the dirt where it circled. As he turned to walk away, he stepped on a thick splinter of board detached from the coop and it snapped under his boot. Micah jerked his head. For a second, he thought it was a distant rifle shot.

Suppose it was a shot. What the hell were you gonna do anyway? he posed to himself, bitterly, to his surprise.

From the coop he went to the pond shore and raked the ground with his light. It was small, but out of place, so he found it.

A yard from the water and away from any brush was a pile of stones. No more than eight inches high, six in diameter at the base, rounded, tapered, rising to a single stone on top. Micah bent to it and brought the flashlight closer, mindful not to disturb it with either his feet or his cane.

The rock at the top was different from all the others beneath and supporting it. Not the gray-brown-purplish stones common to this shore. Nor did it have any flecks of quartz, also common. Yet it did seem luminous in its own way. Deep, dark red was most of its surface, with a single, thin golden-yellow vein. In all, it was about half the size of a golf ball, as were the ones below, each with at least one semi-flat side giving the whole pile a modicum of stability.

She couldn't have done this whole thing last night. She was only briefly in this spot and when I looked again she was gone.

Micah backed away and awkwardly lowered himself to sit on the ground. At first, it was cold on his buttocks but would have to do because he didn't trust his balance to squat. Not for long anyway. And somehow he thought he would be here for a while. How long? For as long as it took.

CHAPTER NINE

With the morning fog came the dampness that Micah felt seep into his bones. A few times he dozed. Briefly, before a twitch or cramp or the quack of a duck snapped him back, he fixed on the pile of stones. Sunlight had started coming through the fog. Single rays, as through a prism, snatching color from the water and trees. One beam, pure white light, thin as a pencil. It was aimed true at the red rock on top. Struck its yellow seam and ricocheted, split as two, red and gold, to end as small blossoms on the side of Kodi's trailer.

It lasted maybe a minute, until more fog evaporated and the mist was gone and when Micah looked out at the pond it was a clear morning and birds were plentiful across the water's surface. Looked directly across the pond. Expected to see the deer again. Didn't, and didn't bother to turn for the coyote.

Gravaroom . . . the birds to wing at Kodi's return.

He was stuck. Left leg useless and unfeeling, right leg tight and achy. Tried with his stick, couldn't get leverage. Felt like a fool. Attempted rolling to his knees, failed, and listed until his shoulder touched the ground.

"Micah, Micah, are you okay?" Kodi approaching swiftly, urgently. "What's the matter? Please tell me you're all right."

"All right," he said. "Got a bit locked up. It'll pass."

"I don't care, Pumpok, you can't stay on the ground." Was beside and above him reaching down with both hands. Camo paint across her face, in hunter's garb, no blood visible this time.

Micah took both hands and allowed himself to be pulled to his feet. When he dropped her hands, she put hers to his shoulders to assure both of them he was steady. Convinced he was, Kodi stepped back, stooped, and retrieved his cane.

"Here. Take your time," Kodi said.

Now Micah felt twice the fool. "You're wondering what I'm doing out here." Leaned heavily on the cane.

"None of my business. It's your land, do as you like."

Nice way to settle it for some, unfinished for Micah.

"I was walking and saw the stones." Pointed to them with his free hand. "Amazing how the sun seemed to find it. The light reflected and . . ." He stopped.

Kodi waited for two breaths so as not to finish the sentence.

"It's a prayer mound. '*Okosu-wacuw.*' Anything else it is or does, you brought to it."

And that's how it was finally settled.

"How'd it go this morning?"

"Two more." Kodi jerked a thumb at the pickup. The edge of the tarp was visible. "One in the valley, the other in Albro Woods. Do you want to see?"

Micah nodded, took a step. Everything, such as it was, was coming back and he followed Kodi to the truck. She untied the tarp and drew it back.

"The gray one's from the Kempenaar. Male, young but still full-grown." Kodi pointed to the one beside it. "The female I took in Albro Woods. Long past bearing pups. Too lean in the flanks, you can tell. Don't think she'd have lasted another winter. But I stole her last summer."

That stung Micah. "Don't say that, not to me. We agreed it was the job. That's all."

Kodi smiled. It was delicate, sweet, and sad at the same time. Then she looked out over the pond. The birds were returning.

"Nothing is ever only one thing," she said. "Like the *okosu-wacuw*. It does something for me and something different for you."

They looked back into the bay of the pickup. As before, it was not a gruesome scene. The coyotes lay side by side with eyes closed. Without asking, Micah knew they had been cleanly shot through the hearts.

"When's Ranger Ferzoco coming for them?"

Kodi replaced the tarp and started tying it off. "She's not, we have to go to her."

The "we" was not lost on Micah. "How come?"

"Got a call from Wawokak. People are starting to fan out and try to find me. Both sides, hunters and animal rights people. Somebody even got arrested for trespassing hoping to see me this morning on private land. Had a camera with him. Last thing Wawokak wants is a Fish and Wildlife truck rolling up to the LaVeck residence at dawn."

And skyline both of us, thought Micah. What he said was, "Good thinking."

"Well," and Kodi smirked, "that's Wawokak's job."

KODI WENT to clean up and change. Micah went in the house to wait for her. He didn't know where the Fish and Wildlife facility was, so couldn't figure how long their trip would be. Didn't mind if it took all day. Used the bathroom and checked his e-mails.

One from Laurie Catlett.

> Micah,
>
> Be on the lookout for strangers as I warned. This operation is gaining a public head of steam. Report anything out of the ordinary.
>
> LC

I go from doing her a favor to taking orders.

RESPOND:

> Roger that – ML

That'll show you who's cozy.

SEND.

He shut down the computer.

Kodi came through the back door and called, "Ready?"

"You bet."

Micah went to the kitchen. He immediately noticed something about Kodi.

"What's that on your nose?" he said.

Kodi felt it with the palm of her hand, wiped, then looked. "Cold cream. Only thing that gets the paint off."

"Guys do that too?"

"Yeah, but they won't admit it. Some even swiped it outta my footlocker."

Might as well tell her. "Wawokak gave me a heads-up to watch out for strangers nosing around, like she warned you."

"She called?"

"E-mailed."

"She must be pissed at you."

"I can handle it." Pause. "Actually, I don't care."

"Check. Let's get a move on. Maybe we can make it to Cranston before rush hour."

MIDDLETOWN TO Cranston was maybe forty-five minutes. Micah was disappointed. At least Providence meant a proper road trip. But Cranston it was.

They drove into Newport and over the Pell Bridge onto Jamestown and then another bridge to the mainland. The sun was up and the water beneath the bridges sparkled.

Riding in silence, there were a thousand things Micah wanted to ask her. All the opportunities before this, he had never pried. The impulse was getting beyond his control. He admitted to himself he cared about Kodi, and wanted to know things about her. But where to start?

From 138, they got on Route 4 and hooked up with Interstate-95 and were moving at a good clip, when Micah suddenly felt sad. He missed driving. Had to give it up a year earlier when his condition manifested itself in his right leg as well. Not that much, no comparison to his left, but enough that a sensible citizen wouldn't take the chance. It was his own choice. A valid driver's license was still in his wallet.

Kodi interrupted his thoughts. "You okay? You fully recovered from this morning?"

"Sure, why?

"This is our exit and you haven't said anything since Route 4. I haven't known you long, and you're not exactly a magpie, but that's close to a record."

She made him laugh and everything melancholy slipped away. They swung up around the exit ramp and into Cranston.

"Know where you're going?" he said.

"Yup, been there twice while this thing was being put together."

This thing, Micah thought, *the hunt*, and remembered their cargo under the tarp.

"You know Ranger Ferzoco before this thing?"

"About two years."

"She Indian too?"

"If she is, it's the Portuguese kind. It's not that, I served with her son in Iraq, Staff Sergeant Vosco Ferzoco. You can guess what we did with that name. Called him Coco."

"Like the clown or hot chocolate?"

Kodi chuckled. "Well, it wasn't for Chanel Number 5."

"Is he still in the army?"

Without missing a beat, "Coco died in an ambush. When I finished my tour, I looked up his mother. The shrinks in uniform call it closure. Personally, I don't know what the hell it was, but it felt right, and Ferzie and I have been friends since. Not that close, we sorta keep in touch."

Micah wanted to ask Kodi if she was with Coco when he was killed, went to, but her cell phone rang.

"Kodi," she said flipping it open. She listened and only said at the end, "Okay, Ferzie, roger that. I'll find it and see you there." Snapped the phone closed.

"Change of plans?" Micah said.

"Fish and Wildlife is staked out with assholes too. There's even a camera truck from some TV station. We're gonna meet in a parking lot before the stores open. Any idea where the Garden City Mall is?"

"Indeed, I have. Turn around."

After several circles around the near empty Garden City Mall parking lot, Kodi cut through an alley to the loading and refuse area behind the stores. By a trash compactor idled a nondescript silver van. As they drew closer, Ranger Ferzoco waved from the driver's side window. Kodi swung around and parked rear to rear with the van, leaving enough room between for the job to be done.

"Sorry this was last minute," Ferzoco greeted them. "My boss is furious, but the gapers and protesters aren't physically on our property so there isn't much he can do."

Ferzoco gave Kodi a quick hug and shook Micah's hand.

"How is it at your place?" Ferzoco asked Micah.

"So far, we're still off the grid."

This time he was allowed to help with the transfer. With his butt wedged on Kodi's tailgate he was able to slide the bottom tarps forward and edge the coyotes up to where Kodi and the ranger could get a better grip and lift them into the van.

They weren't as neat and peaceful-looking in the cramped bay of the van so Micah looked away and Ferzoco covered them with an extra tarp.

Task completed, Ferzoco filled out two receipts.

"Going again tonight?" Ferzoco asked Kodi.

"No, I'm working it every other day and then off for the weekend. Their packs are separate, but they border and communicate. A mission like this is new to them. Every lull and Coyote will think it's over."

"Even at that, with your rate, could be six a week. Be done in two months."

Micah did the math in his head; forty-eight coyotes give or take. *How many are there on Aquidneck Island?*

Kodi was telling the ranger that was only an optimal possibility. "If this local interest gets any worse, that could be cut in half, or maybe even shut down completely."

Ferzoco agreed but said there was a bright side. "Portsmouth, and even Tiverton and Little Compton on the mainland, a bunch of towns are starting to perk up and take this coyote-thinning seriously as an option. Bet you get work for the rest of the year."

"You got that much pull, Ferzie?" Kodi asked.

"Let's say I'm owed a lot of favors and nobody, at least in conservation, wants this turned into a circus."

It's already a media circus, thought Micah, but didn't speak his mind.

Ranger Ferzoco got in to the van. "Ring me on the next one. Unless something happens, we'll meet here again."

"Roger that," Kodi said.

Ferzoco drove away.

Kodi turned to Micah. "Can you put up with me for another two months?"

Micah pretended to contemplate the notion. He had an idea, but wasn't ready to share it. He said, "It's not so bad. And there is the chicken coop we can burn down together."

"Deal."

On the drive home Micah asked what Kodi would like for dinner.

"You don't have to do that," she said.

"I want to. What'll it be?"

Kodi thought a minute. "Your steak and stew are great, but you know what I could really go for?"

Micah couldn't imagine.

"Chicken," she said.

"I can do chicken. How do you like it?"

"Only a hunch, but I bet you got a sweet recipe from Alsace-Lorraine."

Micah felt his face redden because she remembered the story.

They stopped at the Whole Foods in Cranston and Micah bought what he needed. Next, they hit a distributorship for wine and beer. In the lot, Kodi pulled a wallet from her jeans.

"You gotta let me cover some of this."

"When it's your turn to cook, you buy."

"Thanks, Micah."

"I thought I was Pumpok."

On the ride to Aquidneck Island Micah asked Kodi if she had any plans for the afternoon.

"You wrote the manual," she said. "I've got to service my weapon. Clean it by the book."

"Ha, that's one I didn't write. The weapons maintenance manual was written by a sixty-three-year-old lady from West Virginia. Angie was her name, I think."

"Bullshit, an old lady?"

"I swear. Did I mention she is a retired sharpshooter for the West Virginia State Police and former US Marine?"

"No, I think you left that out, on purpose."

Micah only smiled, he was already trying to remember his mother's recipe for roast chicken. So far, all he recalled was an onion and wine.

And garlic too. The only thing Mom didn't put garlic on was ice cream.

CHAPTER TEN

The chicken was decidedly more Lorraine than Alsatian, with as much butter in the sauce as wine, and Micah was certain Mama LaVeck would have approved.

Any awkward newness to their arrangement had vanished. As did all the topics for polite dinner conversation. After cleaning up, they repaired to the parlor. Micah built a fire in the hearth for it was a throwback, cold March night, got fresh drinks for them both, and sensed his resolve fortified. So he asked.

"What is it you want to know?" Kodi replied.

"What I said, who are you, really?"

"You mean coyote hunter isn't enough."

"That's now; I want to know what was before."

"The army? Iraq and Afghanistan?"

"Further back."

"Why?"

"I think you know why. I want to learn about Kodi, the helpful, before she became Kodi, the cold."

"I'm not cold to you," Kodi said.

"You're right, you're not. That's how I know there's another side."

Kodi stared at the fire a long time. When she spoke, it was more at the fire than to Micah.

"My people are Pocasset, a subtribe of the Wampanoag Confederacy. Wampanoag territory starts on the shore of Narragansett Bay and ends at Cape Cod. The Pocasset were mostly in Tiverton and Little Compton for spring and summer. We were one of the first tribes to have a squaw sachem. Her name was Weetamoo, which means Sweet Heart. She was, too. She had five husbands."

Micah hadn't expected Kodi to go that far back; nevertheless, he was enthralled and didn't interrupt the history lesson.

The Indians of New England, all traceable to the Algonquin, through the Narragansett, had no concept of "ownership" when it came to land. The earth was to be shared as the gift it was meant to be from the Great Spirit. The first white settlers were welcomed, and so emerged the true story of the first Thanksgiving at Plymouth colony. But when the feast, and then the severe winter, were over, the European concept of ownership manifested itself. Skirmishes and raids, perpetrated by both sides, ensued. Treaty followed broken treaty.

Kodi stopped. "You know the rest."

"What happened to Weetamoo?" Micah asked.

"She drowned in a river evading capture by the English. She was a strong sachem. They figured if they eliminated her, the rest of the tribe would quiet down or go away."

"Did they?"

"Many."

"Where were you born?"

"Swansea."

"Ah, Massachusetts."

"The Pocasset didn't draw the state line. Somerset and Fall River in Massachusetts were all ruled by Weetamoo along with Little Compton and Tiverton in Rhode Island."

"When you were young, did you get to Aquidneck Island much?"

"Not much. It's kinda expensive over here."

Big yawn. Kodi, Micah realized, had been up since two or three in the morning for her hunt.

"To be continued," he said.

Micah excused himself for another glass of wine. When he returned, Kodi was sound asleep, with her bare feet up on the couch and her head nestled in the crook of her elbow. He went to the spare bedroom and got a wool afghan. After draping it over the sleeping Kodi, he quietly fed more wood to the fire for her, and went to bed.

In the morning, Kodi was gone, the afghan folded neatly on the couch. Micah looked out the kitchen window. The shade was down on the trailer, no light flickering behind it. Micah went to the study.

E-mail from Laurie Catlett. Dated today, early for Catlett.

> Micah,
>
> Emergency session of Town Council tonight at 8:00.
>
> Come alone.
>
> LC

Come alone, another dig. Bitch.

He did not respond.

E-mail from Roger Ohlm thanking Micah for his reply and wishing him speedy progress.

Micah had almost forgotten about Icobar Ohlm.

You want speedy, you read the damn journals.

Again, no reply.

The weather station read fifty-one degrees; the cold front had passed with the night. He picked up the next volume of the journals, Icobar at war.

ALMOST A month's gap from the previous journal's last entry. Icobar was wounded at Manassas. During an attack, his company came under heavy fire from the Confederate line. Icobar was felled by a musket ball in the left knee. Far ahead of the Union line due to the charge, he could not be removed from the battlefield until the exchange petered out when a Yankee flanking maneuver drew the rebel fire elsewhere. A comrade helped him to the field hospital, Icobar using his own musket as a crutch.

Micah sensed the difference in the narrative immediately. It was as if Icobar were now writing in the third person, as if the wound happened to someone else and Icobar was only an observer.

Micah remembered reading *The Red Badge of Courage*, first in high school, then while writing the Confederate general's memoirs. How vividly personal the action was in the book. Emotion in almost every line. It made you feel the fear and dread. All absent in Icobar's firsthand account.

This is somehow important, Micah thought, though unsure why.

He got up and went to his bookshelf. Took the published edition of the Confederate general's book, found a remembered passage, and reread it. The general had been verbose, but precise, as was the style of that day. Exact about troop deployment, staff members, and orders. Yet intertwined with the historical data were his reflections and opinions, desires and fears. Not so much for posterity, Micah always believed, so much as for relief from the onus of command.

Back to Icobar's account. A description of the field hospital where triage, in the 1860s, meant wounded officers first, enlisted men later, regardless of the severity of the injury.

Just like that: officers first. No griping you had to wait into the night bleeding and, with a shattered knee, in excruciating pain. No opinion.

Icobar, who are you suddenly? You, who flew into a rage when the landlady raised your rent one penny a month after you'd been in the boarding house two years. Now, all of a sudden, it's officers first. And that's okay. Icobar, you might lose that leg.

Icobar didn't. It was, however, the end of his infantry service. He was ordered back to Washington with the rest of the invalids no longer fit for duty in the field. Was told the knee would eventually fuse, but be unbendable the rest of his life.

Micah felt her presence, put the journal down, and spun slowly in his chair. Kodi was standing in the doorway. She smiled, so Micah smiled too.

"Good morning," Kodi said.

"There's an emergency meeting of the Town Council tonight."

"Think I'll be fired?" Kodi said.

"I doubt it."

As she had before the last hunt, Kodi told Micah she'd be gone for the day. Same explanation, errands off-island. He didn't want to make a nuisance of himself, so wished her well and said if she needed anything he'd be home until he left for the meeting.

"Be careful tonight," he added.

"You be careful," Kodi said. "I think that meeting is going to turn out rougher than my coyote hunt."

"I meant watch out for prying eyes."

"Which I can split at 1,000 yards."

"I'll warn them of that tonight."

Kodi grinned.

When she left the house, Micah couldn't help wondering.

Is she going to Massachusetts? Does she still have family and friends there?

One part of him hoped she did. A part that wished Kodi more than the friendship of a gangly legged, washed-up writer and the mother of a dead comrade in arms.

After Kodi's truck left the property, Micah walked down by the pond. The *okosu-wacuw* stones were still there, but different. The red top rock was gone, replaced with a greenish stone. It was as smooth as the first, but less luminescent in essence. Micah wondered what it meant.

Different prayers?

Somehow, after everything else, it was a question he could be comfortable asking. Coming from Pumpok, that is.

THE MEETING room at Town Hall was so full, the folding chairs were removed and everyone, except the council and the mayor, was expected to stand. Micah noticed there were three extra chairs set to the left side, off the long conference table, yet still on the platform. Ten years of council meetings, he'd never seen that before tonight.

Around the room, Micah saw the regular attendees, an array of business and religious leaders along with the heads of prominent organizations and clubs: Elks, Kiwanis, VFW, and the like. He noticed Anne Selig from The Potters League, an animal protection society that also operated a shelter for lost or abused dogs, cats, and injured wildlife. Selig only attended council meetings if a pertinent issue was on the agenda. Micah assumed professionally dispatching coyotes met her criteria.

A half-roomful of new faces.

Melvin Sturgis, Aquidneck Wine and Spirit Shop proprietor, was a newcomer. He said hello to Micah, then sidled up next to Ginny Dacosta, also new, owner of the Middletown Cheese Emporium. Micah chuckled to himself. *There's a match made in heaven.*

In a far corner, helping himself to water from a cooler, was Dr. William Mackey, in blue blazer with the Rod and Gun crest affixed to breast pocket, also another first timer. The *Newport Daily News* and the *Providence Journal* had their familiar representatives. These two reporters were huddled with three others with press credentials dangling from lanyards.

Micah took his usual spot, by the exit, careful his cane didn't obstruct anyone passing by. Mackey passed him and nodded once in some kind of recognition. Micah returned the nod.

From the anteroom door behind the dais, Laurie Catlett entered, placed papers on the podium, scanned the entire room with one sweeping glance, and took her place at the extreme right, last seat at the table. She opened her portfolio and began flipping pages.

Mackey came back. He looked at his watch and then at Micah. "Do these damn things ever start on time?"

"Usually," Micah said. He looked to his left where people were still filing through the entrance. "Maybe they're waiting till everybody's in."

All that got from Mackey was a "Harrumph." He shouldered his way forcibly through the crowd back to the watercooler. As he passed, Micah caught the odor of whiskey.

The anteroom door opened again and the council members entered and took their places. Momentary pause. The entrance of Mayor Mary Boyd. Behind her came three people: a man, then a woman, and another man. Micah recognized each, mayors all, from Newport and Portsmouth on Aquidneck Island, and Tiverton on the mainland. The extra chairs were for them.

Boyd called the meeting to order, apologized for the cramped quarters, and moved the reading of the last meeting's minutes be waived as this was a special session on a single topic. It was seconded simultaneously by two council members.

After requesting everyone's patience and cooperation, Boyd read a prepared statement. Questions would follow. A better than average orator, a la Margret Thatcher without the accent, she gave her report, punctuated by crowd eye contact at appropriate intervals.

The coyote hunt was underway with results better than anticipated. Two nocturnal forays had resulted in four animals killed, their carcasses delivered to the Fish and Wildlife Division. There had been no lapse in public safety and no citizenry inconvenienced. To summarize, the operation was virtually invisible to the residents of Middletown and would continue until the proposed impact on the coyote population was achieved. Certainly before the summer tourist season commenced with Memorial Day Weekend.

Micah remembered Ferzoco's estimate and recalculated in his head.

Maybe longer than that, Mayor.

So successful, Boyd continued, similar initiatives were now being considered by neighboring townships. She introduced the three other mayors.

At last Boyd came to the purpose of the special council session.

"Our efforts have raised undue amounts of curiosity and speculation, bordering dangerously close to interference," Boyd said. "Quite frankly, I want it stopped immediately. A full report will be issued by this council at the conclusion of the exercise. And not before," she stressed. "I met today with our chief of police. Anyone impeding the hunt to satisfy self-interest, or advance a cause, will be accountable under the law. Such irresponsibility not only hinders our progress and swift resolution, but endangers public safety. I ask, no, I expect townspeople to conduct themselves with propriety until this matter is concluded. Let the professionals do their job." Long pause. "Any questions?"

There were many, all at once.

"Who's the hunter?"

"Where's he staying?"

"Why can't we get a schedule of the hunts?"

"Send him to my place, I saw a coyote yesterday."

Boyd used the gavel. "Order, order. One at a time and raise your hand."

Out of all the hands, she called on Dr. Mackey.

With obvious high opinion of himself, Mackey waited for quiet before posing his question.

"This project is funded by tax dollars. As a Middletown taxpayer, I demand to know who's being paid for this hunt. And why pay at all? The membership of the Middletown Rod and Gun Club will perform this service for free. You want to give away our money, give it to the schools, the parks, and senior residences."

Unfazed, Boyd raised her hand before Mackey went on. "Which, exactly, is your question, Dr. Mackey?"

Unfazed as well, Mackey said evenly, "Who is the hunter?"

"A temporary contractor for the township."

"That's not an answer."

Boyd treated him to a wry smile. "Let me ask you this, Doctor. What are the names of the men on the crew that pick up your trash? Who's the driver that plows your street in winter? The inspector that checks your sewer or the landscapers of our beautiful parks?"

Mackey lost it. "Dammit, don't be absurd."

"Municipal employees and contractors. That's how they're named. Any further details are spelled out in their contracts and the annual audit. I suggest you, and everyone else, be patient. As for your sports club, it is neither a professional service entity nor insured by the township for liability, and, with no disrespect intended, I'm not certain it would survive the rigid vetting process we apply to all town contractors. Which is why we hired a professional, and not a sportsman, in the first place."

"Harrumph," from Mackey, and he stormed from the room, butting anyone in his way.

CHAPTER ELEVEN

When Micah returned from the meeting, Kodi was not home. That surprised him, eleven P.M., she had not hunted at night before this. Or was she still wherever she had gone? He put up water for tea and read his book. Concentration was elusive. Micah's mind kept replaying clips of the council meeting.

Mayor Boyd's message had been clear. The hunter was not to be bothered. Dr. Mackey's exit did not end the inquiries.

Who is it? Why is it a secret?

Boyd remained adamant. So too were council members. Questions directed at them on the topic met with stony faces, a no comment remark, and deferral to the mayor.

At least she has loyalty.

He put down the book and opened a notepad. He started a list of people who might know about Kodi. It included the mayor, Catlett, and the Town Council. To that he added the Middletown treasurer who would be writing checks to Kodi. Then the Chief of Police Harry Reismann. How many of his officers did Reismann have to tell? Micah put a question mark.

I hope Harry's got loyalty too.

Next came Ranger Ferzoco. Did that mean others at Fish and Wildlife? Another question mark. That made two areas of potential vulnerability.

Micah thought back again to the meeting. Specifically, its aftermath. The motel owners and innkeepers had formed a cluster. It was March, no tourists, business was slow. No doubt they were comparing notes to determine if one of them was unknowingly hosting the hunter. So too was grouped the trio of sporting goods shop owners, the only three that sold guns and ammunition.

When Laurie Catlett passed him, Micah had complimented her on the mayor's prepared statement. Without stopping, she'd said, "Thanks." Then she did stop, turned, and came back to him.

"It's going to get worse," she said.

"No doubt."

"Mary will fucking ruin anyone that leaks, and they all know it. Stay alert down there at the pond."

"I've got an Indian tracker for that, Laurie."

"You can really be a bastard."

Sitting in his kitchen, sipping his tea, it still made Micah smile.

When Micah woke up he knew instinctively it would be one of those rare March days. Didn't need to check his weather station, could feel it in his bones. Normally cantankerous on rising, his bones felt light and strong at the same time. It was contagious and spreading. On his way to the kitchen he opened every window he passed. Still quite cool outside, but would get exceedingly warmer. Micah remembered last year around this very time, a record high of eighty-four degrees.

Records are made to be broken. Micah knew it wouldn't last. After the record breaker, it went back down to the forties. But that did not mean it should be wasted, surely the opposite.

It was two hours to sunrise and Kodi's truck still absent.

Because of the meeting, he'd missed dinner the night before, holding to a schedule that included a forty-five minute walk to Town Hall. Sometimes he took a taxi there and back. And, often enough after meetings, someone would offer a ride. Last night had been too, too . . .

You're a writer, what's the word?

Micah wouldn't have accepted one anyway, or taken a cab. Didn't want someone who knew him, or a bored hack driver, encountering Kodi.

Hunger, that's where his mind was again. He set about making breakfast.

After eating, it was time for a walk around the property. The green stone still on Kodi's *okosu-wacuw*. Green End Pond full of birds. He tested himself. Micah told Mackey he was an amateur bird-watcher. That was true—if not in practice, at least inclination. Started with the ducks. Ruddy ducks and northern shovelers. To the trees. A blue-gray kingfisher, a female cardinal, and right at the edge of his property, in the branches of a Japanese maple, a Cooper's hawk, watching and biding. Wind out of the northeast, warm and light.

The hawk to wing.

"Mr. LaVeck."

Micah turned. A uniformed police officer Micah recognized from around town, but didn't know his name.

"Yes, Officer, how can I help you?"

African American, he was in his fifties, but trim and athletic-looking. Trace of a smile and cool, steady eyes under the brim of his cap.

"Patrol Sergeant Foster." He touched the visor with index finger. "Chief Reismann sent me over." Foster paused to give Kodi's trailer a thorough once-over look. Said nothing about it. "Mind if we talk inside?"

"Not at all, Sergeant."

Foster now took in the whole property with his eyes in a smooth sweep. "Lovely piece of ground you got here, sir."

"It's Micah, and it is that, lovely."

"Elmer. We should go inside."

MICAH COULDN'T believe it and protested immediately.

"I hardly know the man. All we've said in ten years is 'Good morning' and 'Merry Christmas.' "

Foster hunched his shoulders and shook his head.

"You're on the town line, Micah. Technically, he's a Newporter."

"Damn right he is," said Micah, agreeing. Newport, the jewel of the three towns on Aquidneck Island. Home to America's Cup Races, the International Tennis Hall of Fame, jazz and folk festivals, the mansions along Bellevue Avenue, even a Kennedy compound. Middletown and Portsmouth were more agrarian. They benefited from the overflow of tourists, but it was home, not a resort.

"Nevertheless, he has a lawful point," Foster said with exasperation.

"On my own property?"

"You can park a trailer on your own land any time you want, for as long as you want. But you need a permit to live in it, even on private land. Zoning regulations. Otherwise every citizen with a misfortunate relative could plop a camper in their yard and, as they say, there goes the neighborhood."

Micah knew from when they first sat at the kitchen table that Patrol Sergeant Elmer Foster knew exactly what was going on with the trailer. Chief Reismann had handpicked Foster to deliver the news. Other issues loomed as well.

"Do you think he's been spying on her?" Micah said.

"I doubt it. If he knew the facts, the news would have spread by now. Instead he calls the cops. My guess is the trailer's blocking his own view of the pond."

"So it's gotta go," Micah said.

"That's what the chief says. If this guy makes a formal complaint, there'll be a public record. A file with the owner's name. It's best to move it."

"How much time have I got?"

"Seventy-two hours. Can you handle it? The chief is willing to help."

Micah racked his brain. One idea dovetailed into something else he'd been thinking. Maybe a possibility. The legal campgrounds on Aquidneck Island were as obvious and public as the motels. That was not an option.

"Elmer, tell the chief he can do me a favor. Wait the three days and then come back and take it away. Not impound it, with all the paperwork, merely stick it in your impound yard until this is over."

Foster slapped his hands on the table. "I like it, Micah, and I'm sure the chief will as well. You're off the hook, the cops look good, and the neighbor's got his view back. Works for everybody."

Almost. Let's hope it works for Kodi.

So much for the gorgeous day. Sergeant Foster, through no fault of his own, had ruined the mood. Micah went to his study to work. He grimaced when he picked up the journal.

The Icobar Ohlm of the earliest pages, recalcitrant and petty, made Micah think of his neighbor.

Newporter, mind your own business.

Icobar was healing well, though his knee was as the doctor predicted, sore and hardly flexible at all. Icobar wrote that, except for having sensation, it was the equivalent of walking on a tree limb. His nurse suggested a cane.

A brother gimp. I might get to like you yet.

Icobar was offered an honorable discharge along with a citation for his bravery at Manassas. Not a medal, a citation on a scroll. He took the scroll but not the discharge. With a letter of recommendation from his commanding officer, Icobar secured a transfer to the Quartermaster Corps. The war was broadening, able-bodied men were needed at the front. Administration was needed to handle supplies. Clerks, as Icobar put it, didn't have to walk so good. It was better than going back to his uncle's print shop with nothing but a scroll.

After he learned the ropes, it was simple enough. The goods came in from vendors and were meted out by requisitions. Every transaction and movement recorded in immense, bound ledgers. Icobar worked in a building outside Washington in a room with seven other clerks. They recorded bills of lading and prepared manifests and transport orders. Icobar strove to be thorough and precise. On several occasions, the lieutenant in charge complimented Icobar on his penmanship. In a few weeks' time, he was lent out to other departments to write official communiqués. The bookkeeper was becoming a scribe.

Micah actually began to feel proud of Icobar. The young man, aside from being cited for bravery and wounded in action, was starting to achieve something for himself. Micah was not the only one who noticed.

One morning Icobar was called into the lieutenant's office. The officer shut the door and asked Icobar to sit. He took a requisition from his desk and asked Icobar if he could copy it. Copy it exactly to another similar form, just as the original appeared. When he was done, the officer compared the two documents and declared them a perfect match. Icobar was sent back to work with a satisfied clap on his back from the lieutenant.

Icobar didn't get it yet; Micah did.

The scribe is becoming a forger.

The bay of the pickup was not covered with a tarp, empty from cab to gate. Micah looked from his window to his weather station: two fifteen and seventy-four degrees. Back to the window. Kodi got out of the truck. She wore a gray sweat suit, plain, no army markings. Her face cleaned of camo paint, ebony hair fluttered by the breeze.

Kodi reached back into the cab and withdrew the Winchester and a backpack. She went to the trailer, disappeared inside, and came out without the gun or pack. Micah kept on watching.

She walked to the edge of the spit, stooped, and picked the top rock off her *okosu-wacuw*. Though he couldn't see it, Micah remembered it was green. Kodi made a fist with the stone inside and shook it vigorously beside her ear as if the solid thing were made to rattle. She stopped, opened her palm, and stared at it. Delicately she lifted it to her lips and appeared to kiss it. Stared a moment longer, closed her fist, and flung the rock far out to splash in Green End Pond.

Micah did not want to watch anymore, but could not help himself. Kodi stripped off the sweatshirt, then the pants, and stood naked at the shore, the coppery patina of her body framed by the water. Micah caught his breath, not in lust, but in wonder at the pure beauty of it all.

Before he realized it, she was wading into the water a pace at a time, then faster, deeper, until it reached her knees and she lunged forward into a dive below the surface. A long moment later, she emerged, far out, and began to stroke evenly, the ducks gliding out of her way.

She swam almost to the other side. Stood while it was still deep enough so that when she turned to face back, her breasts were settled in pools on the surface, ringlets of ripples forming circles around her. Then she swam back.

Micah stood and clenched his cane. Passing the pantry he grabbed a large bath towel and hung it over his arm. Could he, should he? He didn't know and he didn't care. What had Kodi told him?

"It's your land, do as you like."

I don't think she had this in mind.

By the time he reached the trailer, she was back to the shore. Stood and came from the water. Grabbed her hair from over her shoulder and wrung it like a rag. Beads of water along her skin afire with the sunlight. The red of her skin turned gold except in the darker places beneath her breasts and between her thighs.

Micah came forward, averting his eyes as if looking at the town sign a few yards distant along the shore. Held the towel out in Kodi's general direction.

"Thought you could use this. Warm day, but that water's got to be damn cold."

He felt the towel lifted off his arm.

"Thank you, Pumpok."

He brought his eyes back only as far as the *okosu-wacuw* on the ground.

"What happened to the green stone?"

"It had a journey to make where I can't go."

"Is that a sad thing?"

"No, Pumpok, a very natural thing."

"Then I'm happy for it."

"Look at me."

Micah did. Kodi was wrapped in the huge towel, breasts covered, down to her knees.

He nodded at the pond. "That's the water supply; you're not supposed to swim in it."

Kodi laughed softly. "I didn't pee in it. Can't say the same for the ducks."

"They're not the problem."

"It's only a convenience while I'm on this job."

With that apology, Kodi stepped up into the trailer and held an arm back to keep the door open for Micah. Whatever he expected, this wasn't it. A cot, her open duffel bag on top filled with clothes. A few other garments hanging from pegs on one wall. The camp lantern, as Micah suspected, in the center of a drop-down table by the one window. A counter with hotplate, teapot, and bags of tea. Some tins of food: tuna, chili, a can of bean paste, all no-frills generic store brands. No coffee. At the end, a narrow door Micah assumed was a toilet.

"I know it's not much, but will they take care of it?"

"The sergeant assured me it would be fine. You've got the word of the chief of police."

It had been settled over an early supper while Kodi told him about the morning's hunt.

Only one coyote this time. A male taken on Tyler's Farm, one of the agreeable landowners. Afterward, Ranger Ferzoco suggested an alternate exchange site yet again. Things were still out of hand in Cranston and security had become paramount. Even the mall before store hours was too risky.

They met at Ferzoco's house in Little Compton. Kodi cleaned up and borrowed the gray sweat suit. Ferzoco would deliver the carcass to Fish and Wildlife after nightfall.

"It was a '*cacaw*,'" Kodi said. "In Pocasset that means one and only, a loner, not part of any family or pack. Considering his age, I'd say it means his mate probably died sometime before, like maybe last season."

"You weren't hunting last year. You think Tyler shot it?"

"Creatures die, Pumpok, they don't have to be shot."

When Micah had told Kodi about the sergeant's visit and the neighbor's complaint, he got the impression she was not surprised.

"Maybe it's time to move on," she had said.

"Or move in."

"What?"

"I have a spare bedroom. It's yours if you want it."

Kodi had thought on that a moment. "Indians have great ears. I think I hear Wawokak pulling her hair out."

It was settled. Micah would help her bring whatever she needed into the house. On Monday, the Middletown police would tow the trailer to obscurity. Kodi's pickup didn't pose a problem; no legal gripe could be made against it being parked on Micah's property.

This gave rise to another issue in Micah's mind and one he chose not to pursue for the time being. The trailer and the pickup both had valid Rhode Island registrations. Somewhere, in this, the tiniest state in the union, Kodi had to have a legal address.

CHAPTER TWELVE

The weather held for Saturday. Micah had the same feeling deep in his marrow.

Good, I need to be quiet and not stumbling around.

Kodi was Micah's first overnight guest at 18 Green End Avenue who hadn't slept in the same bed with him. The bathroom separated the two bedrooms, so he postponed his shower until later. Donned jeans and a sweater, and went to the kitchen as quietly as possible and got around to yesterday's newspaper. Full report on Thursday's special town meeting, minus Dr. Mackey's rude departure. Separate article on the success so far of the coyote hunt. Third article on growing acceptance and appreciation of the plan, including a key judiciary step: the injunction had been denied. This meant public property could be hunted with advance permission of state or local authorities.

Open season on public land. He wasn't sure if that was a good or bad thing. *They may expect higher and faster kill numbers.*

Heard the toilet flush.

Her hair was every-which-way and she wore a tee shirt and gym shorts.

"Good morning. How'd you sleep?"

"Like a bear in his den."

"I take it that means you were comfortable."

"Hmm."

"I tried to be quiet," he said. "I suppose that didn't work."

Kodi slid into a chair at the table.

"If this is gonna work," she said, "you can't do anything different. Pretend I'm not here and do your routine. Otherwise I'll feel terrible and we'll have to think of something else."

"On one condition: that you do as you damn well please as well. Come and go, eat and drink, whatever you were doing when you weren't hunting or with me."

"You mean like swimming naked in the pond?"

"I'd advise only through tomorrow. When the trailer's gone Monday, our neighbor will have a full view. Not that I think he'll complain about this particular violation of the law. Newporters pick their battles selfishly. He'll let it slide."

"Is he a dirty old man?"

"No idea, hardly know him. Now, I'd rather not know him at all."

"Are you?"

"Which—selfish or a dirty old man?"

Kodi reflected before deciding, rubbing the back of her neck under her hair. "I don't know why I asked. I truthfully don't think you're either of those. Too easygoing, open, and honest."

"Not to mention, respectful."

"Yes." Kodi nodded. "Definitely that too."

"I'm a lot older than you, Kodi. I haven't learned a lot, but I like to tell myself I've mastered the basics. Young men look at the world one way, older men another. And if an old man tries to kid himself, the rest of his life will have no satisfaction whatsoever."

"You're not that old," Kodi said.

"Old enough and, with my disease, qualitatively older than that. It lends itself to a certain perspective."

"Is that some kind of wisdom?"

"I wouldn't know. Must be one of those manuals I never got around to writing. Still in the research phase."

Micah worked in the study; Kodi cleaned the Winchester at the kitchen table. When she had set out her tools, oil, and cloths, there was something else. A small, but formidable, steel box with keylock.

"What's that?" Micah had asked.

"My sidearm."

"What kind?"

"Standard army-issue; Beretta nine mil."

"I didn't think you got to keep those," Micah said.

"You don't, it's not mine. It belonged to Coco."

"Oh."

Then they both set to their separate chores. At one point, still reading about Icobar's duties as a quartermaster's clerk, Micah heard the washing machine start.

All right, she's getting comfortable enough to do stuff around here.

Coffee break around ten thirty. When Micah got to the kitchen, a full pot was made, and untouched. The Beretta was disassembled on the table on newspaper. Kodi was cleaning the magazine with a wire brush.

"Right on time," she said. "I'll get it."

Kodi poured the coffees and set them on the table. Micah sat down.

"You wanted nothing different," Micah said. "I'm not usually served."

"Then don't get used to it." She moved the gun parts aside and sat down. "Any plans for this afternoon?"

Micah considered it. His life was what it was and he wasn't ashamed of it. "I don't stock a lot of stuff, only the basics, so I usually do a bit of food shopping."

"I'll drive you."

"Think that's wise?"

"We've got the truck; we can go off-island."

"Works for me."

Micah excused himself to go to the front porch for the newspaper. He regained his seat and left it, still folded, on the table. Kodi started drumming her fingers until he looked at her.

"Micah, read your paper."

"What about you?"

"I've gotta check the clothes in the dryer."

I am such an old fart, but he opened the paper anyway.

No Friday hunt to report about, due to the diversion of going to Ferzoco's home with the carcass, yet the *Newport Daily News* was not about to drop the story, even for a day.

COYOTE HUNTER MAY BE MORE THAN MARKSMAN

The *News* had an investigative reporter named Chuck Lewis. He clearly had his sights on a bigger readership than Aquidneck Island. Micah had read him many times and liked his stuff. Micah had once remarked to Melvin Sturgis at the wine store that Lewis could make the tide table in the paper sound like a miraculous event.

This was different. For this story, Lewis had either reached a long-shot conclusion and made his facts work for it, or he had a tip. The citing of sources was too vague to be sure. Micah read it a second time.

Kodi returned.

“They’re still trying to pin you down,” he said. “A writer in the *News* has a theory.”

“What sort of theory?”

Micah recounted the article. Lewis had interviewed everyone who participated in the five necropsies of the coyotes Kodi had shot. Next, he consulted with a dozen sport hunters around the country, each highly skilled with national reputations within that society. Last, he sought out the marine colonel in charge of security at the Newport Naval Base and asked the combat veteran to review his notes. Then he wrote his conclusion, which Micah read aloud for Kodi.

“In the opinion of people experienced to know, it is likely that Middletown’s clandestine coyote hunter is military-trained to an expert degree, and likely a combat-experienced sniper. No confirmation, or denial, was forthcoming from Mayor Mary Boyd’s office, only the often reiterated ‘no comment.’ ”

They drove and shopped all Saturday afternoon. Up East Bay into Warren and Barrington: foods, wine and beer, a book for Micah, new jeans for Kodi, and stuff they didn’t need but took their fancy. On her insistence, Kodi paid for the beer and the jeans. Micah put the rest on his credit card and didn’t keep track, because he didn’t care. They had an amiable spat when gassing up the pickup. Kodi won, alleging it was covered by her expenses billed to Middletown. Micah didn’t remember that part of her deal, but let it pass.

At one point, Micah named a few brand outlet stores in Fall River across the state line.

“I don’t go there for the outlets,” Kodi said.

Micah saw that as an opening. “So what do you go there for?”

"The Pocasset Indian Reservation is in Fall River."

"Is it nice?"

"Ever been on a res?"

"Not that I recall."

"The tourist part is nice; the rest is for Pocassets that got nowhere else to live."

"Bad?" Micah asked.

"I didn't say that, I meant isolated. People my age say that if you go back to the res to live after being somewhere else, you never leave again."

"So where's your home, or is it only your trailer?"

"Might as well be."

The way Kodi's face was set—looking straight ahead out the windshield, her firm two-handed grip on the steering wheel, and a nudge up on the accelerator—Micah sensed the subject was closed.

For now.

"Whatya say we go home?" he said. "I've had enough and I'm starting to peter out."

"Me too, and I'm cooking tonight."

THE IDEA of a home-cooked meal that he didn't cook himself was appealing. He fought off the urge to ask Kodi what she had in mind, content to be surprised.

A different surprise was in store. They had finished putting the groceries away when Kodi's cell phone rang. She looked at Micah before answering.

"I don't hunt on Saturday nights," she said.

"I know, but you can't not answer it."

Kodi flipped it open and said her name. She threw her head back and tapped the countertop with the fist of her free hand. She listened for no more than thirty seconds and answered, "I'll be there." Snapped the phone closed. "Bitch."

"Ah," said Micah. "That would be Wawokak. What did she want?"

"A meeting, tonight. I have to go to Town Hall."

"Only her?" Micah asked, wondering why Catlett didn't simply drive down to Green End Pond.

"No, your mayor too."

Now it made sense. Mary Boyd, as Micah knew, liked the trappings of her office. That included home field advantage in any situation. Then it didn't make sense.

What kind of advantage does she need with Kodi? And why two against one? Catlett's the professional at delivering Mary's bad news.

"If you don't mind," he said, "I'd like to go with you."

"I wouldn't mind that one damn bit."

THEY DIDN'T talk on the drive except when Micah had to give directions. He'd forgotten Kodi had never been to Middletown Town Hall, or ever met the mayor.

For a short drive, he had a lot to think about. Was the hunt over?

No, Catlett would have enjoyed pulling the plug herself, and in person, without deferring to the mayor.

Does the mayor have a new strategy?

Maybe, with the injunction against the hunt denied by the state, Mary would now authorize Kodi to hunt on town-owned land.

Was there some kind of personal complaint against Kodi, other than from that Newporter?

Nobody's seen her, or even knows who she is.

Laurie Catlett?

Laurie Catlett. She's already got some bug up her butt about me and Kodi. When I show up uninvited she's gonna . . .

"Where should I park?" Kodi asked.

Micah told her to go around the back. The front lot was visible from East Main Road. Also, officially, Town Hall was closed at night except for scheduled, public meetings. He was pretty sure the front door would be locked.

The back door was unlocked and the hallway lit. He led Kodi to the main staircase and up to Boyd's office. The door was closed. He rapped it twice with the handle of his stick.

"Good luck," he said to Kodi.

"Come in," Mary Boyd called through the door.

Kodi opened it and strode in. Micah counted to five, and followed.

The mayor was standing to greet her, Catlett was seated.

"Micah, a nice surprise," Boyd said. "I wasn't expecting you too."

Before he could answer Catlett said, "What are you doing here?"

Micah ignored Catlett. "Madam Mayor, let me present Kodi, my friend and your coyote hunter."

Boyd came around the desk and extended her hand to Kodi. "A pleasure, at last, my dear." They shook hands and Boyd escorted Kodi to a chair. Micah grabbed his own, a spare one from against the wall. As the mayor regained her chair, Catlett, Kodi, and Micah formed a semicircle in front of her desk.

"I must note at the start," Boyd was saying, "that we're very pleased with what you've accomplished thus far, Kodi."

"Thank you, Mayor," Kodi said.

Boyd smiled her campaign smile. "It's after hours, no one here but us, it's Mary."

"Mary," Kodi repeated.

Micah wondered if Kodi was already dreaming up a Pocasset name for Mary Boyd.

Boyd continued. "There have been several developments we, that is Laurie and I, wanted to discuss with you face-to-face. However, first I'd like to go on record that not only are you a valued, temporary public servant employed by this township, you are also, officially and personally, my guest in Middletown. Your comfort and safety are always at the top of my priorities."

Classic Mary Boyd, Micah thought.

"That's kind of you, Mary," Kodi said. "Everything's been fine. And Micah's been a real big help."

"No doubt," Catlett muttered.

Boyd stayed on program. "Chief Reismann informed me of a glitch in your present accommodations. That his department, at your request it seems, will be storing your trailer for a while."

"There was some kind of complaint," Kodi said. She nodded at Micah. "It's all been taken care of."

"How is it taken care of?" Catlett demanded. "Motels and inns are out of the question."

Kodi answered, speaking to Boyd. "I'll be staying with Micah, he has a spare bedroom."

"Whose convenient idea was that?" Catlett asked.

Micah also spoke directly at Boyd. "Whether Kodi lives in my yard or in my house, I believe the same purpose is served."

Boyd was nodding. "Well, that was easy enough. You sure you're all right with this, Micah?"

"Perfectly."

The nod again from Boyd. "Good, then let's move on, we've other matters to cover."

Boyd's agenda did include hunting on public town land, as Micah suspected. The new areas covered three parks, two cemeteries, and three reservoirs. One of the areas was Paradise Valley Park with its historic 1815 windmill. It bordered on a campground, still closed for the season, and the neighborhood of Gretchen Miller.

Maybe a coyote did get her kitty.

Next on Boyd's list was security. Public land, by definition, meant public access. Boyd was not about to close any to the public nor employ a curfew other than regular hours, usually dawn to dusk.

"We might as well hang up a sign that says you're there," Boyd said.

"I'll work around it," Kodi said. "There might be only one problem."

Boyd didn't like problems and raised her eyebrows.

"I'm a sniper," Kodi said flatly. "I make my kills undetected. That's how we're trained. So far I've also been retrieving the bodies. That's where I'm exposed. In the future, if you permit, I'll do my job and let Fish and Wildlife pick up the kills. I'll phone in locations to the ranger in charge."

Boyd sat back in her chair and exhaled with relief. "My, young lady, you seem to be settling everything for us." She turned to Catlett. "Don't you agree?"

Micah smiled to himself. Laurie Catlett was a political professional. *When your boss directly asks you to agree, you agree, or go work for somebody else.*

"Fine," Catlett said as if spitting out a bad taste in her mouth.

Boyd clapped her hands. "Where are my manners? Anyone for coffee, water . . . er, Scotch?"

Like beer, Micah hadn't drunk whiskey in years. But the offer and the moment were too good to pass up.

It was too late to think about cooking. At Micah's suggestion, they bought from the take-out window at Burger King. Then the drive home.

"If you don't mind me asking, what's between Wawokak and you?"

Micah wondered how to put it. "I think I broke one of her rules."

"Other women?"

He chuckled at the notion: Micah LaVeck juggling romances. "Not that. It was supposed to be casual, and it was, until the end."

"What did you do?"

"I broke it off before she had the chance to do the same thing."

"That's all?"

"In Wawokak's rule book, a major foul."

"So why did you?"

Micah pointed to his cane. "I was getting worse. Laurie thrives on another's weakness and makes it work for her."

"Bitch."

CHAPTER THIRTEEN

Sunday dawned gray but no rain. Micah knew the sudden taste of spring was only a tease. Kodi was still asleep in her bedroom. Micah wanted it to rain; she wouldn't have to hunt. He thought back to their Town Hall visit. Not about Catlett, he didn't give a damn about her any longer. About the way Kodi had conducted herself.

At the start, she had been courteous and respectful to Mayor Boyd, thanking Boyd for her compliments, concerns, and professing everything was fine. Attesting to Micah's help in the process, and not baited by Catlett. Kodi's tone and presentation put Catlett in sharp contrast, making the chief of staff appear irritable.

Mary was impressed. Even made Laurie agree. Some politicians are run by their staff chiefs. Not our mayor. Mary uses Laurie and their roles are absolute.

Later, there was the other Kodi. Micah was sure that impression wasn't lost on Mayor Boyd. Kodi, the professional, weighing tactics and logistics. She'll do the job she's paid for, let Fish and Wildlife deal with the result. Sadly, for Micah, it always came back to what the young woman was proficient in doing.

Killing.

Whether the rain came or not, the killing would continue. While Kodi did that, Micah was left with Icobar Ohlm. Back to work.

Not uninteresting, this part. Icobar's assignments in "copying" increased. And it wasn't always an exact rendering of the original. Sometimes the lieutenant brought a document, a letter or report, and a stack of blank paper on which Icobar could practice until he got his cursive to pass for the original. So crucial his efforts seemed to his superiors, Icobar was afforded the privacy of a room in the basement to work undisturbed. Icobar liked that, instead of the crowded room filled with scribes where he'd worked on ledgers. No need to feign interest in the chattering of his peers, or rise to salute officers passing through the room. He could do his work and be alone with his thoughts.

One evening near the end of office hours, he was visited by his lieutenant along with a captain and a man in civilian dress. The captain was introduced as Quinn and Icobar saluted him. When the civilian was introduced, the captain, it seemed to Icobar, purposely garbled his name so Icobar gleaned only the first syllable, "Del," and went on to compliment Icobar's work.

This Del fellow opened a satchel and withdrew a folded document and opened it on Icobar's desk. Asked Icobar to copy it onto one of the blank sheets of practice paper. Icobar read the document, some sort of field report detailing the writer's current strength in men and arms, and a request for additional soldiers and artillery pieces to be assembled at a Virginia location. The signature identified the author as a colonel. Icobar didn't recognize the name, didn't even know if the colonel was with the Union or Confederacy. And didn't ask. He copied the report. The two officers and the civilian were impressed with the result.

The captain took the copy and marked it up with a pencil and gave it back to Icobar. The civilian produced a flat piece of paper, blank, but identical in texture to the paper on which the original was penned. Even an apprentice printer knows fine paper when he sees it. Next, a bottle of ink and a stick pen unwrapped from a velvet cloth.

Icobar's orders: copy again onto the fine paper with the provided tools. This time, inserting the changes made by the captain in pencil on Icobar's practice draft.

The date changed, force-strength increased, requested aid doubled, name of town changed.

Simple, and signed.

Everyone was pleased. When the ink was dry, the civilian folded it to match the creases in the original. He put it in his bag and hurried from the room.

While the captain informed Icobar he was being promoted to corporal, the lieutenant burned the original and practice copy on a metal plate.

"Ready for a break?" Kodi asked from the doorway.

Micah turned. "I didn't hear you get up."

"You must be very busy. I'm up, showered, and dressed."

She was in the new jeans, a yellow tee shirt, and sneakers on bare feet.

"I'll leave you alone," she said.

"No, you're right; I'm ready for a break."

He followed her to the kitchen where his newspaper was already on the table, folded by his place. On her side, a laptop was set up and Micah recalled Kodi saying she had a computer, only no printer. The laptop was a bit battered-looking and Micah thought easily ten years old or more.

"You've been busy yourself," he said.

"I know Paradise Valley from my first recon here and Sweet Cherry Farm up the road from there. Remember?"

"I do, when I told you about the bird sanctuary and the protected lands."

"Paradise is not protected now. I was looking at Map-Quest to see if I can do Paradise and Sweet Cherry in one night. Otherwise, the area's spooked for a few days."

"What did you decide?"

Kodi sat down and keyed the computer. "I have to come from downwind in the valley and wait for a shot. If I get one, I still have to stay downwind and cross over to Sweet Cherry by this stream." She turned the screen to face Micah, pointing to the spot. "That doubles the distance back to my truck, me in camo with a rifle as the sun comes up."

"What's your plan?"

"You drop me at Paradise and then meet me at Sweet Cherry when I'm done."

Micah was surprised. He hadn't explained his voluntary suspension of driving. He also didn't own a car anymore and Kodi hadn't figured that out.

"I don't drive much nowadays."

"I'll get us to Paradise and home from Sweet Cherry. You've only got to do the leg in between."

Micah held up his cane. "You're asking me for a leg?"

IT DIDN'T rain, the hunt was on.

After a light supper, Kodi and Micah retired early. Micah set his alarm clock for two A.M. When it went off, he could hear Kodi in the kitchen. He didn't bother to shower and dressed warmly with a sweatshirt over his tee, under a flannel. That and his mac should be enough.

Kodi too, already dressed, in all camo. As Micah entered the kitchen, she finished applying her face paint.

"How do you do that without a mirror?" he said.

"Only got one face. Practice."

Kodi uncased the Winchester on the table, worked the bolt, inspected, and put it down. Into her backpack she put a box of cartridges. That was when Micah noticed the lock-box that was under the pack. Kodi unlocked it, withdrew the Beretta, and ejected the clip. Satisfied, she clapped it home, but didn't slide a round into the chamber. The handgun went into the backpack.

"Now we're ready," she said.

Kodi with backpack and rifle, Micah behind, they went out the back door and got in the pickup, Kodi driving.

"Remember when I told you about *nuhsh-ahta*?" she said. "That's Pocasset for 'killing place,' but only in my mind."

Micah nodded. *A frame of mind.*

"It's real," Kodi said, "and I depend on it."

Again, Micah only nodded his head.

"Except in an emergency, don't talk to me from here on out, unless I talk to you first."

"Why, you might shoot me?"

"Stop it, Pumpok. Now I have to start all over."

Micah said no more.

They backed out onto Green End Avenue.

"When I park, stay in the truck and keep the windows up. If the wind changes, Coyote will smell you for sure. Right about now he's starting to hunt. Coyote's a born hunter. Sees, hears, smells, senses everything."

Another nod from Micah's side.

Kodi drove the pickup around the point of Green End Pond and turned south on Valley Road. At the end, near the beach, a left onto Purgatory Road. The air was salty with the sea, and the stars were bright in the black, cloudless sky above the ocean. Where the road turned away from the shore was the intersection of Paradise Avenue. Kodi turned onto it and shut the headlights at the same time. One hundred feet up, she pulled to the side of the road.

"Gotta check the wind. Stay put."

Kodi got out and eased the door closed without letting it latch. Not a sound.

Micah watched and thought she might wet a finger and hold it up, as he'd seen done, but only in movies. Kodi didn't. Hands at side, she raised her head high and back, turned, and drew deep breaths from the four points of the compass in her head. Completed one revolution, and tested north and south again. Got back in the cab, pulled the door behind her with her shoulder against it until the first "click."

"I'm gonna ease up the road about a hundred yards. When I get out, you'll have to manage getting over here without getting out of the truck. Can you do that?"

Now she asks me. Micah silently mouthed, "Yes."

"Then sit tight till first light. Not dawn, first sunlight. Over there." She pointed past Micah toward the east. "When the sun breaks out, take the truck up to Sweet Cherry, right at the Paradise corner, and wait for me."

Kodi put the truck in gear and, at less than fifteen miles an hour, covered the hundred yards. She pulled to the side once more and killed the engine.

Micah badly wanted to say something, but remembered the rules. Kodi was in her *nuhsh-ahta.*

Now, she was out of the truck with rifle and pack.

Literally a pain in the ass, but Micah managed to get from his seat, across the console, and into the driver's seat. After catching his breath, he planted his left foot as far from the brake pedal as possible, in case it had one of its twitch episodes while he drove. It was only practice; sunrise was more than three hours away.

He wasn't cold, in fact, it was stuffy in the cab.

Windows closed, he reminded himself. He recalled how sweet the night smells in this season. The ground ripe and ready for spring. This was Aquidneck farmland, except for the park and a few houses along Paradise Avenue.

On his left, across the road, was Paradise Valley. He couldn't see it now, but somewhere up ahead on that side was the Paradise Windmill. Bet if he opened the window he would hear its sails creaking as they spun.

Looked right, a few dim outlines of houses. One of which had to be Gretchen Miller's.

Coyote country. Damn, that sounded funny on the shores of New England.

Started to doze.

NOTHING STARTLED him, but Micah knew he had dozed off, maybe only minutes; it was still dark. Looked at his watch. More like three-quarters of an hour. And not really as dark anymore.

He shifted in his seat and banged his knee against the door. Didn't mind it hurt, was concerned he'd made too much noise.

Heard an owl somewhere behind him. Craned his neck that way, saw the trees along the roadside, still bare, limbs bending with the breeze. Heard the owl again.

You woke me up, he said to the owl in his mind. Then added, *Thanks.*

Something moved outside, near, and to his right. Micah kept still. Saw the eyes, first. Golden-yellow eyes with the coal centers. The coyote was barely five feet from the front of the truck.

What have you got?

The coyote obliged, lifted its head, and waved its jaws side to side. A dead rabbit was in its teeth.

No more cats to prey on around here? Never mind, go on, it's okay. She's gotta be way up the valley by now. But stay clear of Sweet Cherry. Or not. That's between the two of you.

The coyote's head tilted and it dropped the rabbit in the road, then grabbed it deeper in its jaws. Sprang and ran, across to Paradise Valley, and out of sight.

Micah was sure he wouldn't doze again. It was getting light enough that he could have brought a book and passed the time. Instead he pondered on Icobar. What would become of the discovered talent for forgery? It would appear, barring some treasonous treachery among his superiors, that Icobar was helping the Union war effort with his doctored copies. What about after the war?

I'll be a son of a bitch, you hooked me, Icobar. I'll have to finish your journals. Still can't promise they'll sell, but you've got one interested reader.

Micah looked right, east toward the hills behind Hanging Rock. The glow of dawn blossoming above the woodland, the first rays vectoring out.

He started the truck. Besides the owl and his banged knee, the first sound he'd heard in hours. As the motor settled to an idle, he heard birds.

Sounds, for then he realized he hadn't heard one rifle shot his whole vigil.

Micah put the truck in gear and started up Paradise Avenue, following the curve, passing the windmill, and on to the corner of Sweet Cherry Farm. Pulled to the side and kept the motor running.

There was a copse of trees right at the corner that edged back onto the farm dividing two fields until a low rock wall finished the job. Kodi in her camo was coming toward the truck in a crouch.

She yanked open the passenger door. “Right on time, Pumpok. Get us out of here. There’s company up the road.”

Micah hit the gas and swung the steering wheel. Kodi kept her head down as he drove.

“What did you see?” he said.

“Green four-by-four nosing along the road back there. Real slow and sneaky.”

Micah checked the rearview mirror. “He’s stopped at the trees.” They went around the curve back toward Purgatory Road. “I don’t think he saw us.”

“I saw him, and got his plate number. My instincts tell me he’s no bird-watcher.”

Micah was inclined to agree.

CHAPTER FOURTEEN

Micah's leg was cramping from all that sitting so they stopped at Easton's Beach to change places. While Micah stretched his legs beside the pickup, he heard Kodi call Ranger Ferzoco. Kodi had shot one adult male in Paradise Valley and a female at Sweet Cherry Farm. She provided coordinates by referencing the road, large trees, and the stream. As Micah got in the passenger seat, she was giving a description and license plate for the green four-by-four.

"How's the leg?" she asked when she hung up.

"Better, a little walk always helps."

"Next time, I'll wait in the truck. You track Coyote."

Kodi laughed and so did Micah. Then he remembered.

"I don't have to track them, they come to me."

Kodi got serious. "What do you mean?"

"Before you came to Middletown, I'd never seen one. Since you did, three."

Kodi started the truck. "I've got to get this paint off and outta these clothes. Be home before the traffic starts, but I want to hear this. Don't forget."

She pulled out of the lot, scattering a bunch of squawking seagulls. They passed two cars but Kodi had pulled off her camo cap, fluffed her hair, and turned away as they came by.

Micah thought of something else. "What about your receipt? You've made two more kills."

"Not to worry, I trust Ferzie and Mayor Boyd."

Micah didn't feel it necessary to point out whom she omitted.

"What I am worried about," she continued, "is that guy in the SUV. He was looking for the hunter, I'm positive, Micah. You think it was dumb luck he came down Paradise Avenue this particular morning before dawn?"

"Don't know, what did Ferzoco say?"

"She can't do anything with the plate number, doesn't have the authority. Said I should call Wawokak or Chief Reismann. What do you think?"

"Neither, for now. The police are taking your trailer today. I'm sure it will be supervised by Sergeant Foster."

"You trust him?"

Kodi pulled into Micah's yard, leaving room to extract the trailer.

"I think you can put him and Reismann on your list with Ferzoco and Mary Boyd. But that's it for now."

Kodi showered first. Micah saw the cold cream jar Kodi had left on the table. Curious, he picked it up and examined the label. No chic fashion blend, a generic from a pharmacy chain.

Exactly like her, he thought. *All the creature comforts, generic.*

"Your turn," she announced, wrapped in one of the huge bath towels from breasts to knees.

Micah always avoided using those towels, they were too big for his liking, but every female that ever availed herself of his shower was drawn to them like magnets.

When he didn't budge, she asked, "What time you figure they'll come for my trailer?"

"No idea." It was a listless response.

"You okay?"

He felt a little foolish. Hadn't done anything except wait in the truck, and even stole a nap. "I think I'm a little tired."

"Lie down awhile," Kodi suggested.

"I'd rather not. A shower will help."

She smiled at him and went to her bedroom to dress. He remembered the sound of the morning birds, and then the owl. Liked living back on the land and not in a city. A pond out his back door. As natural as he ever expected his life to be, especially after he was diagnosed.

"You still here?" Kodi asked. Jeans and black sweatshirt Micah remembered from their first day. Nothing special about it, only he remembered it.

"I was only sitting and thinking," he said.

Kodi sat down across from him. "Think you're ready to talk?"

"About what?"

"Coyote. You said you've seen him three times since I'm here. Tell me, Pumpok, tell me about the three times."

She said coyote, singular, as if it was the same one over and over again.

Micah told the stories. The first one, when he saw the doe across the pond and the coyote spooked her to run away. Then the silver-gray one on the steps of the chicken coop, Kodi sitting in the darkness by her trailer.

"I didn't know you were there," she said.

Micah snorted. "Some Indian tracker you are."

"And the third?"

The coyote in the road, this morning, with the dead rabbit.

"You sure?" Kodi said. "That was downwind of me. I shot the male in the valley."

"I don't know if it was male or female."

"No way to be sure. I shot a female on the farm, but there could be a whole pack in this general area."

"Is this one of those: Why did the chicken cross the road?"

"No, I think you were dreaming."

"Nope, an owl woke me up."

"You heard an owl?"

"A screech owl, they're common around farmland."

"I know that, how many?"

"I think it was only one."

"No, how many times did you hear it?"

Micah thought a moment. "I really heard it only twice, but it must have screeched three times because I think it was the first that woke me up."

"So you only heard it twice."

"When I positively heard it, twice."

Kodi abruptly left the kitchen. Seconds later she returned. In her hand was a sack about the size of a pound coffee bag. It looked to be made of some sort of skin, and secured at the top with a hank of cord.

"Come with me," she told Micah.

He grabbed his cane and followed Kodi out the back door, across the yard, to the spot where he'd spent sitting as he waited. The spot of the *okosu-wacuw*. Since Kodi had thrown the green stone into Green End Pond to make its journey, the pinnacle of the prayer mound was still flat and stoneless.

Kodi opened the pouch. "Put your hand in and pick one, don't look."

Micah dug his hand into the bag. Felt the rocks, almost two-thirds of a bagful. They seemed roughly the same size, but their shapes varied, as did the tactile texture. Couldn't decide, somehow knew it was important, felt one with an edge graze his thumb, seized it. Withdrew his hand.

Micah held it closed in a fist, tight. Released his grip and let the stone sit in the palm of his hand. Held it out to show Kodi: a black stone with flecks of pink quartz, shaped somewhat like a tiny pyramid.

Kodi took it from his hand with her fingertips. She turned toward the pond and oriented herself. Bearings noted, she held the stone high, first north, then east, south, and west, pausing an instant at each point. Micah heard a soft chant under her breath. She eased the stone into her palm and made a fist. Brought it to her mouth and blew on it. Kodi held her hand out.

"Take it."

Micah picked the stone from her palm.

"Make a fist with it. Touch your forehead, your lips, your heart, stomach, and feet."

Micah performed the ritual, relying heavily on his cane and struggling to do the foot part. Slowly, with awkward effort, he straightened up.

"Put it on the top of *okosu-wacuw*."

It pained him to go low again, yet he did it. Setting the stone atop the others, a point of the crude pyramid shape for its acme. Gasped a few seconds, half for breath, some for pain, and straightened up.

"Am I supposed to say something?" he said.

"You already did."

"Will my rock make a journey too?"

"Can't say yet, maybe."

"Can't say, or won't?"

"There's only so much we can know until its time has come."

Micah nodded.

"Are you a shaman?" he asked.

"My people say *moyikow*, and I'm not. It's a simple blessing, when you've heard an owl three times, at one time, in one place."

"It's a bad omen."

"Could go either way, that's why we make a blessing."

SHORTLY AFTER nine A.M. a Nissan flatbed auto hauler backed into Micah's yard. Micah saw it arrive; he was fetching his morning paper from the front porch, his weariness gone. A guy in the passenger seat called out his window.

"You LaVeck?"

"You got it, haul away."

"Can't, gotta wait for the cops with the paperwork. We're civilians."

Micah waved in acknowledgment.

Private contractors for town towing, budget cuts. I bet Laurie was lying about the town pumping out the trailer.

Two minutes later, a Middletown police cruiser showed up, Patrol Sergeant Elmer Foster at the wheel and alone. He got out and yelled, "Morning, Micah," and went to talk with the haulers, clipboard in hand.

Kodi came out on the porch. Dressed as she was, Micah didn't think it a problem. For all the haulers knew, she was his daughter.

After the paperwork was exchanged, Foster came up on the porch and tipped his hat.

"You must be Kodi. Pleased to meet you, ma'am."

Kodi shook his hand. Foster asked if everything in the trailer was secured for moving and there were no valuables left inside. Kodi assured him on both issues. Foster called to the haulers to go ahead with the job.

"You work with these guys a lot?" Micah asked.

"All the time. Usually to tow cars after DUI arrests. With all the prominent people in town that drink too much, they know to keep their mouths shut, or lose the contract."

"Good, but there's another problem."

Foster grimaced, asked what it was.

"Tell Elmer," Micah said to Kodi.

She moved closer to Foster. "Someone was tracking me this morning. He failed, but came close, I got his tag number."

Foster produced a notebook and jotted down the description and numbers. "I got a computer in the car, gimme a minute."

Kodi and Micah remained on the porch. They could hear the clink of chains and the winch working in the backyard. Foster returned from his police cruiser.

"Green Toyota 4Runner registered to Charles Lewis, Newport. Figure you know who he is."

"Chuck Lewis, *Daily News* reporter," Micah said.

"I'll call this in to Chief Reismann. Get Lewis to back off. Maybe lean on the publisher."

The flatbed was coming out of the yard with the trailer lashed down in back. One guy waved and they pulled onto Green End Avenue. Micah was thinking of something else.

"Be interesting to know how Lewis pegged the exact location."

Foster grinned. "Before Harry became chief, he was a detective with the Rhode Island State Police, a damn good one. Lewis will have his hands full."

Foster excused himself to walk around back and make sure the extraction hadn't caused any property damage. Micah appreciated that, and he and Kodi tagged along.

"Seems okay," Foster said.

Micah nodded. "Like nobody was ever here."

"Except for the tracks," Kodi said.

Micah said with a little rain it would be his old yard again in no time. It was never kept like a suburban showplace anyway.

"This should shut up your neighbor," Foster said.

A wicked idea came to Micah and he turned to face the chicken coop across the yard. "Maybe silence isn't what I'm looking for."

"What do you mean?" asked Foster.

"It's illegal to raise chickens on private home property in Newport, but it isn't in Middletown. I'm thinking of filling that henhouse with as many as it holds."

Foster was delighted. "Damn Newporter. And a couple of ornery roosters so he'll always know when it's dawn."

"Good-bye bonfire," said Kodi.

CHAPTER FIFTEEN

Ranger Ferzoco called Monday afternoon to report the two coyote carcasses had been retrieved and she had submitted receipts directly to Laurie Catlett. The rest of the day was quiet and relaxing. Kodi did her usual chores, laundry and rifle maintenance, while Micah worked a while on the Ohlm journals. Kodi was the chef of the evening, and prepared a dish of chouriço, rice, and beans—very spicy. Micah loved it.

"Is this authentic Pocasset food?" he asked.

"My own hybrid," Kodi said, "Indian and Portuguese."

"What's the Indian part?"

"Beans."

With the day and the meal behind him, Micah's second wind blew itself out and he started to nod off while Kodi watched television. He excused himself and went to bed. Kodi finished her program.

Tuesday dawned sunny, but cool. They took a walk along the rim of Green End Pond and down Valley Road as far as the dam. It grew warmer, the sun on the water igniting sparkling ripples. Waterfowl swam in clusters and Micah named as many as he could for Kodi.

On the walk back, Micah had them cut through the patches of woods, searching for a branch to fashion a new cane. Even with Kodi's help, nothing they found was suitable.

"Maybe not today, but we'll find one," Kodi promised.

The cell phone clipped to her belt rang. She plucked it off and checked the ID on the screen.

"Wawokak," she said.

"Answer on speaker."

Kodi pressed that button and took the call. "Kodi here."

"Are you out of your fucking mind?" shrieked Catlett on the other end.

"Excuse me?" Kodi said coldly.

"Excuse you, bullshit. You're finished, you crazy bitch."

Micah grabbed the phone.

"Shut up, Laurie. If you can't be civil, I'm hanging up. Kodi's done nothing to warrant such abuse. I'm ashamed of you."

"Get your head out of your ass, Micah," Catlett came back. "Or whatever other part of your anatomy is calling the shots. That dumb bitch splattered a coyote all over High Street. Half its head blown off, four pups whelping around it, not ten yards from a school bus stop. It's nauseating and infuriating. What the hell was she . . . ?"

"Stop it," Micah interrupted. "Kodi hasn't hunted since early Monday morning. I oughta know. I've been with her the whole time."

"Who the hell else would do it?"

"I suggest you involve the police, immediately."

Micah hit END.

Kodi took the phone back and dialed.

"Who you calling?" Micah said.

"Ferzie. I shot the male in the Kempenaar Valley last week. That's the mother somebody else shot. Those pups are orphans now, and won't last the night with all the other animals."

The call went through and Kodi told it all to Ranger Ferzoco. She was off speaker now, so Micah only got Kodi's side of it. He shook his head.

This was going so well. Why are there so many assholes in the world?

Then he remembered Catlett's anatomy remark.

You're loving it, Wawokak. You may be a smart person, but you're still an asshole.

Kodi hung up. "We better get home, Pumpok, this is gonna be a shitstorm."

First to arrive was Chief Harry Reismann, in an unmarked car and in plain clothes. Micah invited him inside the house.

"I need to see your rifles," he said to Kodi.

She came off a little cool and detached. "Like the papers I filed with you, only got the one, a Winchester Light 22-250. I'll get it."

Kodi went to the bedroom and returned with the gun case. She opened the case, extracted the bolt from the gun, and laid the gun and bolt on the kitchen table. Reismann picked up the rifle, examined it, put it down. He took a notebook from a pocket and compared the serial numbers.

"Checks out," he said. "Now look at this." He produced a cell phone, scrolled through some pictures, selected one, and handed the phone to Kodi.

Kodi stared at the frame. "Downright cruel. Had to be at least a .30-06 or .338 round. You could take down an elk with that load."

Reismann nodded. "That's how I figured it too, but based only on experience. It's not like I can muster a forensic shooting team, at state expense, for the murder of a wild animal."

"Butcher," Kodi said.

Reismann agreed with a grunt. Kodi handed the phone to Micah. Before he looked, the scenes flashed in his mind of the dead coyotes in the back of Kodi's truck, so serene and sleep-like. Looked. Sickening, and he said it again, aloud, "Sickening." He didn't know if the other two heard; they were still talking.

Reismann said, "The Fish and Wildlife ranger now has the carcass. She was also able to round up the four stray pups. They'll be sheltered until somebody decides what to do with them."

"What about the shooter?" Kodi asked.

"I got officers going door-to-door on High Street. See if anybody heard the shot or saw a vehicle in the area. That stretch of road is pretty wide open on the valley side."

Micah remembered their recon of the Kempenaar Valley and had an idea.

"Check video surveillance from the shopping center parking lot. Whoever did this probably parked there and came into the valley past the graveyard instead of from the street."

Reismann was impressed. "Damn good thinking."

Kodi eased up a little on the chief. Micah assumed she simply hadn't wanted to appear tense or guilty at the outset. Now, they were beyond that, way beyond.

"I was home all night, Chief. Micah can vouch for that. All morning too."

Reismann scratched his head. "I was sure you didn't do this, Kodi, not after the kills you've accomplished. This is something else, something sick. But the situation is complicated and I've got a job to do. Whether or not the mayor's on board with me, I'm suspending any further hunts until this is sorted out. I still have jurisdiction over firearms in this township. Agreed?"

"Affirmative, Chief."

Something else occurred to Micah. "What about Chuck Lewis?"

"We should be so lucky," Reismann said. "I ran the registry before coming here. No firearms in his name," and he reached to Micah for his phone back.

NEXT TO arrive, shortly after the chief's departure, was Fish and Wildlife Ranger Flavia Ferzoco. She and Kodi shared a brief embrace.

"Twenty-five years with the department," Ferzoco said, "never saw anything as gruesome as that. And I inspect roadkill at least once a week."

"I see you came in your own car," Micah said.

"Can't be too careful, the whole town's buzzing about this."

"Talk to Wawokak since this morning?" Kodi asked.

Evidently Ferzoco knew the name. Micah wondered if she also knew Kodi's for him.

"Yeah, she called," Ferzoco said. "Screaming on the phone I get over there and clean the mess up, pronto. I told her it wasn't my mess, call animal control or Middletown sanitation. My job is to collect bodies you put down for analysis, not keep the streets clean."

"What did she say to that?" Micah asked.

"Yelled louder with a string of vulgarities. I went and picked it up anyway, and gathered in the pups. I don't take orders from her. What I do for creatures is between the department and me."

"The hunt's on hold, Ferzie," Kodi said. "Chief's orders."

"Had to figure that would happen. The upside is: Reismann asked for a list of Middletown hunters who have been cited for violations or issued warnings in the past. I gave it to him."

"Was William Mackey on that list?" Micah asked.

"More than once."

Ferzoco gave copies of the receipts to Kodi that she had tendered to Catlett yesterday.

"Stay close to the ground and downwind until this blows over, kiddo."

"Thanks, Ferzie."

Ferzoco declined to stay for lunch and left.

"You think Mackey did this?" Kodi asked Micah.

"If it wasn't him, it's reasonable to assume he knows who. I don't know much about hunting, but if you join a club for it, I guess it would be to brag about what you've killed."

"Not many snipers brag; that's for assholes."

"How do you say that in Pocasset?"

Kodi had to ponder a minute. "*Wukak-yocan*, an opening from behind."

"Now do your slang thing."

Almost instantly, she said, "*Wuk-yocs*."

"Indeed," Micah said. "Middletown's got its share of *wuk-yocs*."

"Can I tell you a secret, Pumpok?"

"It's safe with me."

"There isn't even a word in Pocasset for coyote. When the first linguists wrote down our language in 1710, there weren't any coyotes this far east. But they're here now and it doesn't matter."

"What do you mean?"

"Past, present, future—we don't use tenses in our language. We say: Yesterday I hunt, tomorrow I hunt, today I hunt."

"Not today," Micah said.

The morning paper had Kodi's two kills from the previous day along with the now-almost-routine tributes to their skill and humaneness. It had gone to press before the senseless slaughter on High Street. Next to the article was an interesting sidebar with Chuck Lewis's byline: in the last two weeks the frequency of reported coyote sightings had dropped by almost a third in volume according to Animal Control of the Middletown Police Department. Micah pointed neither news item out to Kodi. What he did share was a Letter to the Editor from one "Concerned Citizen" which warned that a freelance coyote hunter let loose in Middletown was a "tragic accident waiting to happen."

Over the years, Micah had written several letters to the *Newport Daily News* on a number of issues. All were published. To the best of his knowledge, the newspaper did not print anonymous epistles. Every day on the Letters page, in a box near the bottom, was a policy statement that all letters, in order to be considered for publication, must include the writer's name and address. In ten years of reading the paper, Micah could not recall a single nom de plume before today's Concerned Citizen.

Policy change, or a deliberate opportunity to incite? Maybe both—the policy box was missing today.

At Micah's request, Kodi read the letter.

"The guy doesn't know what he's talking about," she said. "No sniper, marksman, or even a professional hunter, would be as careless as he says. There's rules, safety classes, licensing tests, enforcement. He's describing some *wuk-yoc* who shouldn't even own a gun."

"It's not the invectiveness that concerns me," Micah said. "It's the anonymity, which is flat-out counter to the paper's previously published policy, and, even more so, it's the timing."

CHAPTER SIXTEEN

Another summons from Mayor Boyd was inevitable and Kodi took the call during supper. This time, Boyd suggested her home for the meeting; staff people were at Town Hall working late on the bad press that would result from High Street, regardless of how unjustified. For a second, that's where Micah figured Laurie Catlett ought to be, setting the course and leading the troops, then realized Catlett would never let Boyd meet with Kodi without her personal supervision. No doubt, Micah thought, Catlett already got in a few cheap shots at the mayor for Boyd's bypassing her chief of staff in hiring Kodi.

The mayor lived on Longmeadow Avenue, four long blocks up Valley Road from Green End Avenue, but Micah suggested they walk anyway. It was a mild night, midforties in temperature, and Kodi agreed. They set out around seven. Good time was made, even with Kodi adjusting to the pace of Micah's assisted gait. And he was pushing it.

Mary Boyd was a woman of taste, but not extravagance. The house was sizeable, but subtle in appointments. Micah had been there for several Christmas parties and the retirement party of Boyd's husband, Jack Landsdale. Boyd was already moving up stones in the political pyramid of Middletown when they married, so she kept her maiden name. Micah was never clear what Landsdale retired from, something in business, but it was a lively party.

Micah knocked on the front door. Landsdale answered, greeted Micah, and was introduced to Kodi.

"They're in the big study," Landsdale said.

That confirmed it. *Catlett's here.*

Landsdale led the way.

The "big" study was a combination of library, office, and sitting room. The "they" was more than a pair. Along with Boyd and Catlett, Chief Reismann was present, all seated near the fireplace that was crackling. Landsdale situated two more chairs, forming a crude circle, and excused himself, leaving the room.

Catlett had her portfolio open in her lap, flipped numerous pages, and barely acknowledged the newcomers.

Without introduction, Catlett began, "The way I see it, we've got one option to nip this in the bud and set the record straight at the same time." She looked up at Boyd, who remained impassive, then back at her notes. She resumed, referring to everyone in the third person as if they weren't in the room. "There's a press conference by the mayor with the chief and Kodi. After the mayor's opening statement, the chief introduces Kodi as Middletown's contracted coyote hunter. He further states that, after a thorough investigation, it has been positively determined that Kodi is not the perpetrator of the crime on High Street. Therefore, that matter is still under investigation. Back to the mayor. She thanks Kodi for her services, praises the manner in which they were rendered, and declares an end to the hunt. Most important," a peek at Boyd, "the mayor cites that coyote reports are down 33 percent, according to animal control. The original goal was to see them drop by 50 percent; that was not achieved, but a damn good inroad was made since there is no reliable benchmark for comparison. Conference concluded. No questions entertained." Catlett looked up and swept the participants with one glance. "Open and shut, answers everything, ends on a positive note, case closed."

As if to underscore the finality, Catlett snapped her portfolio closed as well.

Micah looked at each; no one met his eyes except Kodi. Boyd was staring at the fire, apparently in deep thought. Reismann fidgeted a bit, eyes darting everywhere. Catlett had a tight-lipped, smug smile.

"Any other thoughts from anyone?" Boyd asked without turning around.

Micah said, "In my opinion . . ."

Catlett cut him off. "Sorry, Micah, your opinion doesn't count. This is a political issue for the mayor."

He would not be put off. "Which is why, I trust, she's seeking the opinion of everyone in the room. Politics is funny that way."

Catlett would have retorted, but the mayor turned and held up her hand for quiet.

"Bear with me, Micah," Boyd said, "I promise you'll have your say, but first I'd like to hear what Harry thinks. Law enforcement's perspective is vital in all this."

Reismann's face tightened. "Mary, I'm a cop not a politician. I'll only say what's true, regardless of fallout, and in compliance with my oath. First, Kodi didn't do it. Second, the investigation continues. There is no third. The rest is politics and doesn't concern my department."

Boyd nodded. "Thank you."

She looked again at Micah, briefly, but settled on Kodi.

"I'd like to hear your opinion, Kodi. It would seem you're at the heart of this, through no wrongdoing on your part. Your concerns have certainly earned my utmost consideration."

Kodi inclined her head slightly. "Thank you, Mary." She looked at Reismann, smiled. Looked at Catlett, blank-faced. Looked at Micah, smiled again. Faced Boyd.

"Micah and I had a long talk walking up here. Some of what I'm about to say includes his input. Good input, because he knows Middletown a lot more than I do, and has always struck me as an intelligent and fair man."

There had been no discussion. It was a hike to be on time and Micah's energy was absorbed in making it. But he liked what he heard, trusted Kodi, and may even have blushed a twinge.

"I don't understand politics, I'm Pocasset and we have different ways. I'm also an army veteran and value things like honor and duty. From my tribe and the military, I also understand the role of leadership. Good leadership is proactive, not reactive. That's what Micah and I were discussing."

Micah didn't know where Kodi was going, but his confidence never wavered. He looked at Boyd. The mayor appeared intrigued. Kodi knew animals, now Micah saw she could read people as well. He didn't look at Catlett, but imagined he could feel the heat of her fury from across the room.

"Go on," Boyd prompted Kodi.

"A decision was made to employ my services for the good of Middletown. Now it seems that Laurie would have a violent maniac dictate a change in public policy. That's not the way it's supposed to work. That's not what we do in the face of terrorism."

"Oh, for Christ's sake," Catlett erupted, "you're not seriously comparing what happened . . ."

"Quiet," Boyd rebuked her. "Continue, Kodi."

"We have to be stronger than our enemies, carry on despite their efforts to sabotage or stop us. In Micah's and my opinion, the hunt should continue immediately. Doing that is not only leadership, but, with my skills, demonstrates the difference between what you've contracted me to do and what some *wuk-yoc* did on High Street."

"What's a *wuk-yoc*?" Boyd asked.

"An asshole," said Micah.

The meeting dragged on another hour, even after Kodi's point was made and Catlett was overruled.

Mary Boyd was a lawyer and Kodi had a contract. The contract specified Kodi's identity not be publicized through all reasonable effort.

"Of course," Boyd had said, "we didn't foresee these circumstances at the time."

The clause was inserted so that Kodi didn't garner fame boasting her success in the bars, clubs, and spas of Aquidneck Island, prompting a fan base, or protests, and the resulting circus.

"Or free dinners with Bill Mackey and his buddies," Kodi interjected.

"Exactly," Boyd said. "Naturally this was all written down before we had the pleasure of meeting you and were confident that would not happen. Yet it cuts both ways. You had to respect our aims and wishes, and we have equal obligation to protect yours."

Kodi and Micah walked home afterward as the temperature dropped and the stars multiplied above them.

Micah, at last, could not contain his admiration for what Kodi accomplished at the mayor's house. He paused to catch his breath and rest his leg.

"Who was that woman back there?" he said.

"Which one?"

"You."

"Pumpok, you think all I know are guns and prey and prayers?"

"I think there's a lot I don't know about you."

"Now that's something that really cuts both ways."

They arrived home, Micah lit a small fire to cure the chill, and Kodi suggested a cup of tea.

WEDNESDAY MORNING Kodi went for a recon of Shady Stream Orchards. It was private land, as rural as Middletown can get, and the owner amenable to the plan from the outset. Now seemed the time for a quick, clean score. She asked if Micah wanted to come along. At first he said yes, then changed his mind.

"I'd only slow you down. My leg's a little stiff from last night's hike. If I waited in the truck, it might look suspicious as there's nothing there but fruit trees. You go ahead, I'm gonna catch up on some work."

"You sure?" she said.

Micah nodded.

"Anything you need while I'm out?"

No, with a shake of his head.

Kodi left and Micah got his newspaper from the porch. The leg wasn't only stiff, it hurt like hell in the hip and knee and his left foot felt like a cinder block. He was used to walking, enjoyed it, but last night he pushed too hard, too far, and coming home the chill air drove the point through his muscles and bones.

What the hell? It was worth it.

High Street was front page of the *Newport Daily News.* The photo was staged like a crime scene with a tarp covering the body of the dead coyote, police tape strung around it. The pups were not in evidence. The coyote hunter had been questioned by police and was not considered a suspect in the shooting that violated every ordinance governing hunting and control of vermin. Whoever made the shot had to have been down in Kempenaar Valley, fired up the ridgeline and, if the shooter missed, would have struck a home on High Street. Several homeowners of the area were interviewed by reporters. None had seen or heard anything. No comment from the mayor's office except that it was a police matter.

That prompted Micah to look at the Letters page. The box with submission criteria was back where it had always been.

Convenient.

Micah's hand started shaking and the paper ruffled. Tremors came and went occasionally, often precipitated by stress or fatigue. He couldn't remember one lasting this long. Knew his disease was often misdiagnosed as Parkinson's or Lou Gehrig's. Put the paper down and let it subside. Was glad he hadn't gone with Kodi. Missed it, but the right decision.

When he felt he could manage it, Micah went to his study.

Shortly after his promotion to corporal, Icobar Ohlm was transferred out of the Quartermaster Corps. He was excited about this. The most emotion Micah ever detected from Icobar since his rage when Cecilia Morris married Benjamin Wakefield. Icobar wasn't sure where he was going or for what duty. It had something to do with the civilian stranger in the basement with Captain Quinn, Del something.

Generals George McClellan and Joseph Hooker, with the consultation of Allan Pinkerton, a private detective from Chicago, were forming a new entity within the Army of the Potomac to be called Army Bureau of Military Information.

Intelligence, Micah thought.

For joining this new outfit, Icobar was given an allowance to purchase civilian clothes. He was also instructed to buy a valise suitable for travel of undetermined duration. All of which he did with considerable energy and pleasure.

Next came his first assignment.

The War Between the States was amassing more than casualties; it was gathering prisoners of war. A good deal of the initial fighting was done within a day's ride south of Washington, DC. Confederate prisoners were mustered through the capital and dispersed into the growing POW system evolving to meet the need for stockades.

In 1861 it became illegal to communicate by mail between North and South. With one exception. For humanitarian reasons, captured soldiers could write a letter telling the folks back home they were alive, not unaccounted for among the dead, and were receiving provisions and medical attention, if necessary. The Confederacy had a similar program. These letters were exchanged under flags of truce at predetermined times at designated points between the battle lines.

There was one unforeseen glitch in the charitable logic of the arrangement. The majority of Confederate prisoners came from families of poor dirt farmers, itinerant sharecroppers, and unskilled laborers. Many could neither read nor write.

Enter Icobar Ohlm, the scribe, among other things.

CHAPTER SEVENTEEN

Without reading any further in Icobar's journal, Micah grasped the role Icobar would assume writing letters for captured rebels—agent of misinformation and propaganda.

Misinformation and propaganda.

He remembered the anonymous letter to the *Newport Daily News* warning of a tragedy published the day before the shooting on High Street. Micah opened his e-mail and composed his own letter to the newspaper.

> Dear Editor,
>
> I presume the anonymous writer of the coyote hunt's "tragedy waiting to happen" is smugly satisfied events are unfolding as he/she would want without even considering, as substantiated in your paper, that the careless and inhumane slaughter on High Street was not the work of the professional hired to do the job. Enough said.
>
> What troubles me more is the one-day suspension of your paper's policy regarding Letters to the Editor. As a faithful reader of

> the Newport Daily News, I am confused and disappointed with such a decision in light of the volatility of the subject matter and the cowardice of the author. I had a higher opinion of your commitment to truth, fairness, and public safety. Your publication of that letter proved me wrong. Shame on you.
> Micah LaVeck
> Green End Avenue
> Middletown.

SEND.

Micah felt better immediately, having done something, almost as if he'd come to Kodi's defense in a gentlemanly manner.

He went back to the journal to see if Icobar Ohlm had done as well.

Icobar, in his new civilian clothes, was brought by carriage to an internment camp for Confederate prisoners outside the city. Whatever the scribe expected, it was worse than he could imagine. A pervasive smell of decomposition and sewage polluted every breath. Icobar, uncharacteristically poetic, referred to it as "the stench of defeat." The internees, all enlisted men and no officers, were in tattered clothes, any resemblance to a military uniform long disintegrated. A tent had been set up for Icobar outside the stockade. For a full day, except when he was treated to lunch in an officers' mess tent upwind of the prisoners, Icobar interviewed ten captives separately, under armed guard by a Union soldier.

Icobar had a prepared list of questions to be seamlessly interspersed with the prisoner's sentiments to be recorded by Icobar for the letter home. It wasn't until the fourth prisoner that Icobar got an interpretive sense of the Southern dialects.

At the end of each session he showed each prisoner what looked like a letter going home to the soldier's family, freshly penned on the spot. Since these men were chosen specifically because they couldn't read or write, Icobar wrote the same missive over and over ten times. To underscore the "humanity" of the gesture, Icobar forced himself to shake hands with each filthy unfortunate at the conclusion and wish him well and, someday, Godspeed home. All he really recorded, aside from any pertinent military information inadvertently revealed, were enough personal details to make the letter seem authentic to the recipient.

At the end of a long, distasteful, day Icobar was transported back to his new billet with the Army Bureau of Military Information. The following day, in an office, he penned the letters to be exchanged across the battlefront to reach relatives. Icobar recorded one in his journal to exemplify his duties and their purpose.

> Dear Ma,
>
> It eases my heart to write you I am alive after the battle and tell you not to fret no more. I was captured but not wounded. They moved us North where I will be, I reckon, till the end of this war.
>
> It is not as bad as you might think. We get good food aplenty and cots and blankets to sleep. The wounded are tended good. If we needing clothes or shoes, we get them too. All in all, Yankee boys are not as bad as I believed. Even darkies here, freed men, treat us kindly. Can you beat that?
>
> Makes me wonder what this bloody feud be about anyways. It's not like we own slaves, only rich folks do. Pa and me work the dirt like slaves

> ourselves. Nothing good will come of this and we can't win no-how. On the train we passed other trains with Billy Yanks by the thousands, cannon by the hundreds, all headed towards home. We didn't have enough muskets for our whole company. How we gonna win?
>
> A kindly sergeant from my outfit wrote this down for me to send as you know I never got 'round to learning. They say after Christmas they'll start a school for us prisoners to learn our letters. Won't that be something?
>
> I miss you all. Kiss little Penelope for me and one for Aunt Clara. Tell Pa I'm sorry to miss harvest. I kiss your sweet face in my dreams every night.
>
> Your loving son,
> Caleb.

Naturally, Caleb said none of those things, except the last paragraph for he did have a little sister, Penelope, and an Aunt Clara that lived with his family in South Carolina. What Caleb really wanted to tell his folks was that he had conducted himself honorably in battle, been captured with his whole unit, and couldn't wait to escape and get back across the lines to resume fighting for the "Cause."

In light of the new bureau's own cause, that would not do at all.

The power of the pen, thought Micah. *Or the e-mail.*

THE STORY of Icobar Ohlm had finally gotten interesting enough that Micah began making notes for a possible future rewrite. In all his studies and history reading, Micah had never heard of the counterfeit letter campaign. It didn't matter if it was successful or not as a wartime strategy, it was simply unique and interesting enough to warrant its story being told. His notes included researching the Army Bureau of Military Information to determine if the letters were mentioned elsewhere. He hoped not; that would make the story completely original.

Provided, he cautioned himself, *you're telling the truth, Corporal Ohlm, and it doesn't turn out you deserted back at Manassas.*

He heard Kodi's truck enter the yard and put his notes aside. Looked out the window. Saw Kodi walk to the pond shore. Remembered the Newporter next door. Hoped she wouldn't opt for another naked swim. Gave her a minute, she didn't, so went out to join her.

"How were the orchards?" Micah asked as he drew near.

Kodi never turned away from the pond. "Depressing." She finally turned. Her face looked pained. "I'll do what has to be done, this time, whether they pay me or not." The look went from pain to vulnerability. "Sometimes, Pumpok, aside from you and me, I prefer Coyote to the people in this damn town."

"What happened?"

"They're sick."

"The people? Yeah, I'd say a lot of them truly are."

"No, the coyotes. I found the den. Couldn't believe the mother would let me get that close, but she was nowhere around. Then I understood. Four pups, three stillborn, the fourth so deformed and crippled, I had no choice but to snap its neck and put it down painlessly. Somebody's not waiting for the hunt, they're poisoning them. I'm sure the mother and father are plenty sick too. It's a horrible way to die. I've got to hunt them down and end it."

Kodi's shoulders drooped and her whole body trembled. Out of reflex, Micah dropped his cane, stepped forward, and took her in his arms. She let herself melt into the embrace. He held tight and gently stroked the back of her head.

"You've got to call Ferzoco and tell her," Micah said.

"When it's done," she said into his shoulder, "only when it's done and they're out of pain."

"Then that's how we'll do it."

Micah stooped for his cane, then led Kodi to the house with his arm about her shoulders.

It had not been Micah's intent to join Kodi on the hunt, but he'd said it, and was glad.

As they walked, Kodi said, "I need a spotter. Sick animals are erratic. Will you do it?"

"If you think I can help and not slow you down, of course I will."

"You won't have to move a lot, we'll set up a stand as close to the den as we can get."

Micah wasn't sure what that was, but agreed anyway.

"Good, get plenty of rest," she said. "I want to leave earlier and set up in the dark."

They reached the house. Kodi stopped at the steps.

"Somebody's going to answer for this, Micah, this and High Street. I'm okay with what I do because I do it the right way. This one I'm doing for Coyote, not to clean up after some *wuk-yoc.* When it's over, I'm going to the chief and Ferzie. It's illegal to use poisons around agriculture. They better do something. I'll speak this to you, Micah, and only you. I've hunted more men in my life than animals. Not for any personal reasons, I had my orders. Now it's personal."

The *NUHSH-AHTA* was strong with Kodi that day and Micah gave her plenty of space. She spent most of the time in her room and, once, he thought he heard her chanting. Meanwhile he busied himself compiling more notes on Icobar. At dusk he napped for two hours. For supper they ate bowls of cereal. There was no conversation. Afterward Kodi went back to her room and Micah read his book. The time passed without notice.

"We better get ready," Kodi said soon after midnight.

Micah nodded and she went back in her room and Micah to his to change. Kodi emerged dressed in her camo jumpsuit and cap. Micah in black jeans and black sweater.

"You'll need this," Kodi said. She handed him the camouflage rain poncho she'd worn when she first knocked on his door in the rain. "In the field, keep the hood up and pull the strings to keep it tight around your face."

Micah slipped the poncho over his shoulders. It was snug, but wouldn't be a problem.

"Sit," she said.

From her pack she pulled a plastic case, opened it, and showed Micah. It had separate compartments with the colors of her face paints.

"Turn toward me."

Micah shifted the chair and Kodi sat in front of him. She smeared the paint onto Micah's face.

"Don't worry if you get any in your mouth. It's all natural from fruits and vegetables and peanut oil."

It did smell nutty to Micah.

"Now me."

Kodi turned her chair straight to the table and streaked her face without a mirror. Micah excused himself and went to the bathroom to see his face. What confronted him in the glass was neither fierce nor gruesome, only eerie. With the hood up and tied as Kodi instructed, Micah couldn't tell where the nylon ended and his skin began. Only the whites of his eyes stood out.

"If you're ready," Kodi called from the kitchen, "we can move out."

Micah peed and flushed the toilet. "Ready."

Kodi driving, they went up West Main Road and turned on Oliphant Lane. Shady Stream Orchards was to their left and the property ran north as far as the Portsmouth town line. Kodi pulled off the road to their right. Micah could make out the lines of trees in the orchards across the road. Kodi got out of the truck and did her wind test with four-corner breaths. Got back in.

"South wind, we're in luck. We can leave the truck here. Put your hood up."

"Wait a minute. What am I supposed to do?"

"After we set our stand, you watch my back and flanks. There's two out there; sick, scared, and angry. They won't be together, but they'll be close. All they've got left is each other. When I shoot the first one, it will flush the mate. You'll see it before I do. Tell me where, and hit the dirt, I'll get off a shot as quick as possible. Don't come up until I say so in case I miss and have to fire again."

"You never miss," Micah said.

"This is different."

That was all Kodi said, and got out of the truck. Micah got out on his side and came around. Kodi pointed to a spot across the road and then patted her shoulder that Micah should stay behind her. She took the rifle and pack from behind the seats and gave Micah one last signal, a finger across her lips.

Shady Stream grew several varieties of apples along with pears and peaches. The grove they entered was still marked from the last picking season when people paid to pick their own fruit. Kodi crouched and moved slowly between trees. Micah followed. He couldn't crouch as low because of his cane, but did the best he could and kept up with her. The trees got denser and there were cross trails cut through them every twenty yards or so. Micah could definitely smell the scent of pears, though the trees were still bare.

Deep in the orchard, Kodi took a cross trail west a hundred paces, then back into the trees. There was a tiny clearing right ahead. Kodi slung her rifle and then crossed her arms and rocked them back and forth as if with a baby. Micah understood she meant that ahead was the den with the dead pups. She stepped behind a tree, got down on one knee, and unslung the Winchester. Turning half around, she patted the ground for Micah's spot and pointed the directions he should observe while she sighted ahead.

The ground was soft, as Micah let himself down on both knees. He barely heard Kodi work the rifle bolt.

The wait.

Micah had his assignment so he couldn't watch Kodi, but he could hear her breathing soft, slow, steady. His own felt strained and his heart beat rapidly.

I don't know how long I can do this. I shouldn't have come. I'm gonna screw this up.

He wanted to look at his watch but the dial glowed in the dark. Thirty minutes, forty, an hour? He wasn't sure, but it felt twice as long. His body started to settle down.

I can do this. Then another thought. *Maybe the poison already killed them. They won't come and we'll find them at dawn.*

Movement by Kodi. Heard her take a long, slow breath, cut it off, and hold it.

Crack!

The shot not near as loud as Micah expected. Fought another urge to see, concentrated on his vectors. Heard Kodi work the bolt again. Saw something, wasn't sure. Remembered the eyes of the ones he'd seen. Felt Kodi shifting behind him. Saw it again, ahead, was sure.

"There," he said pointing, and forgot to hit the dirt flat.

"Down," Kodi ordered.

He was frozen, not out of fear. Micah wanted to move. The damn leg, the damn hip, damn knee, damn foot, the goddamn disease. He was stuck.

Kodi coming to her feet behind him; planting her feet she nudged him hard. Micah spasmed.

Crack!

Micah jabbed his cane in the ground, pain more than ever, forcing him to rise. Swayed upright. The top of his head glancing Kodi's chin as . . .

Crack!

Kodi fell with a groan and Micah fell on top of her. Grunting and gasping, Kodi eased Micah off her. A moan from back in her throat.

"You're on my ankle," she said.

"Sorry."

"Easy, I think it's only sprained."

Another groan, not from Kodi, followed by the most mournful wail Micah ever heard in his life.

"Shit," Kodi cursed, "Coyote's not dead."

I muffed her shots, Micah thought, and was sure of it.

Kodi propped herself up on one arm, drew off her pack with the other. Flapped it open and withdrew the Beretta. She lay back again, pumped the slide chambering a round, and released the safety. Another groan of pain. Another from the coyote out in the darkness.

"Pumpok, you'll have to do this."

She held up the gun. Micah hesitated, shuddered, reached for the weapon.

"How?"

"One behind the ear. Do it, Pumpok, Coyote needs you to do it."

Micah took the gun, moved it to his left hand so he could use his cane.

Kodi pointed between the bare trees at a narrow path. "Twenty yards, no more. Coyote's down, he won't get up. Close as you can, then behind the ear. If you can't see it, any center headshot will do."

"No, behind the ear," Micah promised.

He switched hands, gun in right, cane left, and started awkwardly through the trees. Counted his paces, then didn't need to anymore. Saw the coyote on the ground, panting, chest heaving. Got closer. Saw its tongue out, trembling on the dirt beneath its head. Micah noticed a white froth around its jaws. Older froth, yellowed with age, in the higher muzzle whiskers.

Poison, Micah knew.

He drew closer. The coyote shifted its head slightly on the ground, no sound now, one golden eye regarding Micah coming, hovering. Then it looked ahead, away from Micah, down the narrow cut in the trees bathed in moonlight.

Any fear drained from Micah. He got down on one knee near the front paws, dug his cane into the dirt for support, held out the gun at full arm's length. Coyote's head shifted again, and there was the ear, the other side of his face in the earth. Micah leaned forward, eight inches from the spot.

Squeezed the trigger, while he could still see before the tears.

CHAPTER EIGHTEEN

Micah made his way back to Kodi and sat beside her in the dirt.

"It's done," he said.

"I heard it."

Micah handed her the Beretta. Kodi engaged the safety and put it in her backpack. It was still way before dawn.

"How's the ankle?" Micah asked.

"I tried it; it won't take much weight."

"I'll help you."

Micah got to his feet and helped Kodi to stand on her good leg. She threw her arm over his shoulder and, keeping her sore foot off the ground, they limped and staggered back to the pickup.

"I'll drive," Micah said.

"I can handle it."

"No, let me."

He got her around to the passenger side and eased her into the seat.

"We should get cleaned up and changed," Micah said, "then I'll take you to the hospital and have it checked out. Maybe you broke something."

"No hospital, I don't have insurance."

Micah didn't want to argue, not here. "All right, then you think of something."

"Let's get home and put some ice on it. I'm sure it's only a sprain."

Micah started the truck and made a U-turn back up Oliphant to West Main. It was still dark and no other traffic. Every time they hit a bump, Kodi stifled a moan of pain.

"I think your stone can make its journey now, Pumpok."

"Why now?"

"Owl's message wasn't what would happen to you," Kodi said, "it was about what you'd have to do. That's why you only heard it twice. I don't imagine you've ever killed like that before."

"I can't imagine it now, and I've already done it."

"That's why it's time," said Kodi, "to send your stone on its journey."

Micah removed his face paint and then showered. When he was done, Kodi couldn't manage a shower so he filled the tub for her to bathe. She sat in the kitchen, leg elevated on another chair, with a plastic bag of ice on her swollen ankle. She leaned on him again and they got to the bathroom.

"Can you manage from here?" he asked.

"Is that a question or an offer?"

It made him smile for the first time in what seemed like ages.

"Put me down on the toilet seat, I'll take it from there."

"Call me if you need anything." He left the bathroom, closing the door behind him.

As he sat in the kitchen, Micah knew he was going to insist on a trip to the emergency room. Kodi's ankle was swollen to four times its normal size and a dreadful purple and blue. She was also, obviously, in a great deal of pain moving at all. He would be more than glad to pay for an examination and treatment.

Given the circumstances, the bath took a long time. When she finished, Kodi called for him and he found her back on the toilet seat wrapped in one of the huge towels.

He got her to the bedroom and laid out what clothes she wanted on the bed. He started to leave.

"Stay," Kodi said. "You're only gonna have to come back and help me to the kitchen."

Micah stayed, sat on the corner of the bed, and looked out the window at the trees. The sun was finally coming up.

"About the hospital," he said, "you've got to go and I'll pay for it." He could hear Kodi rustling the clothes behind him.

"Got a better idea. There's a free clinic on the res if you'll come with me to Fall River. That way you don't have to pay and nobody on Aquidneck Island has to know."

All things considered, it made a lot of sense and Micah agreed.

"But I drive," Kodi added.

"When do we leave?"

"After I call Ferzie."

"Priorities, I've always liked that about you."

"You would have liked giving me a bath too."

"No doubt."

Micah felt her hand on his shoulder.

"If you don't mind my asking, is that affected by your disease too?"

"Is this that gray area of question versus offer again?"

"I don't know, but I'm curious."

"Then I'll be honest. It's been awhile, but not the last time I tried. So I think everything still works."

"Wawokak would freak."

It was a pleasant thought, but only that for Micah.

"She wouldn't be the only one."

KODI SPENT a long time on the phone with Ranger Ferzoco. Along with the sites of the two kills, so Ferzoco could collect the carcasses, Kodi described the den and its location and what she'd had to do the day before out of mercy for the sick pup. That led to a discussion on the poisoning. At the end, because she had to, Kodi said the final coyote was wounded and had to be put out of its misery with a nine mil to its head.

"Yes, I said nine mil, Ferzie," Kodi repeated. She did not mention it had belonged to Ferzie's son, Vasco "Coco" Ferzoco, before he was killed in action. "No, I didn't register it with Chief Reismann. Dammit, if Coyote wasn't half-crazed with poison, I'd have shot him clean and wouldn't have had to use it. You do what you have to do and I'll do what I have to. But if that farm isn't busted, I'm calling the Environmental Protection Agency myself. Tell that to the chief."

Regardless, the call ended amicably. Two things hadn't been mentioned: Micah's involvement and Kodi's injury. When Kodi hung up, Micah added more ice to the bag on her ankle.

"I'll take the heat for the gun," Micah said. "I'll say I got it years ago from a friend at the DOD."

"Thanks, but that won't work. The army has the serial number and it's probably logged somewhere as missing from when Coco was killed. It'll trace back to me anyway, I was there. It's all in the After Action Report. Let's wait and see; Ferzie has an idea."

"What?"

"Keeping the necropsy closed to all but the vet on account of the High Street media circus. Ferzie claims she's owed a lot of favors. What's the difference anyway? Coyote's dead, and we killed him."

Yes, we did, thought Micah, but it was not a source of pride.

Fall River is a forty-five-minute drive from Middletown, across the Sakonnet River Bridge and the state line into Massachusetts. The pickup was an automatic so Kodi only needed her right foot, but Micah could see she was in pain. He offered once to switch places, Kodi declined, and he dropped it.

She doesn't have to prove anything to me, but she's old enough to make her own decisions.

Past a huge pond, they headed north. The commercial and residential neighborhoods ended and the landscape was farms and woodlands.

Kodi pointed to one farm with a rustic log cabin way back from the road. "He still plows with a horse every spring."

A ways farther, she made a turn onto Indian Town Road. There was a sign.

ENTERING WATUPPA
POCASSET INDIAN RESERVATION
LAND OF THE POCASSET WAMPONOAG TRIBE
POKANOKET NATION
All visitors stop at Security Office

"Check-in is a formality, I got ID," Kodi said.

"I wasn't worried. What does *Watuppa* mean?"

"Where we sit and root. Tiverton was our summer home for hunting and fishing, here for winter."

The road led to a square with a totem pole in the center to drive around. The flanks of the square had the security office, a combination café and minimart, a museum and art gallery, a souvenir shop, and a parking lot. The biggest, the museum, was only about the size of the average 7-Eleven store. Kodi pulled up in front of security. Micah went to get out.

"Wait," she said, "he'll come to us. They like to inspect vehicles."

He did come. A middle-aged Native American in khaki uniform came from the office and approached around Kodi's side. He recognized her immediately.

"*Wiqomun,* Kodi." He waved away her proffered ID card. "Who's the *wanuks*?"

"Good friend, I call him Pumpok. Need his ID?"

"He's with you, I'm okay. What are you up to?"

"Visit the clinic. I screwed up my ankle."

"Then don't wait on me, get going." He stepped back and waved the truck on.

Before Micah could ask, Kodi said, "First he said welcome, then he asked who the white guy was."

They drove out of the square, off the pavement, and down a dirt road.

"Now you're in the community," Kodi was saying. "*Wanuks* usually aren't allowed back here."

They passed prefab modular homes on concrete slabs, house trailers on slabs, then freestanding trailers still on wheels. Some looked no better than the one Kodi brought to Middletown.

In one spot was a woodworking barn. Next came huge propane storage tanks. Finally, another square with another totem pole. The buildings bore Indian names, but Micah got the gist from their other markings: community center, another minimart, tribal council office, and clinic. Kodi parked at the clinic.

"If you were expecting slot machines, you're on the wrong res."

"I'm exactly where I want to be," Micah said. He got out and came around to help Kodi.

They entered the clinic and a Native American, in a white lab coat, greeted them.

"Gray Cloud called from security, told me to expect you."

"Bummed up my ankle, Doc."

"We'll get you into examination and take a look."

The doctor took one shoulder, Micah still held the other, and they went into examination with Kodi slung between them. A Pocasset nurse with clipboard followed. When Kodi was seated on the exam table, the doctor said Micah had to wait back in reception.

Micah said, "Take good care of her, anything she needs, I brought my checkbook if it's not covered."

The doctor nodded and shooed Micah out.

He'd waited twenty minutes when the nurse came out. She looked at her clipboard and then at Micah.

"Ms. Red Moon needs an X-ray. This will take awhile."

Red Moon, Kodi Red Moon. "That's okay, I'm glad to wait."

The nurse consulted her papers again. "Are you from Narragansett too?"

Narragansett, permanent address. "No, Aquidneck Island."

"Oh, so this was closer," the nurse said.

"Closer than what?"

"Than the clinic on the Narragansett reservation in Charlestown."

"Yes, closer," Micah said. "And, well, you are her true people."

That made the nurse smile.

Kodi was given a shot of painkiller and the doctor would not let her leave if she insisted on driving. He gave her a pair of well-used crutches and Micah set the adjustable struts for her height. When Kodi signed the release form, the doctor gave her two plastic bottles of medicine, one an anti-inflammatory, the other, milder pain tablets.

"Come back in two weeks," the doctor said, making a notation on her chart.

"We'll see; thanks, Doc," Kodi said. With a you-told-me-so face, she handed Micah the pickup keys.

They made it out to the truck and Micah settled her in the passenger seat. The shot was working. Kodi seemed relieved for the first time since the orchard. Driving out of the square and onto the dirt road, she pointed ahead to the left.

"Pull up over there," she said. "I need a minute."

Kodi was pointing to the woodworking barn. When Micah stopped, Kodi got out and told him to stay with the engine running. He did as she asked and watched her hobble into the shed. A broad-chested man in carpenter's overalls greeted her and they embraced briefly. Micah couldn't hear what they said. The man left her and went into the barn. When he returned, he had a four-foot stick and was testing its strength. Satisfied, he handed it to Kodi. She tucked it under one arm and crutched her way back to the truck. The woodworker waved at Micah and he returned it. Kodi put the stick and her crutches behind the seat and got in.

"What's that?" Micah asked.

"When you finish it, your new cane. It's a branch of hornbeam, very sturdy. For centuries, my people have used it for tool handles. Should make a perfect walking stick."

"Thanks. What made you remember?"

Kodi reached back and smacked the crutches with her palm. "We're not a pair, we're a four-by-three: four legs and three sticks. Let's go home, before the shot wears off."

CHAPTER NINETEEN

Kodi slept the whole afternoon. Micah gave her an extra pillow to keep her foot elevated and she drifted right off.

Micah tried to work; Icobar was still interviewing prisoners and writing his propaganda letters. Within a few weeks, he was being sent to camps in other states—Michigan and Indiana. Icobar confided in his journal this was probably intended so all the letters didn't come from the same place. No matter, he enjoyed the travel and local accommodations.

Interesting, but not today. Micah closed the journal. *And I don't know why I'm not tired. I've been up since almost midnight.*

In the kitchen he examined the branch of hornbeam from Kodi. He hefted it back and forth between hands. It was lighter than he expected, but when he tried to bend it, formidable.

Perfect. A little shaping, durable stain, and a grip: perfect.

He looked out the window to see if it was still nice enough to work outside. Maybe he'd start right now. There were tools and a workbench in the garage, plenty of room since he'd sold his car, but he preferred to work outside. At least that's how he'd done his privet stick, and that was a success.

As he looked across the yard at the pond, a man came into view. A tall man, with long blond hair, and wearing a windbreaker. The man walked out onto the spit where Kodi's trailer had been parked. He didn't appear to be examining the spot, or notice the *okosu-wacuw*. He simply waited, hands in pockets, and stared out over the water.

"Can I help you?" Micah called from the back door. "This is private land and the pond's a protected watershed."

With no surprise, very casually, the man turned toward Micah's voice. He was young, probably around Kodi's age, which Micah figured as twenty-nine or thirty.

"I'm looking for Micah LaVeck," he called back.

"You coulda tried the house first."

"I knocked, nobody answered. Thought I'd try the yard."

Bullshit, you never knocked. I've been trying to be quiet for Kodi, I would have heard it.

"I'm LaVeck. Who are you and what do you want?"

The man smiled as if pleased with himself. He started walking toward the house. Micah came out and tried to cover half the ground so the man wouldn't be that close to the back door.

As their proximity closed, the man extended his hand.

"Chuck Lewis, *Newport Daily News*."

Micah had to switch cane hands to shake. "I'm the Micah you're looking for. What can I do for you, Chuck?"

Lewis's smile faded. "The *News* isn't going to print your letter."

"I'm not surprised," Micah said. "Doesn't say much for your publisher."

A half smile of sarcasm. "Doesn't concern him in the least. He lives in Barbados, October through April. The paper is kind of a summer hobby."

"Then who?"

"Does it matter? The only excuse you'll get is space. Something had to be cut at deadline."

Lame, probably same excuse for the submission rules. "So why are you here?"

"I'd like to know why you wrote it in the first place."

"It's self-explanatory."

"On face value. I'm figuring there's something deeper." Lewis cocked an eyebrow. "Did Mary Boyd put you up to it? I know you know her, in and out of Town Hall."

"You're good," Micah said.

"Thanks, tell my editor."

"I didn't do it for anybody except myself: a faithful, but disappointed, reader."

Lewis changed gears. "What's your opinion of the coyote hunt?"

You didn't come here to ask me that. "I had my doubts until Fish and Wildlife and the land trust got behind it. They strike me as people who'd know what's best."

"For the environment or Middletown?"

"I'd like to think that's the same thing."

The sarcastic grin again. "What about High Street?"

Micah didn't hesitate. "There's someone that needs to be hunted. Not shot, but held accountable."

"Can I quote you?"

"One man's opinion, go ahead."

From the windbreaker, Lewis took a pad and pen. He scribbled a few lines and looked up. "Can I come inside and continue the interview?"

"I have company."

"Wouldn't be Laurie Catlett, would it?"

I said you're good. Or is this something else? "If it were, I'm sure you'd already know, Chuck. So obviously, it isn't. My niece is visiting, convalescing, actually, from a skiing mishap last month. I'd rather she not be disturbed."

A tinge of disappointment, or mistrust, then resolve. "One last question then, Micah. Do you know who the coyote hunter is?"

"Quid pro quo, you first."

"Shoot."

"I'm a bird-watcher, Chuck. I've been all over the Kempenaar with no luck. Do you know if there are any white-throated sparrow sightings in Paradise Valley or Sweet Cherry Farm?"

Smirk. "Not by me."

"Then we're both out of luck."

Scribbling again. "I'll mark that as 'No comment.' "

"It wasn't, but what the hell. The paper's integrity is trash to me now anyway."

"Sorry you feel that way. I'll make it my goal to win you back."

"I wish you luck. Now if you'll excuse me, I've things to do, and you know your way around front."

Micah planted his feet and cane and waited. There was no standoff. Lewis bid Micah good day and walked around the side of the house, right past Kodi's pickup, without so much as a glance at it.

In the evening, Kodi woke up. Micah heard her positioning the crutches, their rubber tips tapping the wood floor. He thought he should offer assistance, but decided no. On one hand, she wouldn't like it. On the other, she'd better get used to them.

Kodi hobbled into the kitchen. Propping herself as straight as she could manage, she said, "I've only got one word to say."

"I hope it's a good one."

"Pizza."

"A finer word for the circumstances is beyond me."

She lowered herself into a chair. "Know somebody who delivers?"

Micah said he did and knew the number by heart. A discussion of toppings ensued. After their flat-out dislikes were respected, accord was reached on peppers, mushrooms, and anchovies. Micah made the call.

"Thirty minutes," he told Kodi. "Did you take any painkillers since you woke up?"

"No, I hate the stuff. Why?"

"Because there's beer in the fridge."

She gave him a look and smiled. Micah fetched the beer, Kodi dismissed a glass, and he popped it for her. She didn't drink until he poured himself a glass of wine.

As he sat down across from her, Micah said, "Had a visitor while you slept."

"Wawokak?"

"Chuck Lewis, from the *News*."

"What'd he want?"

"A couple of things, so I've concluded he's only fishing."

Micah related his encounter with the reporter. Kodi listened and sipped her beer. Micah finished, pretty sure he recounted every detail. She had but one comment.

"Your niece? Why didn't you say it was your girlfriend?"

"I wanted him to believe it."

Kodi lifted a crutch. "The skiing part does kind of work."

When he didn't laugh, Kodi got serious as well, eyeing Micah in inquiry.

"What are you thinking, Pumpok?"

"Now that I've retold the story, I'm not so sure he was fishing. Or if he was, he's got a pretty good idea what's in the water."

Knock on the front door, their pizza had arrived.

Dawn found Kodi and Micah out by the *okosu-wacuw*. Following her instructions, Micah picked his stone off the pile and held it to the true compass points. As Kodi chanted softly, he breathed on it in his fist, reached back, and hurled it out into the pond.

"What were you chanting?"

"Gratitude," Kodi said.

"For my safety?"

"Many things, that included."

Kodi shifted beside a tree, propped her crutches against it, and used the trunk at her back for support to stand. From her sweatshirt pocket, she took her bag of stones. Unlacing the top, Kodi delved into it and came out with an orange stone.

"Beautiful," he said.

Kodi looked, admired it, rolling the rock in her fingers. "Like fire, good. I need its strength."

She did her ritual, now familiar to Micah, and placed the stone atop the *okosu-wacuw*.

"Better than painkillers?" Micah said.

"My people were healing long before it became an industry. All the forces and spirits of the world are natural. We only need patience to understand them."

Micah thought of the poisoned coyotes. "Patience, not much of that anymore."

"Hmm."

Something else occurred to Micah. "You differentiate between forces and spirits. How?"

Kodi reflected. "Everything in the world is alive, but in different ways. Nature is a living force. All spirits, of which we creatures are the lowest form while walking the earth, have distinct identities, personalities, and emotions."

"You sure you're not a priestess?" Micah said.

"Is every man who prays a priest?"

"I get it."

"Besides," and Kodi laughed, "I'm your niece and you should already know everything about me."

"I wish."

"So, Uncle Micah, tell me about our family. Am I your brother's or your sister's child?"

"Sorry to be the one to tell you, you're adopted. From gypsies, I think."

"Oh, mysterious. No gypsies in the LaVeck bloodline?"

Micah felt a sentimental shadow brush over him. "Possibly. My mother was a bit superstitious. She told me she could read tea leaves. We never did it together, but she told me she knew how."

"I think your mother understood."

"Understood what?"

"The power of belief."

Somehow that made Micah feel calm and comfortable. He couldn't explain it if he tried, but savored it a moment.

"Where do you get the rocks?"

"Bag o' Rocks dot com."

"My sister always said you were a snotty kid."

Micah didn't have a sister, or brother. He said it because he was still thinking of his mother, and when she was young.

THE DAY was mild, many passing clouds, but enough sun. After breakfast, Micah brought two lawn chairs from the garage and set them up on the spit. When Kodi was settled in one, he fetched a footstool and pillow from the house for her ankle.

"Anything you want?" he asked.

"I thought we agreed not to wait on each other."

"I feel like it, humor me. Only for today, I promise."

"In that case, I could use my laptop."

"Good. You can work while I start my new stick."

Micah left Kodi on the spit and went for her computer, the hornbeam branch, and his tools. When he returned, Kodi pointed out to the pond, south, toward the dam.

"There's a rowboat out there," she said. "I thought that wasn't allowed."

Micah looked: a small aluminum boat oared by a lone rower.

"Every month they send a guy out to take water samples. They're checking for pollutants, bacteria, anything that shouldn't be in the water supply."

The boat was slowly coming up the center of the pond. The rower was careless, oars slapping the water.

"Water testing," Kodi repeated. "I'm curious, Pumpok, do they do that with a camera?"

"What?"

"Hanging from his neck."

Micah squinted. It had a fat, long lens.

"Damn it all."

"Let's go inside," Kodi said, already using her crutches to stand.

CHAPTER TWENTY

They played Scrabble most of the evening. During a lull between games, Kodi made her announcement.

"I'm leaving in the morning."

"For where?" Micah said.

"Home."

"You're finished, that's it?"

Kodi reached across the table and put her hand on his.

"Probably only a week, I'll be back when I'm fit to hunt again. Besides, between the reporter and that camera guy in the boat, I think we should give ourselves some distance. Let it peter out because there's nothing here to find."

She was right, but Micah was still angry. Not with Kodi: angry and disappointed with his fellow townspeople. He said nothing.

"Will you tell Wawokak for me?" Kodi said.

"Sure, on Monday."

"Thanks, I'll tell Ferzie myself."

"You think a week is enough time to heal?"

"Don't you want me back?" she asked.

"Back? I don't want you to go in the first place."

"Like I said, I think it's best for now."

Again, he couldn't disagree so didn't comment at all. But there was something else.

"Do you need your trailer back from the police?"

"No, I have a home in Narragansett."

"On the reservation?"

"No, a mobile home park, but my site is reserved."

"Very funny. My niece, the ballbuster, like sis always said."

"It's really a lot nicer than my travel trailer, by gypsy standards, of course. You'll see sometime soon." Kodi gave Micah her cell number. "It's the one from Walmart. I don't own any other. Let me know what's going on, if you don't mind."

"Of course. Anything else I can do?"

She scribbled an e-mail address below the cell number, in case the phone was off, which was its usual condition.

"Besides Wawokak, you could call the mayor too. I'd like Mary to get our version rather than Cunning Crow's."

Kodi left at dawn. Her meager things were packed and Micah walked her to the pickup carrying her duffel bag and computer. Kodi wore her backpack. When she was settled in the cab, crutches wedged across the passenger seat, Micah closed the door.

"What about your rifle?" Micah said.

"In the bedroom closet, I'm coming back. This isn't finished."

"It's safe with me."

"Don't get any ideas while I'm gone."

Not much chance in that, but Micah appreciated her saying it anyway.

"I'm only your spotter," he said, remembering the sniper jargon.

It was more than that, but left unsaid by both of them.

"Stay in touch," Micah said.

"You first."

Kodi started the truck, Micah stepped away, and she backed out toward Green End Avenue. At the edge of the property, she stopped, and beckoned him. Micah walked up to the truck and leaned on the window.

"Here." Kodi handed him a small ball of cloth wrapped with string. "There's two stones in there for the *okosu-wacuw.* If you need one, send mine on its journey. Close your eyes as you unwrap it and pick one."

"How will I know when I need one?"

"I'm only in Narragansett; I'll send a smoke signal."

Micah felt the stones through the cloth. "You'll make a Pocasset out of me yet."

"Last Indian lesson for now, Uncle Pumpok: one way or another, everyone's adopted."

IT WAS still early in the morning with a soft breeze and the pond sparkling in the sunshine. Micah got the hornbeam branch, his tools, and a stool, and sat out on the spit to work.

First, a hunting knife that had belonged to his father, to strip the bark. It raveled off the shaft and fell at Micah's feet. Beneath the bark, cured of sap, the wood was grayish-blue with veins of grain that ran the length. Micah remembered the man in the shed handing it to Kodi on the Watuppa Reservation.

He sure knows how to cure wood.

When the bark was off, Micah took a shoemaker's rasp to flatten out the bumps from gnarls and offshoots sheared away. Micah liked working with his hands. All it took was time and patience.

Time. The time with Kodi had gone quickly. But when he thought about it in units of only one day, each seemed three times longer than any routine one before the hunt.

The hunt.

The on-days, the off-days, the good and bad times, always came back to that: the hunt.

During their discussion of forces and spirits, Micah almost asked Kodi why she did it, why professionally. She certainly had a greater respect for life, all forms of life, than anyone Micah had ever met. But he hadn't asked. Wasn't sure he wanted to hear the answer.

As Micah worked, and thought, and philosophized, a pair of pintail ducks waddled up from the pond. The female was bolder and went right to the bark shavings and pecked at the pile. Micah stopped filing. The duck looked up at him, looked away. Turned and quacked to its mate.

Nothing here, Micah supplied their thoughts, *just some old guy farting around with a stick. I don't think he's going inside anytime soon to get us some bread.*

The drake flapped its wings in agreement. He turned for the water and his mate waddled after him. With a flourish of wings, they landed about a yard out from shore.

Micah started filing again. Paused when he heard a car out front stop, idle, then start again.

Micah's newspaper had arrived.

The *Newport Daily News* continued to shatter paradigms. There were three front-page headlines in equal columns. Unprecedented in Micah's experience—he'd never even seen dual headlines.

COYOTE HUNT CONTINUES WITH TWO KILLS

GROWER CITED FOR POISON USE, EPA INVOLVED

ARREST MADE IN HIGH STREET SHOOTING

Micah scanned the bylines. The hunt and poison articles were by regular *News* staffers. The arrest story attributed to Chuck Lewis. Micah fought off Lewis's allure and decided to be methodical, left to right in order.

The two coyotes shot at Shady Stream Orchards were necropsied per agreed spec. The examination was closed to all spectators. Only the vet and a senior, unnamed, official from Fish and Wildlife were present. The reason given was security, not secrecy. Unauthorized people had been trying to infiltrate the facility for over a week. The commissioner of the Department of Environmental Management, overseer of Fish and Wildlife, had ordered the exclusion of nonessential participants, as there wasn't enough time or personnel for screening of attendees.

A written report was published within an hour of the procedure. Nothing new about the shootings: each cleanly hit, as humanely as possible for the circumstances.

Way to go, Ferzie.

That wasn't all. Each coyote showed signs of poisoning, predating the hunt by at least a month, in the lab's estimate. This information was passed up the chain at the DEM and shared with the EPA.

You got 'em, Kodi, exactly like you wanted.

In conclusion, the reporter noted, despite publicity, interference, and criminal intent, the legitimate professional coyote hunt was still underway with continuing success.

The second article Micah read was a bit sketchier with facts. The DEM and EPA had reasonable evidence that Shady Stream Orchards had illegally attempted to deal with its coyote inhabitants by poisoning store-bought meats and distributing them around the property. Since the method was unapproved, uncontrolled, and unsupervised, all ground wildlife and birds in the area were jeopardized as well as current and future fruit crops contaminated. The proprietor of Shady Stream, Charlie Ochs, claimed no knowledge of the poison and was said to be cooperating with investigators.

You're going down, Charlie.

Then it was Chuck Lewis's turn: investigative reporter, and maybe, the only person with a potential lead on the coyote hunter outside the operation itself. Lewis didn't mention that part.

After following a lead provided by a parking lot security camera, a search warrant was obtained for an undisclosed residence in Middletown. The search produced evidence for an arrest. The suspect taken into custody was a fifteen-year-old male. As a minor, his name was withheld, as were those of his parents and the address. Lewis's anonymous source in the Middletown PD confided a confession was imminent and could likely lead to further arrests. The boy did not legally possess a gun, didn't own a car, and wasn't old enough to drive.

You're welcome, Chief Reismann.

Micah worked on the hornbeam into the afternoon. He sanded the shaft and tapered both ends for the ground cap and to secure a grip.

A bit tired in the late afternoon, he took Melvin Sturgis up on his previous offer and had his wine order delivered. There were still enough groceries left from his shopping spree with Kodi. And there was always pizza with peppers, mushrooms, and anchovies on call. That wasn't the way Micah usually took his pizza, but it was suddenly his favorite.

Why haven't I thought of that combo before?

The driver from the wine shop was a local retiree Micah recognized.

"I thought you volunteered at the library?"

"Still do," the gentleman said, "but this pays, cash."

Micah tipped him well.

All the sunshine and all the effort left him lazy and somewhat chilly in the evening. He built a fire in the parlor, ate a sandwich, had some wine, and reread the articles in the *Newport Daily News.*

The urge would not be denied, and Kodi had said, "You first."

Micah hoped her cell was on, he was too pooped to compose a lengthy e-mail. Kodi answered on the second ring.

"I knew you'd call," she said.

"How's the ankle?"

"Elevated and iced."

"Good, don't push yourself too hard."

A mock exasperated breath from Kodi. "Yes, Uncle Pumpok."

Micah changed the subject. "I'm saving the *News* for you." He read Kodi the headlines.

"Read me the whole thing."

"All three stories?"

"Please."

Micah didn't mind at all. For half an hour he read each article through the phone. When he finished, Kodi started with a question that surprised him.

"Do you think Charlie Ochs is lying about not knowing?"

"Pretty much," Micah said. "Growers are the attentive sort. It's unusual for one not to know what's going on with his own land."

A pause of silence on Kodi's end, followed by a different observation.

"I wish it wasn't a kid on High Street."

"That is a shame," Micah agreed. "But he didn't act alone. Some adult is going to be held responsible for facilitating the shooting, if not prompting it."

"Good," Kodi said. Another pause. "Is that a fire I hear crackling in the background? I miss that. In fact, I'm not sure what I'm gonna miss more being here: your coffee, your cooking, or that fireplace."

"I would have thought the bath towels."

"Definitely those towels." A sigh. "You sound tired, Micah."

"A bit, but one last thing. Ranger Ferzoco did great."

"Now she's owed another favor."

"I doubt she keeps score with you."

Kodi didn't say anything.

"Anyway," Micah said, "I'm off to bed."

"Me too, I'll call you tomorrow."

Micah hung up before he was tempted to say anything else.

CHAPTER TWENTY-ONE

A lot of negative things could probably be said of Mayor Mary Boyd, and the opposing party did so at length, but being a hypocrite wasn't one of them. On that cloudy Sunday morning, Micah called her home at nine A.M. because he knew she was not in church. Jack Landsdale answered. Micah apologized for the Sabbath intrusion. Lansdale dismissed it and put his wife on the phone.

"Everything all right, Micah?"

"Yes and no. I'm fine, Kodi had a slight accident."

Micah played it down, as Kodi would have wanted, without making it seem trivial. During the Shady Stream hunt, Kodi had twisted her ankle, finished the job, and then got treatment. Cut to the chase: there would be no more hunts for about a week.

"I'll gladly send my personal physician over to be sure she's okay," Boyd offered.

"She's not here. She had her own doctor look at it and then went home to recuperate. A few days off her feet is the remedy, along with elevation and cold compresses."

"Sounds like something I once did playing tennis."

I doubt a lame spotter fell on your ankle. Micah said, "Then you understand. She asked me to call you first. Monday, I'll call Laurie. Kodi is alerting Fish and Wildlife herself, so they're not standing by for a kill."

"She's a remarkable young woman, very professional. I sensed it when we first met. Not to worry about Laurie, I'll do that myself. As you say, tomorrow. You've done enough, Micah, and I'm very grateful. I should alert Harry as well, so if there are any kills, he'll know it's not our gal."

"That's why you're the boss, Mary."

Boyd then offered Micah some privileged information.

"No doubt you've heard about the High Street arrest. I feel sorry for the child, but grateful it's put to bed. You've been with us from the get-go, Micah, so I won't insult you by holding back, and I completely trust your discretion."

There was a long enough pause for Micah to ask, "What is it, Mary?"

"The shooter is Bob Mackey's son. The good doctor, if you can still call him that, drove the car himself and owns the rifle. He's agreed to surrender to Harry in the morning, through his lawyer, of course. With all the coverage this has generated, those terms are acceptable. No cuffs at the house, no raincoat over his head, and no Chuck Lewis at the ready with pad and pen."

"For my money, I'd bet Lewis already knows," Micah said.

"He does, but I've had a word with him. It's not in today's edition. Tomorrow it's out of my hands."

"As I said, the boss. Enjoy your Sunday, Mary."

"You too, Micah. Pass along my regards to Kodi and get some rest yourself, we've put you through quite a lot."

When the call ended, Micah asked two silent questions.

What else does Lewis know, and would you tell me, Mary?

Micah had breakfast and then went on his computer to research the Army Bureau of Military Information, 1861 to 1865. There were only a handful of Google hits so he narrowed it down to four with recognizable scholarly websites. Before wading through those, on a whim, he Googled "Icobar Ohlm" and the same date span. Nothing, except the prompt: *Did you mean Ichabod Crane?*

Micah chuckled to himself. Back to the historical websites.

Two hours later, Micah knew a bit more about the BMI, but not the slightest hint of corroboration about the letters scheme. Either Icobar had turned from memoirist to novelist, or Micah had discovered a tantalizing angle to promote future publication.

He considered e-mailing Roger Ohlm with the news, then thought better of it. The contemporary Ohlm was greedy already. Throw him a bone and he might go utterly voracious. Voracious, as in deciding Micah LaVeck was a hack, and a story of this magnitude belonged in the hands of a famous writer. Dollar sign, ka-ching.

There is a sizeable online archive of Rhode Island Civil War information maintained jointly by the University of Rhode Island and Brown University. Micah perused it at great length but found no reference to the BMI. He made a list of its contributors and checked their CVs. He zeroed in on a professor emeritus from Brown, Dr. Nathan Jordan, PhD, and composed an e-mail to him outlining his mission. Some corroboration, any corroboration, could be the key. Dr. Jordan had authored four distinguished books about the war, one which briefly included Allan Pinkerton, cofounder of the BMI.

Click. SEND E-MAIL.

Cloudy, but the rain never came. Micah took a walk out to the spit and stood a moment surveying the gray pond under the gray sky. A north wind was raising a swell and its lapping at the shore was audible. Micah's weather station had indicated a foul spell in the next twenty-four hours. Somewhere up north, it was already happening. He remembered the meteorologists at the Department of Defense. Clipper systems out of Canada always brought storms and snows. More than once, he'd heard them lament, "Those damn Canadians, they're supposed to be our allies."

He looked over at the *okosu-wacuw*, Kodi's orange, fire stone still on top. Made a pointless, personal vow not to need a stone of his own until she was better. Pointless, he realized, for who knew fate? Not Micah, not ever.

Something moved by the prayer mound. First, only colors, then a shape, perfectly camouflaged. It was a toad, maybe six inches from the lowest stones, blended exactly to the ground and rocks of the shoreline. Now he stayed quite still, only a twitch now and then of eye movement. Appeared to study the pile, no, that wasn't the word, eyes now motionless, open wide, meditating on it.

You're one of them, aren't you? Micah asked the toad without a sound. One of what, he wasn't sure. *Kodi would know. Or it's only a toad, and I'm a foolish old man.*

But he didn't feel foolish, about any of it, about anything, anymore.

Micah was about to resume his research and read on in Icobar's journal, when his phone rang. Kodi had promised to call today. He would tell her about the toad.

"Micah, Chuck Lewis here."

"Yes, Chuck?"

Lewis asked if Micah had heard any follow-up on his High Street story, without mentioning Mackey's name.

"I spoke with Mary this morning," Micah said. "Decent of you not to run with it until tomorrow."

"I told you I'd win your respect back for the paper."

"It's a start."

"Any comment on Mackey for the record?"

"Why ask me? Your readers won't care what I think. Ask Mary, Laurie, or Harry Reismann."

Lewis didn't answer Micah's question. Instead, he said, "How's your niece doing?"

"Coming along, thanks for asking."

"Only one skiing spot in Rhode Island, Yawgoo Valley."

"Didn't say it happened in Rhode Island. I'm only an uncle lending her some private space. What kids do these days, I've no clue."

"You're talking to a reporter and I'm on the clock," Lewis said with an edge of sarcasm.

"I know that, I just don't know why we're talking."

"Let me put it this way: How many of your relatives are Native Americans?"

Micah said nothing.

Lewis resumed. "I ran the license plate on the pickup in your yard. It's common knowledge you no longer drive."

"Common to whom?"

"You walk all over town, every errand, town meetings, the library, everywhere. There's even a nickname for you."

"What is it?"

"You know that bird with Wile E. Coyote?"

"Road Runner."

"Yeah, only they call you Road Hobbler."

"Delightful," Micah said, now with sarcasm. *I prefer Walks Tilted,* unsaid.

Lewis didn't miss a beat. "Anyway, the truck is registered to one Kodi Red Moon, of Narragansett."

Micah responded, "It's known you have a source in the police department. You said so in your article."

"Among many other sources," Lewis boasted.

"As I said before, Chuck, why are we having this conversation?"

"Ms. Red Moon is an army-trained sniper. I'd like to get her perspective on the coyote hunter. You know, background stuff on what traits and skills the town's hired gun would possess. One professional rating another."

"You're so full of shit, Chuck."

"Agreed, so let me talk to her."

"She's not here, and that's the truth."

"When will she be back?"

"You got kids? They come and go on their own schedule and we're the last to know."

Sharp change in Lewis's voice. "Don't make me go around you, Micah."

"Around me, Mayor Boyd, the Town Council, Chief Reismann, and let's not forget Laurie Catlett."

"You let me worry about the mayor's chief of staff. I did Mary Boyd a big favor today; she owes me."

"You'd bet your career in this town on that?"

"With an exclusive like this, I can kiss Aquidneck Island good-bye. Providence too. Hello Boston or New York."

"Let me think about it."

Lewis considered it. "My Mackey story runs tomorrow. I want a fresh front-page headline for next weekend. Deadline is three P.M. Friday."

"I can live with that."

"You're welcome. Now take down my cell number. Don't call the paper, call me direct. And deadline means the story is written, so don't waste my time."

Chuck Lewis's call left Micah angry, perplexed, and a little frightened. Not fear for himself, but for Kodi, and that played into his anger. So much had happened in the last three weeks, so much had changed. Micah had gone from a desultory Middletown editor and transcriber to aide-de-camp of the coyote hunter. He was as alive as he'd felt in more years than he cared to admit, even to himself.

Alive, yet far from satisfied. His questions would not rest, and stung more now that Kodi was not here. Ironically, for a hunter, she exemplified for Micah the very sacredness of life. And in due course, everything that is sacred has its rituals. These are the cross paths between the daily and the eternal. Or at least, using Kodi's definitions of life forms, Micah's benchmark for appreciation. The Bob Mackeys and Chuck Lewises of the world would never grasp it. Nor did Micah, until the first hunt. Even now, it wasn't an understanding, more of an epiphany for him.

For one so alive, there was a shadow of death that walked behind Kodi. She knew it, understood it, and accepted it.

Now I'm the knee-jerk philosopher again, he concluded.

I wish she'd call.

Nathan Jordan e-mailed back. The professor admitted that not much historical significance had ever been afforded the Bureau of Military Information.

The BMI had a checkered, if not shady, countenance. Agents were regarded by the generals they served as unscrupulous and unsupervised. There were accusations of misinformation propagated when no verifiable intelligence was at hand. It was disbanded at the end of the war in 1865. There would not be another formal intelligence agency in the US until 1882, with the creation of the Office of Naval Intelligence.

No, Jordan had never heard of the POW letter campaign. That was not to say it couldn't have happened. The idea interested the professor. He proposed that he and Micah meet to explore it together. Jordan lived in Jamestown. Was that convenient for Micah? At eighty-one years of age, Jordan rarely left home.

Kodi finally called. She took the news about Lewis very calmly. Or so it seemed to Micah. He was content merely to hear her voice.

CHAPTER TWENTY-TWO

Monday, the first day of April, it rained steadily.

The day started with mundane chores and the early morning passed. A computer check of his bank account to verify direct deposit of his government pension check. Electronic payment of several bills, two loads of laundry, inventory of foodstuffs, compiling of a grocery list, and the *Newport Daily News* from his front porch.

Back in the kitchen, he opened it to find its expected headline and byline.

He thought, *Nothing's gonna dampen your day, Chuck*, and read the article. As he read, he checked his watch. Nine thirty. If Lewis's timing was precise, Dr. Bob was in the custody of the Middletown Police Department. The accompanying photograph of Mackey, pure Lewis. It wasn't Mackey's picture from the American Medical Association archives; it was his official portrait as president of the Middletown Rod and Gun Club, complete with crossed muskets for background. Formal arraignment would take place this afternoon in Newport County Court. The case against his son, being a minor, was relegated to Family Court.

In the pit of his stomach, Micah knew there would be no real satisfaction, except maybe for Mackey. There was a local saying that if an Aquidneck Islander wanted to commit a crime—he should do it on the island. Except for violent crimes, there was a preponderance of case-dismissed rulings with a "stern" warning for residents. The presiding judge had a nickname among prosecutors and reporters: C. D. Walker, for Case Dismissed Walker, though his given name was Frederick, and friends called him Freddy. Killing the coyote was violent all right, but carried out by a child. And what the heck? The town was officially killing them anyway. Aiding and abetting, corruption of a minor, parental negligence . . . C. D. would have a full plate, and the only blood spilled was the coyote's.

Lewis did provide a glimmer of hope. Depending how the charges were applied, and interpreted, and seeing how the Rhode Island Department of Environmental Management might be inclined to involve itself, the case could possibly go to a higher court. A lot would depend on C. D. Walker's mood at the proceedings.

Micah closed the paper. The tremor returned to his left hand. No pain, only a series of jerks subsiding into a lengthy trembling. He watched it with detachment, almost, he thought, the way he'd watched the toad out by the *okosuwacuw*. And that made him think, again of course, of Kodi.

Besides Lewis's veiled threat to expose her, he'd also told Kodi last night about Mackey's arrest.

She had had only one comment, "Good."

Then they talked about other things. Kodi felt she was healing nicely. How was Micah feeling? Rain coming, maybe three days' worth. Would have washed out a hunt anyway. What did you have for dinner? Nothing. Should I come cook for you? You don't have a car. I'll send a pizza. What kind? You know what kind.

When he looked again, Micah's trembling had stopped.

I forgot to tell her about the toad.

A RESTLESSNESS set in that Micah could not banish with further chores or even Icobar Ohlm. He had never felt lonely, or considered himself to be a lonely man. Micah had always been comfortable with solitude and the freedom of his thoughts, especially after working for the Department of Defense. This was something else, and the rain only heightened the feeling.

At noon he had some cheese and crackers, read the rest of the newspaper, and broke an unwritten, personal policy by having a glass of wine, a comfort normally reserved for after three P.M. during the workweek. That is if he'd accomplished enough work to merit it.

When the glass was empty, he donned his mac and waterproof backpack, containing an extra grip bag, and headed out the back door where he yanked on his mud boots.

As the rain streamed off his hood, Micah hiked up Valley Road to East Main and headed east to the Aquidneck Shopping Center. First stop: Aquidneck Wine and Spirit Shop.

"Crap sakes, Micah," Sturgis said, "if it wasn't for your stick I wouldn't have recognized you. You look like some explorer lost in the rain forest."

"I feel like one." For a second Micah wondered if Sturgis ever called him Road Hobbler behind his back. He dashed the thought; Sturgis was good people.

"You coulda phoned it in," Sturgis said.

"Had to get out, but I'll take you up on a delivery later."

"Be my pleasure."

Micah brought his wine selections to the counter. "And add a case of those Coors Silver Bullets."

"Company again?"

"Not sure, but might as well be prepared."

"That's what I always say."

Sturgis rang it up and Micah paid. Micah added he should be home no later than four. Sturgis wrote it on the delivery order.

"Ain't that something about Doc Mackey?" Sturgis said.

"Only met the man twice, briefly at that."

"Me too. He goes to that fancy wine store down in Newport. Guess he deserves what he deserves. Shame about the kid though."

"Real shame, you'd think a doctor would know better."

"I was drafted back in the day, did a tour in 'Nam. Ain't owned or held a gun since. Got nothing against hunters or sportsmen, but learned a thing or two."

"What's that?"

"Put a gun in someone's hand and one of two things happens: Either they use it for a purpose, or they feel it gives them a purpose."

"You've got something there, Melvin."

"Want my driver to give you a lift home?"

Micah declined, saying he'd other errands, and, well, what could you do about the rain anyway.

From the wine shop, Micah headed across the parking lot to Shaw's Supermarket. Consulting his list, he bought what groceries and meats he could handle on his back and carrying the grip bag with his free hand.

Outside in the rain, Micah decided to cut across into the CVS lot and hike down High Street instead of backtracking Valley Road. As he entered the lot, a line of cars was queued up for the traffic light at the entrance. They were tightly packed, bumper-to-bumper, too tight to squeeze between the way he walked and with his load. Micah had no choice but to wait for the light to change.

The rain continued to pour, and Micah waited. The light changed. The line of cars rolled past him. The sixth one caught his eye—a green Toyota 4Runner. The driver was on a cell phone. Turned and glanced at Micah, quickly looked away, and hit the accelerator. It was Chuck Lewis.

Micah chuckled to himself. *Like I give a damn if you use* News *time to run some errands. Look around this lot. Half these people are probably on somebody else's clock.*

Micah crossed the lot and came out the rear side beside the old colonial cemetery. High Street ran due south from this spot with the Kempenaar Valley on Micah's left. A horn tooted twice behind him. Micah stepped to the side and looked back to wave the driver past him. Another vehicle Micah recognized, a blue VW Passat. It inched alongside him and the driver's window came down.

"Get in, I'll give you a lift," Laurie Catlett said.

"I'm fine, thanks anyway."

"Don't be a damn fool, it's fucking pouring."

"I'll be any kind of fool I want, damned or otherwise. And I'm still cognizant enough to know it's fucking raining."

Catlett smirked. "Suit yourself. I hope you and the Indian maiden wind up very happy as trailer trash."

Micah was finished and posed no retort. He didn't need to anyway. Catlett gunned the engine, gravel spread like buckshot, and the Passat was off down High Street.

THE MAC came off and dripped a pool of water beneath its peg. The mud boots stayed by the front door. In his soggy socks, Micah took his groceries to the kitchen. His normal precautions were not in play. The cane tip didn't grab, the slick left sock had no purchase—he went down in a tumble of soup cans, dish detergent, and dairy. His backpack hit the floor like a sack of potatoes. He lay there a minute, sore and embarrassed, feeling like a hockey goalie who failed to block the winning shot. All that was missing was the gasp of the crowd, and the jeers to follow.

There was a tightness in his chest. Micah tried to cough it away, but only managed a few wheezy huffs. So he lay there and waited some more. However many minutes passed, he didn't know. In his mind, the fragility turned to stupidity.

Get up, he willed himself.

His right leg answered and recruited his right arm. Micah rolled that way. Up to one knee, a kitchen chair within reach, a deep breath, and a long pull. The coughing came back in earnest. A feeling like damp cotton lodged at the back of his throat. Finally feeling his heart tick down in pace. Attempting a swallow.

There, not so bad.

Another few minutes of rest.

Okay, clean up this mess.

He gathered the spilt goods and put them away. Opened his backpack, and divided his purchases among freezer, fridge, and pantry. All together, about a half hour's labor.

See, time and patience. But the cough was not patient. Came back insistent, rude, and, in the end, painful.

Knock on the front door. A cheery voice called, "Mr. LaVeck? Island Wine and Spirits."

"It's open, come on in."

"I'm soaking wet."

"So am I, join the party."

It was the retiree from the last time. In his arms were the case of beer and a bag with three bottles of Micah's wines.

"Where do you want these?"

"On the table is fine."

The man put them down. "You okay?"

"Yeah, working up my second wind."

"Can I get you something, a glass of water?"

More good people. "That'd be great, thanks."

While the man filled a glass from the drain board with tap water, Micah pulled a ten-dollar bill from his wallet.

"For your trouble," Micah said, exchanging the bill for the glass.

"No trouble, it's the job." The man pocketed the money. "You sure you're all right?"

"No trouble, it's just me."

"I hear you. Take care."

The man retreated from the kitchen and Micah heard the front door close behind him. Micah drank the water and hoped he wouldn't cough again. He didn't have the energy.

When he was up for it, he went to the fridge and got the open bottle of wine he'd started at noon. He poured half his empty water glass full. Sat back, took a deep swig, and undid the buttons of his soaked shirt. Took it off, balled it up, and threw it in the general direction of his laundry room. Another swallow. Reached for the socks, and threw them too.

You happy, Laurie? I'm trailer trash now. Laundry piled up, wine in a water glass, jeans soaked through to my crotch like I wet myself. All I need is a cheap cigar and a blind dog.

The back door opened. Sound of rain and wind. Kodi standing there on only one crutch. The poncho she'd worn the very first day, dripping as then, hood up. Black paratrooper boots laced to the top. Black jeans. Ominous, one might say. The most beautiful vision Micah ever had in his life.

CHAPTER TWENTY-THREE

"How's the ankle?" Micah asked weakly from his chair.

"Getting better, but you look like hell."

Kodi one-crutched it to the table and put a hand to Micah's forehead.

"You're running a fever."

"Caught in the rain, that's all. It'll pass."

There was water all over the floor where Micah sat, so Kodi stripped off her poncho and slung it over a chair. Next, off came her boots. Again, Micah noticed, she wore no socks. Barefoot she walked to the bathroom with her crutch and returned with two towels. Starting with his hair, she used one briskly, dried him off, down his bare chest and back. She put that towel aside and held the fresh one wide.

"Out of those pants," she ordered.

"I'll get to it."

"I'll do it myself, if I have to."

He didn't doubt her for an instant. Micah undid the buckle of his belt, squirmed in the chair, and Kodi yanked his jeans off by the cuffs. Hovering over him, she draped the towel over his crotch and boxer shorts.

"Those too," she said, and turned around.

Micah removed the shorts and wrapped the towel around his waist.

"Now off to bed," Kodi said, turning back.

Micah pointed to his glass. "I haven't finished my wine."

"Uggh," she moaned. "All right. Have you got a robe or something?"

"There's the afghan. I think it's still in the parlor."

Kodi went to get it. The minute she left the room, Micah started coughing again. He tried to hold it down, not to alarm Kodi. It didn't work, so between hacks he took a slug of his wine, still holding the glass when she returned with the blanket.

"Musta drunk too fast," he said.

"Don't bullshit me, Pumpok. That last one came all the way up from your toes. You need a doctor."

"We'll see in the morning." He drained the glass, held it out to her. "Please, one more, to sleep better."

Kodi considered it, shrugged, and took the glass. Micah wrapped the afghan about his shoulders. It smelled faintly of Kodi, as she'd used it last. He wasn't damp or cold anymore, but did feel a twinge of fear. He had to admit to himself, he was afraid to lie flat. The idea of the heaviness in his chest being level and spreading out was unnerving, rational or otherwise. He pulled the blanket tighter.

Kodi brought the glass back half filled with wine. She placed it on the table instead of handing it to him.

"Thanks. By the way, I stocked up on beer. It's in the fridge. Help yourself."

"So you figured I was coming," Kodi said.

"No, the guy in the store told me it would help me pee better."

Kodi ignored that. "You want some soup or something?"

"No, the wine is fine."

"Okay, so I'll have a beer with you and then you're off to bed."

"Tomorrow's Tuesday; we've got things to talk about. Chuck Lewis isn't going away."

"Fine, we'll talk about him, tomorrow."

Kodi got her beer and joined Micah at the table.

"One more thing," Micah said. "Remind me in the morning. I saw Lewis and Wawokak in the CVS parking lot this afternoon. Not together, but within five minutes of each other. It didn't occur to me then, but now I think that's strange."

"Why, it's a small town?"

Micah tried to put his thoughts together. "Lewis lives in Newport. They got their own CVS down there on Bellevue Avenue. And when I was dating Laurie, she always shopped in Walgreen's. She had one of their discount cards. I think I stumbled on them meeting together. Someway, they're in cahoots."

"I wouldn't put it past either of them. Drink up, bedtime."

At Micah's request, Kodi piled three pillows at the head of his bed. He claimed the incline would produce less coughing, without confiding about the weight in his chest. Kodi tucked a quilt up under his chin. She was barely out the door when he started dozing off. In the haze of half-sleep, his mind settled on the image of the toad by the *okosu-wacuw*. It was joined by the doe he'd seen across the pond. Then came a coyote, silver, docile like a pet dog, that lay down beside the toad. Beyond the trio, there was splashing in the water out from shore. Kodi was swimming. Micah tried to lift his eyes, but they were too heavy. He wheezed out a sigh, and fell asleep.

IT WAS daylight; Micah knew it before he opened his eyes. Opened them, a bright window, blinds filtering the light.

No rain, I was wrong. Everybody was wrong. It had lasted only a day.

Micah took a shallow breath through his mouth to test his chest. The weight was still there, but not as heavy and painful as yesterday. Took another, deeper, and held it to the count of ten. Exhaled. Definitely more than half better.

His leg and shoulder were sore from the kitchen fall. Without checking, he assumed there were bruises. Micah folded the quilt back from his chest. He was in tee shirt and boxer shorts. Did not remember getting changed. Last he recalled, he had a towel around his waist and the afghan around his shoulders—a crazy combination of prizefighter and peasant woman.

Micah's legs responded and dipped off the edge of the bed to the floor. Found his cane against the headboard in easy reach. Made it to his feet on the first try. Always an encouraging sign.

From down the hall, he heard the washing machine running.

Out of a drawer he took a sweat suit. Sat back on the bed to dress. Rose again, and went to the window. Drew up the blinds. He was looking for something from last night, but couldn't remember what it was. Gave up, and followed his nose to the kitchen.

Kodi was at the sink washing some utensils.

"Welcome back," she greeted him.

"From where?"

"You tell me. For the Pocasset, where we go in sleep depends on what spirits we've prevailed upon, or provoked, during the day."

"That could become complicated."

"That's why there's so many spirits."

The idea of spirits made Micah think of something else. "What's that I smell?"

Kodi stepped from the sink and opened the oven door. "Cornbread. You had everything, so I figured I'd try. What are you doing with cornmeal anyway?"

"Don't remember, but glad you found it."

Kodi closed the oven. Her crutch was against the counter. Micah realized she was barely using it.

As he sat at his place, he said, "You're making good progress."

"I don't like being sick."

"If only it were a frame of mind."

"A lot of it is, and you know it better than anybody I know."

"That's because I'm adopted Pocasset."

"From before that." Kodi changed the subject. "The bread's got another seven or eight minutes. You wanted to talk about Lewis."

"Later, after your cornbread. Something else now. I've been meaning to tell you about this toad I saw. It keeps coming back in my mind."

The cornbread was better than its aroma foretold. Micah had his slathered in butter, always having to dab his chin with a napkin as the liquid drooled. Kodi had hers with honey and, though not a dainty eater at all, consumed it with less mess. Between slices, Micah told her about the toad at the *okosu-wacuw*. Kodi listened with interest, never uttering a word until he finished.

"Beautiful," she said, "but you've made a mistake. Despite its coloring, which is known in both, it was a *kopayahs*, a frog."

Micah pretty well knew his birds, but not marine life at all. Wondered why he kept saying it was a toad.

"You sure?"

"I am. We call her Frog Mother. She watches over fresh water and wetlands and the creatures that live there. It is she who appeals to the Spirit and brings the water and keeps it flowing."

"Is that what she was doing at the *okosu-wacuw*—praying?"

"Frog Mother doesn't need a prayer mound; the pond is her *okosu-wacuw*."

"She must be well regarded."

"Very. In fact, Frog Mother has only one enemy, Coyote. Coyote is a trickster and greedy. He likes to drink more than his share of water. If not checked, he can cause a drought. So Frog Mother builds a dam to cut off his supply until he goes away. We have a dry spell for a while, but when Coyote's moved on, Frog Mother breaks the dam and the water comes back."

"Amazing," Micah said.

"Of course, these are only legends of my people. Some adopted from western tribes when the coyotes first came east. There probably was a drought at some point and Coyote got blamed."

"Wait."

"What?"

It had all come back to Micah.

"Last night I saw the frog in a dream, and a coyote came and laid down next to her. It was peaceful. A deer was there too. And so were you. I couldn't exactly see you, but felt you there."

"Pumpok, you had a fever, and drank two large glasses of wine."

"So what? Don't your people have sweat lodges and herbs to bring on visions?"

Kodi raised an eyebrow in skepticism. "So it was a vision, was it? I think maybe I teach you too much too fast. Visions are not as common as outsiders think."

"What if it was, what would it mean?"

Kodi grew serious, as if the doubt was draining out of her. "Coyote and Frog Mother together, that means they made peace between each other. The deer represents innocence, and is there to validate the treaty with no treachery. Where was I that you couldn't see me?"

"Out in the pond."

"In the waters that give life, hmm, I'll have to think about that one."

Micah had his own idea. "Maybe what you're doing, the hunt, is forging the peace and ultimately protecting life."

"Slow down, visions are rarely that explicit. I said I will think about it."

Micah was already convinced.

As THEY had to, it was time to talk about Chuck Lewis. Micah reiterated what Lewis had said on the phone. He was going to expose Kodi with, or without, their involvement, and write it before the end of the week for a weekend edition headline.

"Isn't there some kind of reporters' law that he has to confirm with two sources?" Kodi asked.

"I'm guessing if the primary source is unimpeachable, probably not."

"And you're thinking the unimpeachable source is Wawokak."

"After seeing them in the same lot yesterday, yes."

Kodi frowned in thought. Then said, "It's obvious she doesn't like me, and she tried to shut down the hunt at Mary's house, but what's in it for her to betray the mayor's confidence?"

It sounded ridiculous even as Micah said it. "I think it's something between her and me—spite, payback, I don't know."

Kodi didn't find it that ridiculous at all. "Okay, so what if you confront Lewis with that? He's hanging his career on the motives of a jilted girlfriend."

"In this neck of the woods, the story's big enough he won't care."

"What about confiding in Mary? She puts pressure on Lewis and fires Wawokak."

"The story still breaks and you're finished," Micah said, "only without Lewis. Catlett calls the *Providence Journal* and gives it to them. The harm she wants to do is still done."

"At the cost of her career? Micah, you're a hell of a guy, and dearest to me, but is hurting you worth all that?"

"Thanks, I love you too."

"Get serious, you know what I mean. There's an angle here we're missing. Wawokak is a ruthless professional. Someway, somehow, she's got her ass covered."

"That's what we've got to find out."

"And bust it apart," Kodi added.

"How?" Micah asked.

They lapsed into silence, each thinking about what variables there were, and what vulnerabilities. After several minutes, Kodi abruptly stood up. She left the table without her crutch and walked slowly to the back door. She came back at twice the pace. She did four deep knee bends, followed by four jumping jacks, a grimace of pain on her face.

"We move now," Kodi said, "before Lewis's deadline gets any closer. Call Mary and tell her I'm back in town and all better. Perfect, in fact, and tomorrow night I resume the hunt."

CHAPTER TWENTY-FOUR

Micah called Mayor Boyd and passed on the news Kodi was back and ready to hunt. Boyd was delighted. She promised to alert Catlett and Chief Reismann. Micah said Kodi would tend to Ranger Ferzoco.

"That's done, now what?" Micah said to Kodi.

Kodi unfolded her tourist map on the kitchen table. She pointed to a large patch of green. "What's this place?"

"Wanumetonomy Golf Club. It's private, members only."

"It's got farmland on both sides and good water. Everything Coyote needs. We should check it out."

"Like I said, it's private, very exclusive. We'll need permission."

"Call Mary back and ask. You can triangulate the golf course with Shady Stream Orchards and Tyler's Farm. That will clear Coyote out of the whole northeast area of Middletown."

"You sound like a general planning a military operation," Micah said.

"Exactly," Kodi said. "I want to make a statement. Lewis is looking for cheap thrills and sensationalism for a story. I want to prove it's a business, with a business plan, and a business objective. Going forward, we'll work our way east and south from there. Don't know why I didn't think of this before."

"Because this isn't Afghanistan or Iraq?"

"Hmm. Make the call."

Caught up in the "we," "we'll," and "our," Micah dialed the mayor again. Boyd assured him the area would be fine. Her husband, Jack Landsdale, was on the board of directors for Wanumetonomy. All it would take was a phone call.

"We're on," Micah said to Kodi after hanging up.

Kodi hesitated. "We'll see."

"What's that mean?"

"Wawokak has a master plan concerning you and me. Chuck Lewis has one too, and is on a deadline. He doesn't need to wait for us to tell him what he already knows; he has to catch me in the act. He wants live-action exposure. That's top-notch investigative reporting. Suppose the golf club doesn't work for them. It's private, high-class, and has a direct connection to Mary Boyd's husband, Jack. I'm also sure Wanumetonomy doesn't want to be on the front page with a picture of the coyote hunter. Mary and Jack would be furious."

Micah pondered that a moment. If the ritziest club in New England was embarrassed, and Jack Landsdale on its board, Boyd would make it her mission thereafter to destroy Catlett and Lewis.

"What do you think is going to happen?" he said.

"Wawokak will either cancel the hunt, or change its location to one that suits their plans. Despite that, I still want to check it out. All right with you?"

"Let's do it."

Burma Road has some of the most scenic views of Narragansett Bay. From McAllister's Beach one could see the bridges, all the lighthouses, and Prudence and Dyer's Islands. Kodi wasn't interested in scenery. From the McAllister parking lot, she worked her way east, with Micah right behind, onto the ninth hole of the golf course. At the edge of the fairway, they held back while a foursome of retirees, prosperous-looking in attire and with a proliferation of caddies, played through, and up to the green. All clear, she beckoned Micah to follow.

They cut across the fairway into some thickets and trees. Kodi studied the dirt beneath her feet.

"Good ground," she said, and pointed to a paw print. "Fisher cat." Moved a little farther into the trees. Found a dead rabbit, raggedly gnawed. "Definitely a fisher cat."

"Not a coyote?" Micah said.

"Too much left. Coyote's greedy, eats everything but bone and feathers."

"Maybe there's none here," Micah said.

"Doubt that, but it doesn't matter if the hunt is changed. We'll keep this in reserve for another time."

BACK AT home, Kodi was quiet and subdued. Micah left her to her thoughts as they walked out onto the spit together. Even though they both expected the golf course hunt to be canceled, the *nuhsh-ahta* seemed to have taken hold of her.

Staring out at the pond she said, "There's only one way to suppress a sniper if you can't muster artillery support: force him to move to make his kill. Don't look for the window, create it."

Kodi turned to Micah and grabbed his cane in one swift move. She put the cane over her shoulder like a soldier on the parade ground. Standing at attention, she looked Micah straight in the eyes.

"We don't stand a chance together, do we, Micah, you and me?"

Micah knew this was not about coyote hunts, so there was no answer to that question.

"No, I'm sorry."

Kodi shrugged. "Don't be, it's me." A shake of her head. "What about the other stuff, Catlett and Lewis?"

"Now there, we stand a real chance."

Kodi sighed. "I'm sorry I did this to you, I didn't mean to. It kinda happened and felt right for us."

"I know."

"You know what? Fuck it. Let's go swimming."

They stripped down to nothing and Micah took his cane as far as the water's edge, tossed it back, and limped out into the pond, following the copper half-moons of Kodi's buttocks.

It was damn cold, but felt great. Twenty yards from shore, they spat water at each other from their mouths in comical arcs.

It was the best thing, but also the worst thing, Micah could have done. The cough returned. He half swam, half dog-paddled to shore. In knee-deep water, he could not get to his feet. Felt Kodi come up behind him, put her arms under his shoulders, and lift. Her hard nipples against his bare back. Wanted to feel, but could not feel more than that. It was enough. Damned the fates for their cruelty, and also thanked them in the same labored breath. He wanted to die at that moment, couldn't think of a better way, but felt it pass. Saw his life ahead. Sighed deep, deep into another cough.

Despite Kodi's objections, Micah insisted on making supper. Nothing special: his recipe for meatloaf with macaroni and cheese on the side. Kodi finally got in the mood.

"I suppose you have an Alsatian secret for meatloaf."

"Yes," Micah said. "Two eggs in the mix and a drizzle of red wine over the top."

"You think red wine cures everything." It was said in jest, not a cut. They were beyond that now.

"Doesn't it? I'll let you judge."

"Bring it on."

Micah did. As the loaf was baking, they played the soldiers' mess-hall game of name-that-meal.

"Wop slop," Kodi said.

"Spaghetti and meatballs," Micah came back. "Horse cock."

"Friday night's cold cuts, with bologna." Then, "SOS."

"Shit on a shingle: creamed chipped beef on toast. How about sticks and stones?"

"Chop suey with fried noodles."

"Tommy and mush."

"Turkey, stuffing, and gravy," Kodi said. "How do you know that?"

"Who do you think printed the daily menus?" Micah said.

"All right, smart ass, meatloaf and mashed potatoes."

"Cow pucks and plaster."

"Got me."

"No plaster tonight."

"Better not be."

Forty-five minutes later, the meatloaf was done and the mac and cheese thickening in a saucepan.

Kodi's cell phone rang. She didn't budge.

"Going to get that?" Micah said.

Kodi didn't answer him or the phone. Six rings later, it died.

"I saw the number," Kodi said. "It was Wawokak."

The house phone rang. After three rings, Micah picked up.

"Hi, Laurie. No, she's not here. I mean, she's here, but not in the house." Pause. "Out for a run. Training, she does stuff like that." Listening. "She's freaking army, that's what they do." Listening again. "Let me get a pen. You sure? Fuck you too. She had other plans. Why is this so important?" Scribbled notes. "Okay, I'll tell her." Call over at Catlett's end. Micah hung up.

"What's the deal?" Kodi said.

"Change of venue. She insists you hunt Tillsbury Farm tomorrow night. It's off lower Paradise, north of the bird sanctuary. Says it's a political priority. Karl Tillsbury is a big campaign contributor and has a coyote problem. He breeds horses and they're spooked, so Wawokak says. Whatya think?"

"Sounds like the set-up we're expecting."

"That's my take. It's where they want to spring their trap."

"Then it's perfect."

The meatloaf in the oven was overdone. Cow pucks after all.

Oddly, what Micah remembered, and savored most, was the swimming. He'd been naked, in a pristine pond, with a beautiful woman, and it was his own decrepit body that filled his presleep thoughts. In the deepest water, he hadn't cared. They weren't cranky legs beneath him, they were natural fins, and as long as they moved, even every which way, he was afloat, master of his environment. It made him feel as free as he had in too many years to remember.

Remember. Remember what? he thought. *There is something. Something critical. Not the water, not the freedom. The Tillsbury hunt. Do what, call Mary? No, that brings into play a confrontation we're not ready for, not yet. So it's inevitable.* The feeling in the water came back: cool, soothing, free. *Nothing is inevitable until it's already happened. That's the paradox. Kodi knows this. Everything is in the present tense.*

She'd said as much at dinner. "The concept of time is human; it was, it is, will be. In the universe, there is only—it is."

Micah had said, "Are you Pocasset, or Buddhist?"

"The Pocasset don't have all the answers. Nobody does. Besides, where the answers come from is the real secret, not what those answers are."

It was then that Micah faltered. "I didn't want it to be this way between us."

Kodi was ready. "I know, and it isn't, really. We'll find a new path."

CHAPTER TWENTY-FIVE

Together they scouted Tillsbury Farm at dawn. The horses were still in the stable barn. While they stood at the rock wall marking the property line, a friendly sheepdog bounded up to them. Kodi reached over and patted his head and scratched his neck. The dog's tail wagged fiercely, but he made not a sound.

"Some watchdog," Micah said.

"We're not posing any threat." To the dog she said, "Good boy, you know your job, don't you."

She stopped petting and picked up a stick, threw it, and the dog bounded off to fetch it.

"Watch him," Kodi said. "It's all in the breed. If the horses were in pasture, he wouldn't have time for us. Unless, of course, we invaded the horses' space."

The dog returned with the stick and Kodi threw it again.

"What time is it?" she asked.

Kodi had never asked that question before, not even once. Micah checked his watch.

"Six forty-five."

The dog was back. Kodi took the stick from its mouth, laid it on the wall, and resumed petting.

"Sun's been up a half hour," she said, "and all this dog wants is attention. There're no coyotes in wind of this place. He'd know if there were."

Micah was puzzled. "How can they set a trap with no bait?"

"Spring it before we figure that out."

"To hell with them. Call Wawokak and tell her you did your recon and there's no coyotes to hunt."

"Could do that, but is it even the point?"

From an outbuilding across the pasture, closer to the stable than the house, a young man in overalls and ball cap came out and whistled for the dog. Kodi waved to him. He waved back as the dog raced to him.

Micah squinted at him. "Looks barely thirty, not like some rich contributor."

"He doesn't live in the house. Hired help, he's gonna let the horses out to pasture."

As Kodi and Micah watched, that is exactly what the young man did. At least two dozen beautiful horses came, one by one, out of the stable. Micah was no horseman, but each one looked like a thoroughbred.

"They look spooked to you?" Kodi asked.

Micah didn't need to answer. They walked to the pickup and headed home. Kodi took the long way, down along Sachuest Beach.

"If not here tonight," she said, "Wawokak will make it somewhere else tomorrow. Might as well get it over with and move on, one way or another."

Again, no want of a comment.

THERE WAS an e-mail from Nathan Jordan, the retired professor. It had slipped Micah's mind and he hadn't responded. The e-mail didn't gripe about that; Jordan even wrote he assumed Micah was a busy man. No, he wanted to share something else he hoped would help.

Jordan's interest piqued by Icobar Ohlm, he'd launched his own research. Unfortunately, nothing popped up regarding any Icobar Ohlm and the Bureau of Military Information. Jordan did, however, find obscure references to one Icobar Ohlm: an agent with the Bureau of Indian Affairs, circa 1870s. Was any of this of interest to Micah? Jordan would gladly continue his research.

Micah remembered he'd kept his own search to the war era and not broader. He e-mailed back starting with an apology; he wasn't normally a busy man—something had come up. He confessed to Jordan he was only two-thirds through all the journals, and had not reached any part coinciding with Jordan's find. By all means, please, anything the professor uncovered was worth attention. After all, how many Icobar Ohlms could there be? A meeting between them to be arranged as soon as possible, as in when Micah's situation calmed down. Apologies, again.

SEND.

"Work stuff?" Kodi asked from the study door.

"Letter from a former history professor." Micah's hand patted the pile of journals. "He's helping me research this project."

"You told me once, the Civil War, right?"

"A man's life, and it may turn out the war is only part of it. The professor may be onto something."

"What's his name?"

"Nathan Jordan, from Brown University."

"No, I mean the guy in those books." She pointed to the stack. "What's his name?"

Micah picked up the top volume and opened the cover as if he really needed to consult it.

"It's a classic: Icobar Ohlm."

Kodi's eyes widened and her mouth puckered into a circle. "Say again?"

"Ohlm, Icobar Ohlm."

She blinked. "You're messing with me, Pumpok. I know somebody with that name. Only it isn't what he calls himself. He uses an Indian name."

Now Micah's eyes widened. "Who? What Icobar Ohlm do you know?" He came to his feet using the cane. "It can't be."

"Tell him that, he'll be amused."

"Who is it and how do you know him?"

"You've seen him too. Remember the woodworker on the res? The man who gave me the hornbeam? His birth name was Icobar Ohlm, but he had it legally changed to his Indian name years ago. Since then he's White Oak Brother, *Pakahcumus Nimatak*, or as he's called, Pakamatak, Paka to his friends."

Micah could barely grasp it all. "What about his folks? Do they live on the reservation too?"

"Not that I ever heard."

"What about relatives, white relatives?"

"Slow down. That's not something a brave on the res would own up to easily."

"Kodi, this is fantastic." With the excitement, Micah brought on his cough again. He sank back into his chair.

Kodi went to the kitchen for a glass of water. When she returned, Micah was spitting into a handkerchief. She put the water down beside him.

"You've got to get that checked," she said.

"Soon, right now there's too much to do."

"None of it worth dying for."

"All right, after tonight, after the trap." He drank the water.

"Deal," Kodi said. "If you go to the doctor, then do as he says, and when you're up for it, I'll take you back to the res to meet Paka."

Kodi went to prepare for the hunt, which they both knew was no hunt at all, unless Kodi was considered the prey. Micah sat back in his chair and tried to relax. He knew going to the doctor wasn't going to do a hell of a lot of good, he simply didn't know how to say it to Kodi yet. In the course of his disease, things acted up, miscommunicated, and then eventually got frustrated and shut down. It hadn't occurred to him it might be his lungs next. That revised the whole timetable completely.

He was also excited about the new information concerning Icobar Ohlm, both from Jordan and Kodi. There may well be a link between past and present, a blood link at that. He quoted Kodi's wisdom in his head.

Past, present, future are all in the now.

Micah picked up the journal he'd been working on last. He had an impulse to dash ahead and leaf through the rest for anything related to the Bureau of Indian Affairs or an intermarriage, or liaison, with Indian blood. The writer-scholar in him forbade it. Then he thought of Roger Ohlm.

Does he know? Are they cousins of some kind?

Which brought Paka to mind. He remembered the big man, tall, broad-chested, wearing the overalls of his trade. He'd even waved to Micah. Yes, a big man.

Like an oak tree, Micah thought. *White Oak Brother. Paka.*

White? Icobar Ohlm of the present generation, however far removed from the original family tree, was White Oak Brother.

What was the Pocasset Paka to the *wanuks* Roger Ohlm?

Micah intended to find out.

THEY PASSED on supper and both took naps. Kodi awoke first and brought a steaming cup into Micah's bedroom, gently rubbing his shoulder to awaken him.

"Time to get ready," she said.

Micah saw the cup. "What's that?"

"Indian medicine for the cough."

"Any snakes or bugs in it?"

"Both, but you won't taste them. Drink it."

He propped himself up and accepted the brew. Blew across the top, sniffed it, and tasted.

"Drink it as hot as you can stand," Kodi said.

It was very hot. He sipped again. Could taste honey, cloves, and sage. Micah had a reasonably sharp palate. Maybe a dash of ginger, definitely some mint.

"Drink," she coaxed.

The more he drank, the smoother it went down. He might have imagined it because of the heat, but his chest pressure seemed to lighten.

"All done, Doc," he said handing the empty cup back.

Kodi took it to the kitchen and returned with the camo poncho. She laid it on the edge of the bed.

"Dress warm, but loose; layers not thickness."

"Do we really even have to do this at all? Why don't we simply drive up and yell, 'Boo, gotcha.' "

"I'd rather make them work for it."

Sounded fair. "Roger that."

"When you're ready, I'll paint your face."

Kodi withdrew and Micah dressed as instructed: First, a black tee shirt, then a black cotton turtleneck, and finally a mild-weather, light black sweater. Black jeans and the poncho completed the ensemble. He went to the kitchen.

Kodi was finishing up her own face paint at the table, as always, without a mirror. Her rifle case and backpack were on the table. Micah sat next to her. She turned and began on his face.

"What's my job?" he said.

"Same as the orchard, you're my spotter. We'll park close to the beach and hike up. Can you handle that? There'll be no rush, slow pace; we're on our schedule this time, not Coyote's."

"Not a problem. I'm not sure exactly what was in that elixir, but I feel great."

"Good, but don't push yourself. Here's my plan."

Positive that Chuck Lewis was going to be at the farm, Kodi figured he had to park somewhere. Probably as close as he could to the widest angle of sight he could observe. If they came up behind his SUV, he would be somewhere in front of them.

"You've thought this out," Micah said.

"It's what I do. Different tactics for different prey. Unless you're hunting a pro of equal or better skills, man is the easiest."

Micah's face was finished.

"Now the important stuff," Kodi said.

She unzipped the gun case and took out the Winchester. Worked the bolt and ejected four cartridges, lined them up on the table. Worked the bolt again, nothing happened, slid again and left the chamber exposed. Dipped the rifle for Micah to look inside.

"Take a good look," Kodi said. "If anything happens I want you to be able to swear I left here with an unloaded weapon and carrying no ammo."

Micah looked and nodded. Kodi put the rifle down and removed a half-full box of Winchester 22-250 REM cartridges from the case. She put the four loose bullets in it and handed the box to Micah.

"Put that away somewhere in your bedroom, don't tell me where."

Micah got up and took the box to his room. He put it under some socks in the dresser, then returned to the kitchen.

"Done," he said.

"Now check the case for any strays."

"You're too professional for that."

"Check anyway."

Micah searched the empty gun case thoroughly, no loose rounds.

"Put the rifle in the case and close it."

Micah did.

"I saved the best for last," Kodi said. "Now pat me down for any."

By now he fully realized Kodi wasn't kidding about any of it. They both stood up. Starting at her neck, down both shoulders and arms, around her breasts, down her back, each leg, and crotch. The only things he found were an ID wallet and the keys to the pickup. She wasn't even carrying her hunting knife.

"The Beretta's in the bag and it's loaded. You're to keep it with you at all times."

"Do we have to bring it?" Micah said.

"There's always a 'just in case' and you're mine."

"Check."

Through the entire procedure, except for the best-for-last part, Kodi had been completely professional. Yet Micah sensed something missing. Didn't want to ask. Suddenly realized what it was.

She hasn't sunk into the nuhsh-ahta. *This is only an exercise.*

CHAPTER TWENTY-SIX

Kodi pulled the truck into the deserted beach parking lot. She took the rifle from its case and Micah shouldered the backpack. Kodi in front, they walked single file up the cross-road that bordered Tillsbury Farm. The moon was in its last quarter, but it was still dark in the road with trees to either side. Kodi's pace was leisurely and she kept to the west side of the road, in the rough where the pavement turned to gravel. Micah had no problem keeping up.

In less than a quarter mile, the trees on the east side ended and the rock wall began. Kodi hand-signaled over her shoulder to stop. Micah saw her crouch down, so he did too. They waited and it was very quiet. So quiet, Micah heard himself breathe. He realized now why Kodi had taken the long way home from the recon. It was unlikely anyone with business at Tillsbury Farm would approach from the south where there was only the beach and a roundabout way back to town. No, they would come from the north, a shorter trip by more than half.

Now it wasn't his own breath he heard, it was a car engine, low and steady. He peered past Kodi but could see no headlights; they must be off. Next he heard the crunch of gravel as the vehicle pulled to the shoulder. The engine was cut off.

The sound of a car door closing.

Not very stealthy for an investigative reporter.

Then another door.

In front of him, Kodi flashed a V-sign indicating two people. Watched her raise the empty rifle and peer through the scope, using it in absence of binoculars. Lowered the gun and inched back along the ground until next to Micah.

She whispered, "Lewis and another guy, a photographer loaded down with cameras. Pretty sure of himself."

They stayed still waiting for the pair to cross the road. Kodi checked several times through the scope. Micah thought he heard muted conversation up the road—Lewis and another male. A grunt was audible. Kodi checked with scope.

"They're over the wall," she said.

That's when Micah realized, he didn't know Kodi's full plan. Was she going to surprise them? Confront them?

Kodi was moving again, Micah right behind. They crossed the road and knelt beside the rock wall. Could still hear undecipherable chatter as the two men on the other side walked out into the pasture. When their voices completely faded, Kodi peeked over the wall.

"Looks like they're headed for the stable barn. Probably want to hide there and catch me coming up through the farm."

It made sense to Micah. If there actually were coyotes around, they'd probably nose around the stable drawn by the horses' scent.

Kodi could now risk a long, steady look over the wall. "Almost there."

"Are we following?" Micah said.

"No, still some time till dawn. We sit tight."

Two or three minutes passed. It grew a little lighter in the predawn.

"They're at the stable, checking it out."

In the next instant Micah heard the sheepdog go crazy. Growls and barks louder and fiercer than any pit bull or Doberman Micah ever heard. It was joined by a second, perhaps a sibling or mate, absent yesterday morning.

Micah rose up and looked over the wall, shoulder to shoulder with Kodi. The dogs had Lewis and the photographer pinned against the stable door, snapping at their ankles and knees, one dog to each trespasser.

A light came on at the outbuilding and the door opened. The young man, in his sleeping shorts, came out. He carried a rifle. Instinctively, he fired a warning shot straight up in the air.

Micah looked back at the stable. Lewis was frantically trying to climb the plank wall away from one dog. The photog panicked worse, and did the stupidest thing possible: With arms for leverage, he was trying to kick in the stable door and gain entry for refuge.

There had to be a couple of million dollars in horseflesh in that barn, and the young man was responsible for all of it. His second shot was no warning.

Micah saw his target lurch forward, splayed against the barn door. His head was suddenly misshapen, and his body slid down the door into a heap. Both dogs started barking again. Lewis was screaming hysterically.

The man lowered his rifle and whistled. The dogs took one last appraisal of their intruders, turned, and trotted toward him.

Kodi saw the whole thing up close through her scope.

"Cranium-splitter," she said. "He's gone." No emotion: toneless, cold. She turned the scope on the shooter. "He's on his cell, probably 9-1-1."

Lewis stopped shrieking and sank into a fetal position at the base of the wall beside his dead associate at the bloodied barn door.

Micah suddenly felt cold too. "Not the headline he wanted."

"We can go now," Kodi said. "Stay low."

Micah led this time, half crouched, relying on his stick, but making steady progress. Where the wall ended and the trees began, they stood and walked upright the rest of the way. At their backs, out of the north, sirens were descending on Tillsbury Farm.

In the pickup, Micah asked, "What do we do now?"

"Get cleaned up and call Chief Reismann. We're witnesses to a fatal property invasion."

"I suppose we should."

"Even if it weren't the right thing to do," Kodi said, "there's at least three people still alive that know I was supposed to be there. You're one of them."

And Chuck and Laurie, Micah said to himself.

WITH THE crime scene to investigate, Chief Reismann was late getting to 18 Green End Avenue. He took a lot of notes. When asked, he responded that Chuck Lewis was in Newport County Hospital, in such a state of shock, no statement could be taken. The shooter had said very little. The last was: get old man Tillsbury's lawyer.

Kodi gave her statement first, a recounting of exactly what she and Micah observed together. Then Micah gave his in complete agreement.

Next came the interrogation.

"So what were you both doing there anyway?"

"It was scheduled to be a coyote hunt," Kodi said, "but there was never really going to be one."

"I don't understand," Reismann said.

"It was a setup," Micah said. "Chuck Lewis wanted to catch the coyote hunter in the act and unmask Kodi for the public."

"Who set it up, Lewis?"

"Wawokak," Kodi said.

"Huh?"

Micah took over. "I don't know if my word alone is enough for a court, without Lewis's corroboration, but Laurie Catlett made the arrangements. For whatever reasons of her own, she wants the hunt over and Kodi gone. I also don't know if Tillsbury is involved. Never met the man. Catlett said he's a big campaign donor and had a coyote problem. Trust me; there were no coyotes on his property."

Reismann snorted. "For purposes of this investigation, your word is all I need, Micah. As for Karl Tillsbury, he's in Dubai buying horses. Has been for two weeks. Though he owns the farm, he's not even a registered voter here. His official residence is in Kentucky. Got a huge horse farm there. Keeps this little piece of Aquidneck as a hideaway for special horses for select buyers. From what I've learned this morning, you can't keep a secret about a horse in Kentucky. Calls Tillsbury Farm his safe house."

"So those horses are actually worth a lot," Micah said.

Reismann still hadn't said the young man's name, and Micah respected him for that.

"According to our shooter, he's got bloodlines in there back to Secretariat, Seattle Slew, and Northern Dancer. I don't follow the horses, but I've heard of those ponies."

"What's going to happen to him," Kodi asked, "the shooter?"

"Most likely, nothing," Reismann said. "He was protecting private property from exactly as it appears—an aggressive assault. He couldn't possibly know Lewis's agenda. He was protecting the owner's investment from invasion and possible harm. Old man Tillsbury will probably give him a bonus."

"But they weren't armed," Micah said.

"How's he supposed to know that from fifty yards away in the middle of the night? It's private property, and at least one of them was seeking forceful illegal access to valuable horses." Reismann threw up his hands. "Life sucks, is that what you want to hear? You mess with the wrong kind, you take your chances." Reismann tapped his pen repeatedly on his pad, writing nothing. "Let's get back to you guys." He paused and took a long look at Kodi. "With Tillsbury in Dubai, and trigger-finger in charge, you know, you might have been shot instead. Our shooter claims no knowledge of any coyote hunt, after which he invoked counsel."

"Did they ever have any coyotes?" Kodi asked.

"Two years ago," Reismann said. "Our boy dispatched a few of them, under the radar. They never came back. I guess they got the lay of the land."

It became clear to Micah. "So if Kodi wasn't exposed in a pop of flashbulbs, she could have been shot by Tillsbury's farmhand."

"Didn't I say that?" Reismann said.

"And that's not a crime?"

"What hasn't happened isn't a crime," Reismann said. He turned to Kodi. "You about done with all this?"

"No way, I'm hunting Wanumetonomy tonight. Tell the mayor."

Reismann shook his head. "No offense, young lady, but you surely are the persistent sort."

Kodi only nodded.

"Lewis will be brought up on charges," Reismann said. "They trespassed on his initiative. The photographer's death is on his head."

"So be it. I've got a job to do."

Reismann looked at Micah. "You okay with this?"

Micah nodded. "All of it."

"I hope you know what you're both doing."

"Doesn't really matter anymore," Micah said. "You'll see to Catlett?"

"That's my job." Reismann opened his cell phone and speed-dialed. "Elmer, bring in Laurie Catlett for questioning regarding the Tillsbury shooting." He looked at the ceiling. "Yes, that Laurie Catlett." He hung up.

"That's gonna start a shitstorm," Kodi said.

"The storm's already here." Reismann left.

THE CHIEF was gone an hour before Micah brought up the subject.

"Why'd you say you're hunting tonight?"

"Because I am," Kodi said. "If I don't do it, it doesn't seem important. If the hunt's not important, than neither is my being in Middletown. I've got work to do."

Micah asked why the Wanumetonomy Golf and Country Club? All they'd found there was evidence of a fisher cat. Maybe the club's groundskeepers had cleared the coyotes out of there as well.

"Doubt it," Kodi said. "We did our recon too late in the morning. Coyote had already eaten and gone home. I have a hunch about that place. It's too damn perfect not to attract Coyote. Even if it's only a *cacaw* that comes and goes as he pleases."

Loner, Micah remembered. "You'd know better than anybody else. All right, we'll do it."

"Not we, Pumpok. Sorry, I've got to do this one solo."

Micah was taken aback. They'd been referring to themselves as a team since Paradise Valley and Sweet Cherry Farm. He was her spotter, if only in name.

Kodi sensed what he was thinking. "Take a break from this one. You've been sick lately, and still haven't called the doctor like you promised. Then there's Wawokak to consider. You said her problem might have something to do with you. Why feed into it? Let me go this one alone. If she's not arrested or fired by now, and this goes on, I want to be her target on my terms, for what I do, not because you had the good sense to cut her loose before I ever met you."

Micah gave that some thought. Kodi had a valid point, he had to admit. If he truly was Catlett's primary problem, for whatever nonsensical reason of her own making, then his constant presence with Kodi only exacerbated the situation.

Damn it all. He started to cough again. Hacked until he could hardly catch his breath.

"Time for more of my snake and bug tea," Kodi said.

She guided Micah to a chair, got him some water, then started to prepare her brew.

It wasn't only the coughing and the renewed chest pressure. Micah suddenly felt an intense weariness throughout his whole body. Could barely feel his arms and legs. What he could feel, felt too heavy to lift. His head felt light, but his mind stayed clear, and for that he was grateful. Wanted only to think, and then express himself.

"You're right," he managed to say, "right about everything. It's your contract, your livelihood, and I know you'll do well. We'll do it again some other time, or something else together."

Kodi smiled at him from the sink as she filled the kettle. "Of course we will. And you're right too. Especially about the things you've only begun to question."

For Micah, that was a good and bad thing at the same time. His life would never be the same. Glad it wouldn't be. Grateful, even. But if symptoms were omens, the learning need come faster.

When the potion was ready, Kodi brought it to the table. Micah needed both hands to lift the mug.

"I'd better alert Ferzie," Kodi said. "You drink."

CHAPTER TWENTY-SEVEN

After Kodi's hot toddy and three glasses of wine, that Micah insisted was medicine too, he was ready for bed. Stick on one side, Kodi on the other, Micah staggered to the bedroom. Stripping him to shorts and tee shirt, she laid him down and covered him up.

"Don't get up until I get back in the morning," she said.

"What if I have to pee?"

"Let yourself go, I'll have wash to do anyway."

"I can't do that."

"Well, you can't walk. Hold on."

Kodi left and came back with an empty mayonnaise jar from Micah's recycle bin.

"Use this, but stay in bed. I mean it."

"Be careful tonight."

"Always am."

She felt for a fever, or was simply brushing his hair back, Micah didn't know, but it felt tender. Pictured her kissing his forehead, but she didn't. Closed his eyes and heard her leave the room, closing the door.

Ah, now for my vision, he thought, remembering the last one when he felt like this.

There was no vision, only flashbacks. The sheepdog chasing a stick. The man waving when he whistled. Crouching by the rock wall. The vicious barking. Two desperate, terrified men. A gunshot, then another.

No visions tonight. Just as well.

MICAH SLEPT the whole night and well into the next morning. The first conscious sound he heard was the shower running. Propped himself up. His chest was not so bad and he had no urge to cough. Looked at himself sitting up and realized his arms were back to normal. Tried his legs. Right one fine, left cantankerous as expected. To the closet for jeans and the dresser for a sweatshirt.

In the kitchen, the coffee wasn't made so he set to the task. Heard the water stop in the bathroom. Kodi appeared, wrapped in Micah's ladies' towel of choice.

"How you feeling?" she said.

"Good, better than good, fine. How'd it go?"

"There was a *cacaw*, like I thought. A male, older, lots of experience. Toyed with me awhile in the woods, darting and dodging. He'd seen a lot of people in his time and the fear was gone. When he got tired of it, made his mistake. Figured he could outrun me across the fairway. Of course, it wasn't me he had to outrun. All I needed was a second to sight." Kodi sighed to herself. "I stayed until Ferzie came to get him. Didn't want some dawn golfers gawking at him. He's dead, and that's the way it is. He doesn't have to be a sideshow."

As she walked from the kitchen, Micah remembered her putting him to bed. Wondered if he'd ever return the courtesy.

"Heard anything?" she asked.

"I've been asleep for almost twelve hours. You?"

"Ferzie says it's on the news and in the papers."

"I don't think I care anymore."

"About which part?"

"The selfishness, the senselessness, the stupidity. There're important things people should be concerned about."

Kodi looked at him. "Did you have another vision?"

"Ha! I think this time it's more of an epiphany."

She then said something that took Micah by surprise.

"Why don't you write about it?"

Again, "Ha," though not as humorous and cynical as the first time.

"I'm sorry. You said you don't anymore. All right, so what are you up for today?"

Another surprise. "Don't you need some sleep?"

"I'm good for the day. Tonight will be another story. The day is all yours, if you want to, that is."

"I want to, and I say we get the hell out of this town for a few hours. I know a nice little place in Port Judith and we can drive over there for lunch. It's right on the water."

"Surf and turf?"

"Best in the state."

"Great, one thing first."

"What?"

"I'll show you."

Kodi led Micah outside to the *okosu-wacuw*. She picked the orange stone off the top, did her ritual, and threw it out into the pond. From her pocket she took out a little packet. It was the one she'd given Micah before she left for Narragansett.

"I saw it on your desk; it's your time again."

Kodi opened the pouch and Micah delved in with two fingers. Of the two within, one felt perfectly round. He drew it out. It was solid cobalt blue.

Kodi admired it. "Strong magic."

"Good or bad?"

"The best."

Kodi wrapped Micah's fingers around the stone, and then hers over his. Together, they faced the four corners one by one. They breathed on it. She moved their combined fists to her heart, and then to his.

"Put it on the pile," she said.

"Isn't there more?"

"Not for this one."

They opened their hands and Micah stooped and put the stone on top. Straightened up, watched the sun catch the stone.

"Did we get married?"

Kodi giggled. "No," then stopped giggling. "But as close as we'll ever get."

"Then, indeed, we must celebrate."

As THEY drove over the bridge onto the island of Jamestown, Micah thought of Professor Nathan Jordan. Despite the madness that seemed to have Aquidneck Island in its grip, Micah had one clear objective still intact.

I still have my work. I still have Icobar Ohlm.

He turned to Kodi. "Tell me about Paka. Do you know him well?"

There was hesitation on Kodi's part. It appeared to Micah she suddenly gripped the steering wheel with excessive force. It passed, and she took a deep breath.

"Paka and I go back," she said. "That's why I'm known on Watuppa. I never wanted to live on a res, but he insisted. It was his calling. Like changing his name."

Micah realized what she was saying, did not need her to elaborate.

"Paka was in the army too, but we met afterward. He was Special Forces, all classified stuff. He never talked about it."

Micah asked how they met.

Kodi grinned. "Don't laugh, at a powwow. The term isn't what most people think, no war councils and secret oaths. These days it's a cultural event, like Saint Patrick's Day for the Irish, or Columbus Day for Italians. Lasts about three days. There's food, music, crafts, and a decent share of outright partying."

"Sounds like fun," Micah said.

"It is; I'll take you sometime."

They crossed the Jamestown Verrazzano Bridge off the island onto the mainland.

Kodi came back to her story. "Anyway, Paka had enough of military life. When he came out, he didn't know what to do. It's hard to understand, if you've never been in the service. Army life is all-consuming. There is no real downtime. It's where you're sent, live, eat, sleep, fight, and relax—always with fellow soldiers. Then suddenly you're out and the world is a big vacuum. Nothing is planned for you, regulated, given as an order, or in some manual—no offense."

Kodi turned south through Saunderstown. Soon they would be in Narragansett and Micah's thoughts drifted a few seconds. Somewhere in the vicinity was the trailer park that was Kodi's home. He didn't mention it.

Her story kept unfolding. Paka filled the void with his heritage and took up woodworking, a trade of his forebearers. At the powwow he was working, carving birds and miniature totems, pretty much anything that would sell for a few bucks as genuinely crafted by a Native American. Kodi had stopped to browse his carvings. She wasn't working the powwow, simply a visitor enjoying an autumn Saturday.

Even if they've served in different wars, generations apart, there's a mien, a countenance, which all former military people instantly recognize in each other. Kodi and Paka sensed it before ever speaking a word to each other.

"One thing led to another," Kodi said. "You know how it goes."

"I do," Micah said.

"Later, if it's not to be, it unravels and you're left with loose ends. But we're still friends, always will be."

"So it's a good thing after all."

"After all," and her voice trailed off.

THE RESTAURANT overlooked Point Judith Harbor and Block Island Sound. They watched the ferry come and go—eating oysters on the half shell, followed by the surf and turf, fillet mignon, and a lobster tail. A bottle of Malbec wine was shared. Kodi asked if Micah ever drank white wine. He said no; it gave him a headache.

"I thought wine was wine," she said.

"I used to think people were simply people."

"What's that mean?"

"I don't know, I haven't completely worked out the details of my epiphany."

"Are you thinking of leaving Middletown, moving somewhere else?"

Micah hadn't considered it. "I don't want to, I always thought Green End Pond would be the proverbial last stop. Right now, a part of me is disgusted, but a deeper part has a sense of place. Know what the Rhode Island state motto is? Hope."

"I like that," she said.

There was no room left for dessert. Micah paid the bill and they made the drive back to Green End Avenue.

THE RESPITE was brief. Micah had two phone messages on his machine. Both requested a soonest call back. Neither detailed the nature of the matter. The first was Chief Reismann. The second from Mayor Boyd. Micah was tempted to call Boyd first; they had a good relationship, even friendly. A little more thought, and he decided not to put her ahead of Reismann. Boyd was a politician, and also Laurie Catlett's boss. Kodi had described it as a "shitstorm," and Reismann agreed. Which is precisely when politicians seek damage control. Micah wanted no part of it. Reismann, on the other hand, had strenuously admitted, at the mayor's home, he was no politician, only a sworn officer of the law. Micah didn't know Reismann as well as he did Boyd, but what he did know, he liked. If anyone was going to sort this out and justly assign blame, the chief seemed the better option.

Kodi went to do her laundry and Micah dialed the phone. Reismann's first question did not surprise him.

"Have you discussed the Tillsbury shooting with anyone since we met?"

"Aside from Kodi, no. But I have a message to call Mayor Boyd."

"Nothing from Catlett?"

"I just got home and haven't checked my e-mail yet, but otherwise, no."

"Check, I'll hold," Reismann said.

Micah took the cordless handset to his study and powered up the computer. Only an e-mail from Nathan Jordan.

"Nothing from Laurie, Chief."

"You going to be home this evening? I'd like to come over."

"Come right ahead. Only one question."

"What's that?"

"What do I do about the mayor's message?"

"I'm not telling you what to do, Micah, but if it were me, I'd wait on returning that call."

From the tone of Reismann's voice, it sounded to Micah like good advice.

AT THE kitchen table, Kodi and Micah went over their previous statements with Chief Reismann. Reismann kept referring to his notes from the first interview, but did not make any fresh ones. From his arrival, Reismann had insisted on no questions from either of the pair until his confirmation process of the original statements was concluded.

When it did end, Micah asked, "What's Chuck Lewis got to say?"

"Nothing," Reismann said. "Soon as he was off the tranquilizers and in his right mind, he lawyered up."

"And Catlett?" Kodi said.

It was strange to Micah, not hearing her say Wawokak.

Reismann exhaled with resignation. "Ms. Laurie Catlett, the mayor's chief of staff, is a whole nother story. At the time of the shooting she was out of town. Left around one A.M. to drive to Bennington, Vermont. A family crisis, she says. Some vague reference to her sister's health. Finally reached her by cell, after it was turned off for a considerable length of time."

"Laurie's never turned her cell off in her life," Micah said.

"She did this time. Conveniently, you might note. Whatever the case, she told me she'll be back in Middletown on Monday. Without a formal charge, I can't compel otherwise. And I don't have enough for that charge, not yet."

"Did she say anything about Tillsbury, why she set it up?" Micah pressed.

"Do you mind if I quote her exactly?"

"Please do."

Reismann found it in his notes. " 'That bastard LaVeck is a goddamn liar.' "

Micah and Kodi were stunned.

"How the hell can she say that?" Micah said.

Reismann looked at Kodi. "During the time in question, did you speak to Catlett on the phone?"

"No. She phoned, but I didn't take the call."

"Why not?"

"Chief, Catlett and I have not been very compatible. I prefer dealing directly with Mayor Boyd or through Micah. Catlett and I always wind up antagonistic."

"Too bad," Reismann said. He looked back to Micah. "It's your word against hers she told you Tillsbury."

"Mine, and Lewis's."

"Then the best we can hope for is his lawyer convinces him to cut a deal. Put all the blame on Catlett."

"Is that a possibility?"

"I've been a cop forty years, Micah, anything's possible."

"When should I call Boyd back?"

Reismann looked at his watch. "Coming up on midnight. I'm pretty sure she won't be on the tennis court this particular Saturday. After your breakfast should be fine."

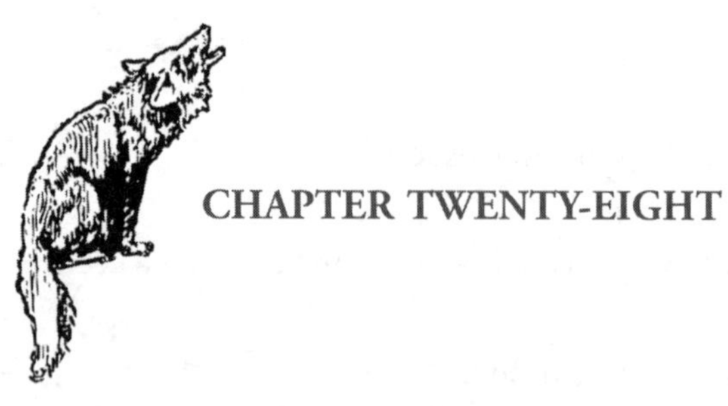

CHAPTER TWENTY-EIGHT

Kodi had been up twenty-four hours and was exhausted. After Chief Reismann left, she excused herself and went to bed. Micah wasn't ready. He made a cup of tea and sat back at the table. Two unread issues of the *Newport Daily News* were on the table. Their very presence irritated Micah. He got up and threw both papers in his recycle bin out the back door.

What they represented could not be recycled. Lives had been ruined, and one ended tragically. Why? Micah thought on that drinking his tea. What he came up with wasn't much of an answer.

Because one person was officially sanctioned to kill on public and private land, and paid to do it at taxpayer expense. And that lone hunter wished to remain anonymous, do her job, and move on with her life.

It hadn't sat well with Bob Mackey: now he was under arrest and his son's life marred as well. It hadn't sat well with Chuck Lewis, who asserted the public's right to know, only for a byline and train ticket to New York. Now a man was dead, and Lewis arrested soon. As for the farmhand, Micah didn't know. He did his job as he saw fit, and the law stood behind him.

And Laurie Catlett, Wawokak. Forget about her for a second.

There was other damage as well. A townspeople still divided by their opinions on the hunt. Also, Micah heard, and he couldn't remember from where, perhaps Reismann mentioned it—Shady Stream Orchards wouldn't open this spring. Charlie Ochs had been impatient and taken matters into his own hands and poisoned his livelihood. Tons of soil, and the trees rooted in it, would be bulldozed and carted away. All at Ochs's expense in fines. Bankruptcy was certain to follow.

Back to Laurie Catlett. *Her career is ruined and she'll be arrested—eventually, I imagine.*

"That bastard LaVeck is a goddamn liar."

Why? Because of a hostess at the Chart House Restaurant? We were already over and done. Because I'm the one who called it quits?

Micah had said as much to Kodi, but didn't fully believe it. He wasn't that prize a catch for the likes of Catlett, and realized it. Besides, the relationship was on life support anyway, only needed one of them to finally pull the plug.

Is her ego that large?

Micah didn't know the answer. Then he remembered what Kodi had said.

"Wawokak is a ruthless professional. Someway, somehow, she's got her ass covered."

If that's the case, it isn't about me, which leaves Kodi or Mary Boyd.

Micah washed his teacup and went to bed. In the morning he'd have to make that phone call.

THERE WAS an icy edge to Mayor Boyd's voice that Micah only heard at town meetings when she retorted to a snide question. She'd never used that tone with him.

"We have a dilemma, Micah."

Damage control. "Actually, Mary, we have a crime and somebody's going to be held responsible."

"For the time being, that's Chuck Lewis."

"For the time being," Micah repeated.

Long silence before Boyd said, "Harry has informed me there's a discrepancy in recollections of a phone call between you and Laurie."

"Laurie's lying."

"I have to consider that, but, and no offense meant, at this stage it's still under investigation."

"Have you spoken to her?"

"She left me a voice message she had an emergency at her sister's in Vermont. Sudden illness, it was. That being the case, family and all, I thought it considerate not to bother her."

"Bother her . . . ?"

Boyd cut him off.

"Micah, as Harry has no case to go up there and arrest her, I think this can all wait until Monday to be sorted out on her return. Provided the sister's condition doesn't necessitate Laurie extending her stay."

"There's nothing to sort out. Once Lewis fully appreciates his situation, he'll fold."

"There's always more than one situation to appreciate."

"This isn't politics; a man is dead."

"That's most unfortunate, I realize that, truly. But what is done cannot be undone, so my priority now is for the best interests of Middletown."

Micah had enough. "Why are you protecting her?"

"Until proven otherwise, she's earned it, that's all."

"I don't think we have anything further to discuss."

"There is one thing," Boyd said. "The arrangements to hunt the golf club the first time were made through me and my husband. If Laurie did change the plan, why didn't you or Kodi notify me?"

"Because it wasn't the first time an order or message was passed to us through your chief of staff. There was no reason to question it."

Micah hung up.

Kodi heard Micah's side of the phone call from across the table.

"Didn't sound like that went well," she said.

Something had come across in his conversation with the mayor that Micah couldn't put his finger on exactly. A nuance, something below the surface. Unsaid and unintended on Boyd's part, but definitely present.

It struck Micah. "Mary's afraid of Wawokak."

"You're wrong. You saw the way Mary shut her down the night at the house. The night Wawokak wanted me fired."

"That was business. This is careers."

His excuse for not calling the doctor was that it was Saturday. Micah said he didn't need emergency treatment; he would call his regular doctor on Monday during normal office hours.

Kodi set up her laptop.

"Whatcha doing?"

"Checking my account. Want to be sure I got paid for the golf club *cacaw.*

"They direct deposit your fees?"

"I didn't want them mailed since I'm not home. And it wasn't like I wanted to go up to Town Hall and collect the checks myself."

He waited while she checked her account.

"Paid in full," she said.

There was an ominous hollowness in the words. Kodi realized it herself.

"Think that's my last?"

"Definite possibility," Micah said. "High Street, Shady Stream, Tillsbury; I'd bet Mary wants this to end and go away. You with it. Part of the damage control."

"Wawokak wins in the end."

"If you call dodging a murder charge winning."

Kodi didn't comment.

"You can't hunt again until tomorrow night. If it is over, you'll hear soon."

Kodi closed the laptop. "The hell with it, let's go out to the pond. I need some air."

Micah felt he had forgotten something. Something about Chief Reismann. No, it wasn't about the shooting. Something with Catlett. Check e-mails.

"In a minute," Micah said. "I just remembered Professor Jordan sent me an e-mail. Let me read it first. Come on into the study."

Micah powered up his computer and retrieved the e-mail.

> Mr. LaVeck,
>
> We're definitely referring to the same Icobar Ohlm. Honorably discharged 1865. Joined Indian Agency same year with a letter of recommendation from Allan Pinkerton, authorized and countersigned by General McClellan.
>
> N. Jordan.

Micah started composing an e-mail thank you. He stopped typing and looked up at Kodi.

"Should the hunt really be over, you still going to be around next week?"

"Why not? I'll be unemployed."

"Good, I mean, you know what I mean."

Micah added to the e-mail a proposal to meet Jordan in Jamestown on Wednesday. As long as it wasn't an imposition, he'd like to bring his research assistant, Ms. Kodi Red Moon.

SEND.

"How did you know my last name?"

"From the clinic on the reservation. That's what the nurse called you. Also, Lewis said it after he'd run the plates from your truck."

"You never mentioned it."

"Didn't I?"

"No."

Micah couldn't tell if she was piqued or amused.

"There should be no secrets," he said, "between sharers of the blue stone."

It was amusement.

"*Nihtuhto wusomi kipi*," Kodi said.

"Which means?"

"You learn a lot, fast."

Officially, the call came on Sunday at eleven a.m. to Kodi's cell phone. At least Mayor Boyd had enough character left to do it herself. Under the circumstances, not enumerated by Boyd, the coyote hunt was concluded. This was no reflection on Kodi, who had done a superb job, but other recent matters tainted the initiative beyond repair. Was Kodi paid in full? Good. Have a safe trip back to Narragansett.

Chief Reismann had called at nine a.m. to Micah's home phone. Micah put it on speaker for a three-way conversation.

"The mayor has shut down the hunt," Reismann said.

"We anticipated that," Micah said.

"She'll let you know in her own good time. Kodi, I didn't want you gearing up for tonight, my knowing it isn't going to happen."

"Appreciate that, Chief," Kodi said.

"Will you be leaving then?"

"Not for a while. I've signed on to do some Native American research for one of Micah's projects."

"Good for you. In any case, your trailer is fine where it is, for as long as you want to leave it."

"Thanks."

"Any word on Lewis?" Micah asked.

"He can't leave the island. The grand jury will indict him tomorrow and I'll bring him in afterward."

"Did he mention a deal?"

"Not yet. His lawyer will wait for the specific charges; then he'll know what sort of deal to argue. If I can pin it on Catlett, he could walk away with criminal trespassing, a hefty fine, and community service."

"And Catlett?"

"She chose the site and the time, knew it was illegal without explicit permission from the landowner, and set it in motion. That's at least a manslaughter charge."

"What if Lewis doesn't cooperate?"

"He takes a hard fall and we get Catlett on conspiracy charges. I don't see it playing out that way. Lewis has only one chance to salvage his life."

"Sounds like you've got the matter well in hand, Chief."

"Only following the book. Tomorrow's going to be a long day for all of us. After which, the DA will want to talk to both of you, depositions and all that stuff. Kodi, if you haven't figured it out already, by sundown tomorrow your cover will be blown. As the legal process comes together, you'll be identified as the coyote hunter of Aquidneck Island."

"Thought so," Kodi said.

"One more thing, and I never said this."

"What's that, Chief?"

"Get that nine mil out of my town as soon as you can."

"How'd you know?"

"In Middletown, nobody puts a bullet in anything that I'm not eventually aware of, how and why."

Micah spoke up. "For the record, I fired that shot."

"There is no record, ditch that gun."

Micah had made up his mind. It was the right thing to do. Wished he could have said to himself "noble thing," but it wasn't. It was only a matter of being fair and objective. A matter of accepting another truth about life, his life and life in general. He waited until they were out by the pond, right at the shore, the *okosu-wacuw*, crowned with the blue stone, behind them.

"This is your last night of anonymity. Tomorrow you'll be known across Aquidneck as Kodi, the coyote hunter. Someone else will write the story instead of Lewis. All of it: a woman, Pocasset Indian, former army sniper, ten confirmed coyote kills—every detail they have, and some they'll invent."

"What are you trying to say, Pumpok?"

"Go out tonight without me. Do what single people your age do. Dress up, hit a club or bar, drink the current cocktail fad, let a half-dozen good looking guys buy them for you, dance with them, and if the right situation presents itself, and you want to, go home with one of them."

"Pumpok!"

"Seriously, all right, maybe not the last part. For one night don't be the coyote hunter. Be Kodi, the beautiful, single, unattached, interesting female with a night to kill, instead of prey."

"What about you?"

"I'm still me, and that world is behind me, but it's still your world. Enjoy it, make the most of it, live a little in the skin you have. In the morning, we'll still be friends, more than friends, and start the next phase of all this together. Tonight, do this for yourself, and if you make me say it, do it for me."

They stared at each other. Then Kodi flinched and threw her arms around Micah. He dropped his stick and embraced her. They held long and tight, no impulse to kiss, only clinging to each other, as the sun set on Green End Pond.

"This is all I have with me, how do I look?"

Kodi wore a black sweater, lower cut than Micah had seen before, tight black jeans, silver sandals. What Micah assumed was some Indian talisman hung from a silver chain about her neck.

"Something's missing," she said. "I haven't a clue what it is. I don't do this often enough to know."

To Micah's eyes, she was perfect. Yet he had enough experience with women to understand this self-doubt. If there wasn't a solution, even the simplest one, it would linger all night.

"I think I've got it," he said.

He went to his bedroom and returned with a charcoal gray vest from a three-piece suit in his closet. He held it open and she slipped into it.

"Go look at yourself in the mirror. I think it completes the ensemble."

Kodi went to her bedroom to check, and came back.

"Good choice, Pumpok. It does provide a little dash, doesn't it?"

"Dash? It races. Now get out of here and have some fun."

Micah pressed $100 into her hand. She resisted, he insisted. Told her it was advance pay against her research job. She might want something to eat, pay a cover charge, and especially, if necessary, cab fare home if she had one too many enjoying herself.

CHAPTER TWENTY-NINE

It was very dark out by Green End Pond. When he stayed still, Micah could hear bass slap the surface, snatching bugs. He'd never been a fisherman, wondered why. Never did anything in his life that involved catching, snaring, or killing another living thing. Wait, he thought about that some more. Worked for the Department of Defense for twenty years. In one aspect, with no disrespect to its mission, a killing machine. Then there was the coyote he'd put down at Shady Stream, humanely ending its suffering. His hands were not clean, but neither were they soiled. They were tools that attended to the job as the work presented itself. There was no fun or sport or craft or profit, only necessity. One could be at peace with that, surely.

Felt the heaviness in his chest creeping back like a consuming sadness. Refused to cough and break the stillness. Realized there was no such thing as absolute stillness. The insects, the bass fish, tiny star flickers above. There was only a peace to be found amidst the constant motion of the universe. If you could find it, or let it find you.

Heard a car out on Green End Avenue. It passed, stopped, backed up. The crunch of gravel and then a car door.

Micah walked up to the house. Was through the back door when the knocking started at the front.

"Sorry to bother you on a Sunday night, Mr. LaVeck. My name is Paul Sturgis. I believe you know my father, Melvin, who owns the wine shop in town."

"Of course." Micah extended his hand. "Nice to meet you, Paul. What can I do for you?"

"I'm an attorney with a firm in Providence. We've been retained by Chuck Lewis. I was hoping we could have a word with you."

"We?"

"Chuck's in the car," Sturgis said. "It will be off the record, and I assure you there's no impropriety. I've spoken with the DA and Chief Reismann. Neither has any objection if it will help adjudicate this mess. You can call the chief, if you like."

"I'll take you at your word. Go get Chuck and come inside."

Lewis looked different. He was pale and aged. Stress lines creased the corners of his mouth and eyes. A slight tremor in his lips. Blank, hollow eyes, as if having witnessed a holocaust beyond description.

Micah assumed his host duties.

"All I have is coffee, tea, wine, or beer. If you want something stronger, we'll have to call your dad."

Paul Sturgis laughed at that. "I guarantee you he's at home watching television, and I don't have the keys to the shop. Whatever suits you suits us."

Lewis hadn't uttered a word, and didn't now.

"Wine it is," Micah said. "I've got a feeling I'll need it."

There was no conversation as he opened a bottle of Cabernet and poured three glasses. Sturgis realized Micah couldn't handle carrying all three, and use his stick, so he went to the counter and carried two. Micah nodded in appreciation. They sat at the kitchen table. Lewis drank off half his glass with the first sip.

Sturgis came to the point. "Regardless of the specific charges handed down by the grand jury, you realize we're going to plead this out."

Micah nodded again.

Sturgis continued. "Everything begins and ends with Laurie Catlett. She was the schemer, she was the motivator."

"Point of exception," Micah said. He looked directly at Lewis, and said, "Your client made direct threats to me, not of harm, exposure. I was to give him Kodi last Friday, or he'd run with what he had. I want that clear. Why he jumped the gun at Tillsbury Farm, I have no idea."

Sturgis was not fazed. "I won't apologize for my client's exuberance, come on, he's an investigative reporter. You, sir, are the wild card. A good source, but not necessarily a dependable one."

"What the hell does that mean?" Micah said.

"You had an affair with Catlett. There's no denying it."

"I'm not denying anything."

"Good, then we can move on. You also have established a unique relationship with Kodi Red Moon, the coyote hunter." Strange accent on "unique" that Micah noticed.

"Why do you say unique?"

"For instance, nude swimming."

That fucking Newporter.

"You've spoken with my neighbor," Micah said. "Let me assure you, that incident is out of context. I'm old enough to be Kodi's father." He tapped the tip of his cane on the floor. "There are other issues as well."

"Nevertheless, things are as they are. Or, as the lawyer side of me will point out, as they seem to an objective observer."

Micah became irate. "You have no right, no business assuming anything about a private relationship."

"Please forgive my bluntness; you'll probably hear worse if this goes to trial, and I can't help that. My only concern has to be my client. I want you to hear what he has to say, and then do whatever it is you have to do. Fair enough?"

Micah drained his wine. Poured another for himself and Lewis. Sturgis hadn't touched his glass.

Over his shoulder from the counter, Micah said, "Fair enough, so far. I want to hear what he has to say."

Sturgis finally sampled his wine. "Everything that's said remains in this kitchen. Eventually, you'll be my witness, not theirs. At least on the stand, where I'll present you as a hostile witness. That part, any trial lawyer will tell you, is theater. For your benefit, if you want to bring down Catlett, this is your only option. Can we proceed?"

Micah indicated Lewis. "Is he ever going to talk?"

"Again, off the record, yes," Sturgis said.

"Let's have it."

Sturgis nodded at Lewis and said, "In your own words, tell it all." He looked to Micah for confirmation when he said, "We're among friends, and this is crucial for all of us."

Lewis took a deep sip of his wine.

"It was all Laurie's plan," Lewis said. "A long-range plan. She's done with small-town politics. There's no action, and no money. Mary Boyd was a stepping-stone in a soft market. Middletown is nowhere. When no other candidate, higher up the food chain, was interested in her, Laurie looked for a cause. The coyotes gave her one."

"How?" Micah said.

"She wants to be a lobbyist in Washington for an animal rights political action committee. Sabotaging the hunt in Middletown is her bona fides. Her defeat here is a victory for the animal rights people in DC. I'm as expendable to her as you are, and Kodi is, and Mayor Boyd. Funny thing, as smart and sharp as Boyd is, she never saw it coming."

"Catlett can't do much from jail," Micah said.

"Except gain martyr status in a cause that loves martyrs," Lewis said. "And what are we really talking about anyway? A year, eighteen months? It was a tragedy, I was there, but how criminal will people see it? Her future employers will bring in the best legal defense they can muster. According to Catlett, they've got the bucks, megabucks—eccentric philanthropists, movie stars, soccer moms with coin jugs at 7-Eleven. All that money—which is why she wants to work for them. Look at the obituaries in my own paper. Every day someone's leaving a chunk of their estate to protect animals, and urging mourners to do the same in remembrance. Not cancer, heart disease, or autism—lost and abused little doggies and cats, beached whales, and turtles. It's a lobbyist's meal ticket."

Micah understood it all, but there was something he couldn't resolve for himself.

"Did she ever mention me?"

"Sure," Lewis said. "The mild-mannered, dying romantic. She says you should have been a poet. Maybe then, your life would have had some meaning."

That cut deep, and Micah drained his wine.

WHEN LEWIS and Sturgis left, what, if anything, had been accomplished? He heard Lewis's side of the story, but not much else. A man was still dead, Kodi was still out of a job, and Laurie Catlett had a career waiting in Washington. So what?

It was eleven P.M. Kodi not home. The night yet young, for that generation. Micah washed his guests' glasses and poured another for himself. He had a lot of catching up to do to reach where Nathan Jordan was in the 1870s.

The Bureau of Military Information was losing what little credibility they ever had. Even Icobar could see this. He applied for transfer after transfer, but his association with BMI proved to be a stain on his record. No one wanted him. The letter campaign was phased out. After Gettysburg, the South was beaten. It was only a matter of time until they accepted it. Icobar was transferred back to Washington. He spent his days transcribing dispatches into intelligence reports he wasn't confident anyone read anyway. Even Allan Pinkerton was done with BMI. He was lobbying the War Department to set up a new security agency, the Secret Service. Rumors of assassination plots by Confederate sects were rampant. When the War Department dismissed him, he turned to the Treasury Department. They would gather intelligence regarding threats and provide round-the-clock security for the commander-in-chief, and his successors.

Last page of this journal: LINCOLN SHOT.

It was after one A.M. when Micah put down the journal. Kodi was not home. He wasn't sure how he felt about that, honestly. He sincerely wanted her to have a good time; she'd earned and deserved it. This is what young people did. A part of her life that wasn't his to share.

His left leg started tapping involuntarily. Heel-toe, heel-toe. Not as if music were playing and picking up the beat—almost as if it wanted to walk on its own. Micah couldn't exactly feel it; it was the bobbing of his knee that caught his attention. Tried to stand. No purchase. Sat back down to let it pass.

Now he could stand, and even though he couldn't feel the leg, it came along to the bedroom.

MICAH WAS up, showered, had breakfast, and was deep in research work at his desk when Kodi came home about ten A.M. He stayed in his study, affording her whatever time she needed. Heard her go to the bedroom and then the bathroom. Finally she came to the study.

"Did you call your doctor?" she said.

"Waiting for my coffee break."

"You thought I'd forget."

"One could hope."

"Not a chance."

"That's why it's only called hope."

Kodi was wearing the jeans she left in, but not the sweater or vest. She wore an oversized man's button-down, blue-and-white-striped shirt. Micah came to his feet.

"Good time last night?" he asked.

Kodi started for the kitchen and Micah followed.

"Very good. Only not sure if it's the smartest thing I could have done."

"Stop it," Micah said. He walked to the counter. "You let your hair down and cut loose for one night. You're a grown woman. What's the issue?"

Kodi sat at the table. "Remember about the strings? I might have tied one back together."

"Huh?"

"I didn't go to a club. It's not really my thing. I went to see Paka. It was a little familiar, but much more different. A little of the old, but a lot that's new for both of us. You know, it might be . . . could be, hell, I don't know. Have to wait and see."

Micah turned from the counter. "You sound confused, but you sure look happy."

"Do I?"

"Yes, and I'm happy for you."

Kodi rose up. She came to the counter and nudged Micah aside with her hip. "You go get your doctor's number."

Micah called the doctor's office and was given an appointment for Friday. He hung up, folded his arms, and looked at Kodi.

"Done. All right?"

"When you keep the appointment, you're done."

Micah changed the subject. "Had a visitor last night, make that two visitors."

"Real people or one of your visions?"

"It was only one vision, and then one epiphany."

"Tell me."

Micah told the story of Chuck Lewis and his lawyer. Kodi's jaw dropped in surprise at one point, followed by anger.

"Animal rights? That bitch."

"Don't know much about PACs, so I did a little research this morning. Sounds like there's a lot of money in it. You have to realize, Wawokak's closer to my age than yours. The motivation to sock some dough away gets pretty strong."

"First there's jail for Wawokak."

"Chuck said a year to eighteen months. His lawyer didn't comment, and I think that's because Chuck's estimate is an overstatement, but the lawyer didn't want to minimize the jeopardy of Chuck's situation prior to the plea bargain. With the right lawyers, I personally don't think she'll do any time at all. She's not a lawyer herself, so there's no license to lose either. Undermining the coyote hunt, from inside no less, and she walks right into the open arms of the animal people and a big paycheck. Probably write a goddamn book about it and make twice as much. There are stories like it all over the Internet."

"A man was killed."

"Neither she, nor Chuck, pulled the trigger. Mark my words, in the hands of the right defense attorney, that's all it will come down to in the end."

"You really think so?" Kodi asked, aghast.

"I do. Want to know how I really know?" Kodi nodded. "It was something Boyd said on the phone yesterday morning, not exactly said, something she asked about you and me. They've figured out we knew Tillsbury Farm was a trap. Like we told Chief Reismann. But we went ahead anyway. The chief didn't pursue that line because we weren't involved in the shooting at all. Wawokak will. One of us is going to be up on the stand under oath and asked: Why?"

"How does that help Wawokak?"

"She tried to trick us, we were ready, and we tried to trick her back. We could have simply called it off, refused to go in the first place, and a man might still be alive."

"Oh, no, Pumpok."

"That's why lawyers make the big bucks."

CHAPTER THIRTY

Micah walked by himself to the wine shop. There was plenty of beer left for Kodi, but his supply of reds was low. Kodi meanwhile drove to Narragansett to get more clothes and personal items from home. Aside from their trip to Jamestown to see Nathan Jordan, they didn't discuss the reasons she was going to continue staying with Micah for a while, it was merely a given between them.

"Heard you met my son," Melvin Sturgis greeted Micah.

"Yes, last night."

"He always lets me know if he's coming to town. He's not a bad sort, for a lawyer, he's done a lot of good for people."

"Paul is doing his job," Micah said, "and doing it well. You must be proud of him."

"Kind of you to say. I'd hate to lose your business because of all this."

What is 'all this'? Micah thought.

"Not a chance, Melvin. There's a bond between a man and his trusted wine merchant that supersedes anything else."

"Amen."

Micah made his selections and put them on the counter.

"How'd you get mixed up in all this anyway?" Sturgis asked.

All this, again. "The usual way, trying to do somebody a favor."

"And got bit in the ass. You read today's paper?"

"Haven't read the *News* in days."

"Then I'll not mention it again."

"All part of the bond."

Sturgis rang the sale; Micah packed his backpack and paid.

"Did you come up Valley Road?" Sturgis said.

"Yeah, all the way."

"Go home High Street. Since you ain't read about it, there's some kind of demonstration gonna happen in front of the police station at three o'clock."

"Demonstration by whom?"

"Like either one of us gives a crap."

Now Micah said, "Amen."

He trudged down High Street, deserted this time of day. Maybe he imagined it, but his pace felt slower than normal, especially for only a wine run and nothing to carry from the supermarket. Slower, and High Street seemed longer.

Should be past the clambake club by now.

The straps of his backpack, with the shifting weight, added a measure of stress to the vague tightness in his chest. Unslung the pack and rested a minute on his stick. Looked across the valley. The grass was getting greener with the season. Birds about, but too deep in the valley for Micah to recognize.

Guess I never will see that white-throated sparrow. Ha, never thought I'd see a coyote and look what happened. Never heard of Frog Mother, but met her too. Never imagined I'd see a naked woman in Green End Pond. Or go in myself, in April no less.

Perhaps it was the memories, something; Micah felt refreshed enough to hoist his pack and head on home.

There was a cluster of a dozen people in front of Micah's house as he turned onto Green End Avenue.

Oh shit, he thought. His despair was quickly supplanted by ire. He walked on with as much purpose as he could muster and reached his driveway.

"Mr. LaVeck," one called.

Another, "Does the coyote hunter live here?"

"I'd like to interview Kodi Red Moon."

They parted to give him passage, their questions and prompts never abating.

Micah raised his free hand. "Excuse me; I have no comment for you. Please respect that this is private property or I shall have to call the police."

Micah walked through the middle of them. No one hindered his progress. One tried to follow him up the path; Micah sensed it and spun around.

"Private property, I said. Remain at the curb or I'm dialing 9-1-1. Don't make this an ugly scene and embarrass yourself."

The reporter backed up.

The phone was ringing when Micah opened the door. He didn't answer it, switched the message machine to "Answer Off," and set about putting his wines away. No sooner did the phone stop ringing, when it started again fifteen seconds later.

There were nine messages on his answering machine. Micah clicked through them, deleting as the callers identified themselves. Two were reporters from the *Newport Daily News*; Micah figured they were competing to replace Chuck Lewis. Also calls from journalists affiliated with papers in Boston; Hartford, Connecticut; and Portland, Maine. Two were TV news reporters, and one a talk-radio host. The last one claimed to be a celebrity agent offering to represent Kodi and Micah for book and movie deals. Micah would have been amused, if he wasn't so disgusted.

During a lull between more ringing, he called Kodi. When she answered, he could hear she was driving and a radio in the background.

"The press is in the street by the house and the phone hasn't stopped ringing. Where are you?"

"Coming up on the Pell Bridge."

"They're gonna surround you when you get here."

Kodi paused to think. "Got a better idea."

"What?"

"Old Indian trick, it's a surprise."

"For me or for them?"

"Both. Be home in an hour."

Kodi rang off.

An hour? The Pell Bridge was ten minutes by car from Micah's house.

He disconnected, then unplugged the phone.

It was a little more than an hour when Kodi came through Micah's back door lugging an overstuffed duffel bag and backpack twice the size of the one she took on hunts. She let them both slip to the floor.

"How'd you manage it?" Micah asked.

Kodi beckoned him to the door and pointed out to Green End Pond. Up on the shore of the spit was an aluminum rowboat.

"You told me they test the water a lot," she said. "Figured they had to have a boat nearby. Sure enough, in a little cove down by the dam. It's got a Newport Water Division tag on the stern."

"Where's your truck?"

"Easton's Beach lot; walked up to the dam from there. How's it going out front?"

"Haven't bothered to check."

Kodi went to the parlor and parted the window curtains a crack. Micah came up behind and peered over her shoulder.

"I count four," he said. "There were a dozen two hours ago."

"I could get the Winchester and scare them away."

"That would make a great news photo."

"Only kidding. But we can't live behind closed doors and drawn curtains."

They retreated to the kitchen. He told her about the demonstration Melvin Sturgis mentioned, adding that he didn't know what it was about.

"It was on the Newport radio station while I was driving. Wawokak had a meeting with Chief Reismann at three o'clock. A couple of animal rights groups got together to show her support."

"Is she under arrest?"

"They didn't say she was. Maybe there really is something to her future plans. Somebody's backing her to pull off a rally on a Monday afternoon. Doesn't anybody work for a living on this island?"

Kodi's cell rang and she answered it. It was Reismann. He wanted to speak with Micah but couldn't get through on Micah's landline.

"It's for you, the chief." Kodi handed Micah the cell.

"Promised to keep you in the loop. Catlett claims it's all a misunderstanding and miscommunication," Reismann said to Micah. "Maintains she was only suggesting Tillsbury Farm, not ordering Kodi to do it, or when. Says she thought it might lure old man Tillsbury into taking an interest in Middletown politics and fork up some bucks for Mary's next campaign."

"That's bullshit."

"Of course it is. We've got Lewis on record with a completely different story. I wind up with a three-way: he said, she said, he said."

"Lewis was here last night," Micah said.

"I know. Young Sturgis was smart enough to ask me first. I ran it by the DA and it was immediately approved. Mary's putting pressure on everybody to make this go away. You can bet Judge Walker got a call too. He's up for reelection this November."

"Case Dismissed Walker," Micah said.

"That would be the magistrate I mean."

"Nothing's going to happen to anyone, is it, Chief?"

"They'll float some charges and then tell me my job is done. Catlett and Lewis will walk or cut their deals. The upside is Catlett gets the hell out of my town. She sent Mary her resignation by e-mail before the mayor could fire her."

Talking about Catlett prompted Micah to ask, "How'd the demonstration go?"

"Not much of a demonstration, more like an ad campaign for animal rights and a convenient backdrop for Catlett's appearance. Probably look good on the six o'clock news, not that I'll be watching."

"I've got my own little demonstration out front," Micah said. He told Reismann about the reporters and Kodi's trip up Green End Pond.

"That gal is amazing," Reismann said. "If they're still around tomorrow, I'll send Elmer by to run them off. They can't be on your property, and I won't let them block the street. Call me if you need me."

"Thanks, Chief."

Kodi made a hand-signal asking for the phone. Micah passed it to her.

"Chief, that nine mil is out of your jurisdiction," she said, referring to Coco's service sidearm that Micah used to kill the poisoned coyote at Shady Stream.

"Always a pleasure doing business with you, Kodi."

"One more favor?"

"If I can."

Kodi told Reismann her pickup was parked at the beach and would be left overnight. There was a beach parking policy against that. Reismann said not to worry; he'd alert the sector patrol to ignore it.

"Then the pleasure's all mine," Kodi said. "Good night, Chief." She shut the phone and looked at Micah. "You know what tonight is?"

"What?"

"Pizza night."

"It'll be front page news in the morning."

"So what, there won't be any left for anyone else."

Micah placed the order using Kodi's phone. She carried her bags to her bedroom and unpacked.

By the time the pizza was delivered, all the reporters were gone.

Eating their pizza, they decided to spend tomorrow going over the Icobar Ohlm material and Micah's notes, in preparation for meeting Nathan Jordan on Wednesday. Micah was reluctant to share bits and pieces as they ate, saying it was important, and proper research protocol, for Kodi to absorb the story in chronological order.

"If you insist, Professor," she teased him.

Micah blushed. "It's the way I was taught."

"Were your parents teachers?"

"Nope. Pop was a mining engineer and, since we traveled a lot and lived in various places, my mom did lots of different things. In Colorado, she was a sales clerk, in West Virginia, a secretary. Whatever was available where we found ourselves."

"Did you like moving around?"

"You know, I kinda did. That's strange for a kid, I realize, but I really didn't mind."

"I bet it's because you make friends easily," Kodi said.

"Not so much anymore. I've grown very particular when it comes to friends. Anyway, it prepared me for working at the DOD. They sent, you went."

"Sort of like the army."

"Without the combat," Micah said. "Plenty of political infighting, backstabbing, and jealousies, but we never came to blows."

"How does a guy like you survive in that racket?"

Micah found himself amused at his own answer. "Curb your ambition."

"Go along to get along."

"Something like that."

Kodi's cell phone rang. As she answered, Micah glanced at the clock: nine P.M.

After her "Hello," she covered the mouthpiece with her hand.

"It's Paka. I'm gonna take this in my room."

"I'll leave," Micah said.

"No you won't. Be back in a few minutes."

Kodi headed to her room. Micah heard the door close. He got himself more wine.

Good for her, and knew he meant it.

Micah started his new book, the one he'd bought on their shopping spree together. He didn't get far. Kodi was back in less than five minutes.

"That was quick," he said.

Kodi made a face. "We're not teenagers."

"Right."

"He asked me out Friday night. More of an official date than last night."

"I like his style."

"I hope you like him."

"I'm sure I will, but it doesn't matter. It's your life, and if this is right for you, there's no more to be said except by you and him."

"And I like your style."

It popped into Micah's mind. "Did you by any chance on Sunday, or tonight, mention to Paka the Icobar Ohlm connection?"

"No, it's your work, I thought it would be better coming from you."

"Because it involves the possibility of his having some non-Indian genes?"

Kodi grew serious. "Do you know how many Native American wives and daughters were raped in the white man's conquest? Too many to even try to count. Odds are we've all got a little pollution in the gene pool. But if we live today as Indians, we don't talk about it."

"Sorry, I didn't mean it to go that far."

"Don't be sorry. We can't undo history. Everything in the present, remember?"

CHAPTER THIRTY-ONE

They started early. Kodi brought a kitchen chair. Micah showed her the volumes he'd read, separated from those he hadn't. Of the former, the last few had Post-it notes protruding from the closed pages.

"Those are reference markers to entries I want to revisit if I ever try to pull this all together," he said.

Next, he printed his Word document notes. He began the story from memory.

"Icobar Ohlm was a printer's apprentice a year before the Civil War. A petty and taciturn young man. The war changed everything, especially him."

Consulting the notes on the covers for time periods, Micah gave her a synopsis of the events in each volume. Kodi followed along using his notes. Two hours later, she arrived where Micah had left off. Micah picked up the next volume and the one after it.

"It would help," he said, "if we cover his years with the Indian Agency before meeting Professor Jordan. I have no idea how many pages, volumes, or years that is. So we'll alternate volumes." Micah placed a pad of paper on the desk's edge along with a pencil. "You don't have to read it word for word,

I won't either. There isn't time. We're only interested in places and events. I can go back later and be more thorough. Icobar rambles sometimes. We're not interested in what he ate or the weather. Skip over that. Oh, yes, and record any name, especially if it has a rank or title."

"Check," Kodi said. "Places, events, and names."

"You sure you don't mind doing this?"

Kodi took a volume from his hand, and set to work.

They broke for lunch at twelve thirty. Since neither had eaten breakfast, Micah whipped up an omelet with scallions, mushrooms, and cheddar cheese.

As they sat to eat, Micah asked, "How's it going for you?"

"Plenty of names and places. I'm trying to be thorough. Doesn't sound like he's thrilled working for the Indian Agency."

"You're right, my volume gets into that much deeper. Good work."

Icobar Ohlm wasn't exactly an Indian agent. You needed political connections for that job. His new position was back to being a scribe. He wrote letters, memos, and reports dictated to him by the actual agent. Not that he minded all that much, at the beginning. In a Pullman car with his own private compartment, Icobar went to Oklahoma, Florida, Texas, California, and the Dakotas. As time, distance, and exposure accumulated, his perspective changed about what was going on and what he was privy to in his role. He encountered more than two dozen different native tribes, the length and breadth of the country. Chickasaw in Oklahoma, Seminoles in Florida, Washoe in California, Apache down in Texas—he met them all. They fascinated Icobar and he began developing a sincere appreciation for Indian life and ways.

In 1866, his first official report dealt with the combined wisdoms of Generals Philip H. Sheridan and William Tecumseh Sherman as they pondered the westward expansion and how to defend it as they encroached on Indian lands. The generals determined the buffalo in America should be exterminated. Without buffalo, the Indians of the West and the Plains would have no hold on their way of life. Icobar quoted Sherman as saying, "Kill the buffalo and you kill the Indians."

Land for settlement was only part of what white men wanted out West. They also coveted what was under the land.

Early November of 1868 found Icobar at Fort Laramie in Wyoming. For two years, bloody battles had raged between the Indians and the settlers, prospectors, and US cavalry over an area the Oglala Sioux revered as sacred hunting grounds. Unfortunately for the Sioux, sacred or not, the Bozeman Trail, the route to the Montana gold fields, cut right through the middle. A massive troop buildup and the superior firepower of the army finally decided the dispute. The sixth of November was set as the day for Chief Red Cloud to sign a peace treaty with General Sherman. In mid-October, Icobar was summoned to Fort Laramie to commit the terms of the treaty to a document.

With his growing affinity for the Indian peoples, Icobar wanted nothing in the treaty that could not be clearly understood by Chief Red Cloud. To this end, he enlisted the help of one of Red Cloud's young nieces, Morning Dew. Morning Dew had been partially educated by white missionaries who had lived and preached in peace among the Sioux for more than a generation. Her English was excellent. Not so, the terms of the pact.

In exchange for an end to the fighting and safe passageway, the US government ceded parts of Wyoming and the Dakotas to the Sioux. Boundaries were marked and enforced by the army and their interiors managed by the Indian Agency. The system of reservations for Native Americans was created.

Icobar wrote the document as ordered but with disgust and foreboding. Without any options, Chief Red Cloud inked his sign beside Sherman's signature.

Three days later, as Icobar's train left Wyoming, and despite the misgivings of the Indian agent and scornful stares from other passengers, Morning Dew was on board, newly designated as Icobar's Indian interpreter. Of course it was presumed by all, even if fictitiously for appearances' sake, Morning Dew slept in the baggage car, and not Icobar's compartment. In his journal, Icobar wrote that the only one to wish the pair well was Chief Red Cloud, himself, described by Icobar as having eyes filled with wisdom as if he could see the future of his people and was sparing Morning Dew.

"We have our connection," Micah said.

It was not strict scholarship but all they had time for before tomorrow: Micah and Kodi forged ahead into the next volume together.

Managing the Indians, according to Icobar, became a big business. The Indian Agency quadrupled in size and was renamed the Bureau of Indian Affairs. Everywhere across the country, lines were drawn on maps and reservations created without any consultation with the tribes. Locations were merely delivered to them in deed-like documents with deadlines for them to move.

States wanted their own share of the business and Washington gave them more say in the management of reservations within their borders. This had a curtailing effect on Icobar's and Morning Dew's travels. Ultimately, he was reassigned to Washington in a clerk's role at bureau headquarters.

The couple rented the upstairs floor of a sympathetic widow's nondescript house in a quiet neighborhood. Icobar took a horse trolley to work each morning. If Morning Dew ever complained, Icobar made no note of it.

"Had to be tough," Kodi said. "I wonder if she adopted white dress and cut her hair, or whatever she'd have to do to fit in."

"Maybe she didn't want to fit in. Perhaps they simply wanted to be left alone. Three times this week he talks about quitting and moving back to Rhode Island."

"Why Rhode Island, do you think? They'd seen almost the whole country."

"Because of Roger Williams's legacy: freedom and tolerance. The state was founded on it."

"Nice premise," Kodi said.

They read on and found another answer, the entry comprised of all of three words: Wife with child.

"So there was a child," Micah said.

"With Indian blood and the Ohlm name."

They pressed on to the next volume. It started to rain outside.

Despite a father-to-be and not mentioning any other prospects for employment, Icobar resigned from the Bureau of Indian Affairs. His comments here were introspective and insightful at the same time. No one in the bureau tried to dissuade him. His appreciation and respect for Indian cultures, and his contempt for the government's treatment of the tribes, had not gone unnoticed by peers and superiors.

Icobar was as frugal in domestic married life as he'd been as a bachelor. Using some of their savings, Icobar bought a wagon and draft horse to bring his pregnant wife and their belongings to his home state. Both, he reasoned, could be sold upon arrival.

"Where do you think they'll wind up?" Kodi said.

"No idea."

"The Ohlm family that hired you, where do they live?"

If he ever knew, Micah couldn't remember. Everything had been arranged through the original antique dealer. Since then, there had only been e-mails between Roger Ohlm and Micah.

"It must be on the contract," Micah said. He delved into his file drawer. "Here it is. Portsmouth."

"Aquidneck Island," said Kodi.

The rain was still falling and, with dusk, it was time for a beer and a glass of wine. A reward for their accomplishment. The intent was to cover Icobar's Indian Agency years, the period of Nathan Jordan's research, and that was done. A wife and a baby along the way were bonuses.

"I haven't studied like that since I dropped out of college," Kodi said.

A revelation. "You went to college?"

Kodi made that face. "Don't sound so damned surprised."

"You're smart and articulate, but you never mentioned college. What happened?"

"I joined the army. Which wasn't why I quit school. I dropped out because I was broke. Enlisted because the army didn't care I was broke."

Micah let it go, for now.

In the back of his freezer, Micah had a store-bought frozen lasagna from who remembers when. He wiped off the frost and preheated the oven. Held up the box for Kodi's approval.

"Italian two nights in a row," she said. "What the hell, why not? Neither of us feels like cooking."

"Later, a fire in the parlor. It feels damp in here."

She agreed again. “What do you suppose is happening in our world, as opposed to Icobar’s?”

“Don’t really give a damn. Another beer?”

Kodi nodded. “We have to row to the truck in the morning, you know.”

“You have to row. I cooked dinner.”

“Fair enough.”

Yes, Micah thought, *I honestly don’t give a damn about it anymore. We have food, booze, a warm fire, our Icobar work, and I’m taking a pond cruise in the morning. Not a bad life.*

So delightful and relaxing to contemplate, Micah didn’t hear the first raps. Kodi did.

“Someone’s at the front door,” she said.

“I’ll go see, you stay here. The official household response is: No comment. This is followed by: Get the hell off my property.”

Kodi raised her beer in salute. Micah left the kitchen. The knocking came again.

At first glance, Micah didn’t recognize her. She was out of uniform and her hair was down.

“Ranger Ferzoco, what brings you out on a night like this? Come in.”

A dripping Ferzoco entered. “I didn’t see her pickup. Is Kodi here? Her cell must be off.”

“She’s in the kitchen. We’ve been bothered by reporters and keeping a low profile. Give me your coat and go on in.”

Ferzoco shed a soaked rain slicker, which Micah hung up, and then both went to the back of the house.

Kodi was surprised, rose, and they embraced.

“What’s up, Ferzie?”

Micah offered a chair and the two women sat. He asked Ferzoco if she preferred wine or beer.

“Wine. And stop calling me ranger. It’s Ferzie.”

Micah was at the counter as Ferzoco spoke to Kodi. "Are you retired from coyote hunting, or are you up for a little work?"

"I've been shut down," Kodi said. "I thought you'd have heard by now."

"Yeah, in Middletown. I'm talking about Little Compton. Riverside Farm, 100 acres of fields, another acre of greenhouses. It's privately owned and it's a private contract on the down low. A family called Shaw owns it. They've been farming Little Compton for three generations. The police chief and the mayor over there already said okay. Like I said, private, under the radar, one night's work."

"How many coyotes?"

"They're pretty sure only one, but a mean son of a bitch, a loner."

"*Cacaw,*" Kodi said.

"Right, you told me once."

Like most farms, Ferzoco explained, the Shaws kept a few cows, chickens, pigs, and rabbits. None of which were the commercial side of their farm, which was all vegetables.

"At least three times a week, it's been a chicken, a rabbit, or some other critter from the fields. Your *cacaw* even raids their garbage cans. These are good, solid farm-stock folks, but now they're getting scared."

"How much?" Kodi said.

"Farm-stock, but not poor. One *cacaw* for one grand."

Kodi glanced at Micah, didn't wait for a signal, looked back at Ferzoco.

"Deal. Thursday night, I'm busy tomorrow and Friday. Otherwise, next week."

"You sure they can keep a lid on this?" Micah asked.

"They want a lid on it as much as you. The last thing they need is animal rights and news people all over their quiet town. Little Compton is as rural as Rhode Island gets, and just as New England. Ain't nobody gonna say nothing. That's the way they like it." Ferzoco looked at Kodi. "Thursday it is."

"You got a map?" Kodi said.

Ferzoco took one from a hip pocket and unfolded it on the table. "Like you'll need a map. One old coyote, hell, I could find him."

"You're with conservation, I have to kill him."

Micah invited Ferzoco to stay for dinner, there was plenty of lasagna. She declined, and rose to go.

"Call me and let me know where, so I can retrieve the carcass and tag it," she said to Kodi.

"One coyote, 100 acres, you said you could find him yourself."

Ferzoco laughed heartily.

Micah got her slicker and walked her to the door.

Back in the kitchen he asked Kodi, "You sure you want to do this?"

"For a thousand bucks, I'd shoot Wawokak."

CHAPTER THIRTY-TWO

It was a day of sun and water and boats. Also no reason to hurry. Nathan Jordan's invitation was open for the whole day. He wasn't going anywhere and had no particular plans, so his guests could come when it suited them.

After breakfast, Micah collected his notes and stowed them in a book bag along with two sample volumes from Icobar's Indian Agency period to show Professor Jordan what he was working with in the original format. Then Kodi and Micah went out to the spit.

Kodi angled the rowboat half in, half out of the water and set the oars.

"Get in," she said. "I'll push off."

Micah sat on the bow bench, Kodi slid the boat out farther, gave one solid shove, and frog-leapt over the stern to the center bench and took up the oars. She rowed straight for the center of the pond before steering due south.

A little past eight A.M., Green End Pond was teeming with birds. With fishing banned, the pond was full of fish, which made it a prime dining spot for the feathered species. Micah watched them and named for Kodi as many as he recognized: terns, sandpipers, and a drifting pair of egrets.

"When did you get interested in birds?" Kodi said.

"As a kid, from my father. Every mine has a pair of mascot birds, usually canaries or doves. It's a tradition out of respect for the miners of old. They kept birds in the mines to detect poison gases. If the birds died, the miners knew the air in the shaft was getting toxic. We also kept birds at home. It sort of evolved from that to birds in general, all kinds."

Micah drifted off in his thoughts. Kodi was proficient at the oars, the blades slicing the surface with barely any sound and no splash.

Two-thirds of the way down the pond, Kodi stopped rowing. They had come into the current created by the water gate at the dam and she let it guide them until the cove she remembered came up on the port side. Kodi pivoted the boat left, then used both oars together rowing into the cove, propelling the rowboat up onto shore. Micah got out and, best as he could, yanked it up a few feet more, lost his balance, and fell on his ass. He was the first to laugh.

"Maybe not graceful, but got the job done," Kodi said.

Micah came to his feet and brushed sand from his butt. Kodi handed him the book bag and his stick and pulled the rowboat completely out of the water.

They hiked down to the end of Valley Road and were soon at the beach parking lot. Kodi's pickup was where she left it and, as Chief Reismann promised, there was no summons on the windshield despite what the sign at the entrance warned. They got in and Kodi drove to Newport.

At the end of Memorial Boulevard, she turned onto America's Cup Avenue, passed Sayer's, Bannister's, and Bowen's Wharfs, turned onto Long Wharf, and parked in a public spot outside the gated Newport Yacht Club.

A shorter walk this time, to the Marine Terminal. As of April first, the seasonal water taxi to Jamestown was back in operation. They could have driven across the Pell Bridge and been on Jamestown Island in fifteen minutes, but what was the pleasure in that on a gorgeous spring day?

Micah paid the agent in the booth for two roundtrip passages.

"Ten minutes," the woman said, handing Micah the boarding passes.

"Thanks," he said. "We're in no hurry."

"Local?"

"Middletown."

That got a smile. She obviously had all the impatient tourists she could handle between Memorial Day and Labor Day. This odd pair, a lame older man and a much younger, pretty Native American girl, were fellow Aquidneck Islanders. Odd, but neighbors.

As they walked to a bench to wait, Micah said to Kodi, "I assume she doesn't read the newspapers."

Two minutes to the hour the Jamestown Water Taxi nudged the bumpers on the pier and the mate leapt to the dock and tied her off. Next he set the gangway and two women, with shopping totes slung from their shoulders, got off and strolled away toward the shops of Newport.

Micah and Kodi walked over, showed their passes, and boarded. The skipper at the helm was a white-haired, sun-leathered sea dog with an Irish grin.

"Welcome aboard, sit where you please, it's the slow part of the season."

"Nice day for a sail," Kodi said to him.

"'Tis that, young lady. Mind, there's a breeze on the bay, so if you sit out from the canopy, you might catch some spray."

"Sounds like fun."

She led Micah to the stern and they sat in the last two seats, no cover over their heads. The mate hauled in the gangway and cast off the ropes. As the captain reversed the boat out of dockage, the mate recited the safety precautions per Coast Guard regulations.

Kodi put her hand over Micah's in his lap and squeezed. She was enjoying the whole thing immensely. Not that Micah wasn't.

In compliance with its contract with the City of Newport, the taxi headed first to Rose Island, a cluster of rocks with a vintage lighthouse. They tied up briefly; the mate didn't set the gangplank. Nobody was getting off or on: it was for tourists later in the season, but the stop was mandatory.

From there they headed out into Narragansett Bay. It was definitely breezy and there was a light swell. Though he never felt any spray, Micah could taste salt on his lips. When he mentioned it, Kodi said she did too. Within fifteen minutes they were entering the harbor at East Ferry, Jamestown.

When the taxi was moored, they thanked the captain and mate and said they'd see them again on the return voyage.

"We'll be here," the skipper said.

Kodi and Micah went down the gangway. A young couple with backpacks was waiting to board.

Kodi carried the book bag, for no reason except she wanted to, and they walked south on Walcott Avenue. They found Noanett Street, walked east directly toward the water, and came to the last of three houses.

"This is it," Micah said. "You ready?"

"Roger."

They walked up the pathway and knocked on the door. It was opened by a pleasant-faced, middle-aged woman, in jeans and a yellow scrub smock.

"Good morning," Micah said. He introduced himself and Kodi. "We have an appointment with Professor Jordan. He didn't specify a time, only said to drop by today."

"Nathan is expecting you. I'm Sylvia, his home health aide and, if you ask him, his housekeeper and drill sergeant," she said with a smile.

She led them into the house, modestly furnished with bookshelves situated everywhere possible. If it wasn't for the few pieces of compulsory furniture to make it a home, it was much more a library. Kodi and Micah soon understood the scant furnishings as they were led into a study and presented to Nathan Jordan. He was in a wheelchair and spun around from a desk.

"Micah LaVeck and Miss Red Moon, I presume."

Jordan had once been a big man, one could tell from his shoulders and hands. Now he was sunken in the chest and narrow in the neck and limbs. He wore a gray beard, a tad out of control, and thick spectacles.

"Nathan," he said.

"Micah and Kodi. Thanks for seeing us."

Jordan held Kodi's hand an extra few seconds and the magnified eyes behind the strong lenses of his glasses twinkled in amusement.

"Kodi," Jordan said. "Kodi Red Moon, I know that name. You're the Pocasset dealing with the coyotes in Middletown."

"Was dealing," Kodi said. "The job is over."

"So I've read. Been studying and teaching history for over sixty years and all I've learned definitively is to never trust a politician."

"Or anybody who works for them," Micah added spontaneously.

Sylvia had left the room and now returned with two folding chairs. Jordan was gracious.

"Do you mind if we work in here? It's a bit cramped, but I have everything at my fingertips."

Micah assured him it was fine, and he and Kodi sat.

Jordan was still full of mirth. "Want to hear something funny, Kodi? In South Korea there are scientists cloning coyotes, successfully too. Rhode Island doesn't know what to do with them, and Korea is growing them. In a perfect world our two countries probably could have worked something out."

Kodi and Micah laughed.

"All right," Jordan said, "amusing interlude over and time to get to work. Let's address Mr. Icobar Ohlm, hero of Manassas, formerly of the Bureau of Indian Affairs, and late come home to his native Rhode Island." Jordan couldn't resist after all. "And walks with a stick like his biographer, Micah LaVeck."

Micah had always considered himself a resourceful researcher, but was the first to admit, aloud, he was outclassed by Nathan Jordan.

"When you're old, on four wheels, waited on by a good woman, what else you gonna do?" Jordan said.

They went at it for two straight hours. Without being asked, Kodi took copious notes, even requesting pauses to pursue clarification. Jordan and Micah were both impressed.

Jordan was fascinated by Ohlm's journals. Stroked each leather cover almost as if it were a beloved housecat.

"Rare," he said, "that a middle-income civil servant would go to such lengths."

"Maybe he got rich," Kodi suggested.

"Perhaps he did," Jordan said. "I'm not that far along and running out of new avenues, so," he held up a volume, "if it's not in the rest of these, there's only one way to find out. The answer has to be in the archives of the Portsmouth Historical Society, if it exists at all and has survived. They're not that well-funded, little of the archives are online."

"So Icobar did live in Portsmouth," Kodi said to Micah. "And the family's still there."

"More precisely," Jordan said, "Icobar lived on Prudence Island. Through a simple property and directory search, I've determined no one of the Ohlm name currently resides on the island. Unless by now, it's only a maiden name and not in the registries."

Sylvia prepared lunch for the four of them. Jordan wheeled himself to the small dining table, one chair missing for him to position himself. Micah, Kodi, and Sylvia took the three chairs. After lunch, it was back to the study.

They stayed at it until Micah and Kodi left in time to catch the five o'clock water taxi to Newport. After apologizing to Sylvia first, Jordan said it was the most enjoyable day he'd had in quite some time.

The sun was starting to set behind them over Jamestown as they cruised the bay. In this direction, the taxi's mandatory stop was historic Fort Adams. Like Rose Island, a formality until high season, nobody on or off.

Motoring up the harbor coast of Newport, they passed the yacht clubs and wharfs full of shops and restaurants. In another month, they would be crowded with tourists. This early in the season, it was mostly locals going about the pre-summer preparations. The water taxi had to navigate around three immense private yachts anchored in a row, too huge for dockage at the yacht clubs.

"Wonder what it's like to live like that," Kodi said.

"I'm certain I'll never know."

“Do you care?”

“Hell no. Those behemoths guzzle more fuel than I do wine. Totally impractical.”

“That’s not what I meant.”

“I know what you meant, and the answer’s still no.”

They passed a small, set-back dock of commercial fishing trawlers.

“What do you think of Icobar?” Kodi asked.

Micah was expecting the question, only he didn’t know when.

“I think he did what he thought he had to do. He was a family man with responsibilities.”

“And Morning Dew?”

“Life can be hard, can be unfair, can even be cruel. I’m not sure what love was like back then,” Micah said. “Not even sure what it is these days. But Icobar and Morning Dew were a team, and that makes you stronger.”

The water taxi slid smoothly into its berth at the Marine Terminal. The captain thanked Kodi and Micah for their patronage and wished them a good evening.

The pair walked over to Long Wharf and down to the pickup. They didn’t talk on the way home to Middletown. They had learned a lot in their research, a good deal more from Nathan Jordan, and had more work ahead of them.

A good team, Micah thought again, *makes you stronger.*

CHAPTER THIRTY-THREE

Icobar Ohlm wasn't the only business to attend to on Thursday. Kodi had to prepare for a hunt.

"There's a great café in Tiverton, right on the river," Micah said. "After you check out the farm in Little Compton, we can stop for breakfast on the way back."

It didn't have to be said he was going with Kodi to Riverside Farm for recon too, but Micah wasn't sure about the hunt to follow. His track record as her "spotter" was not stellar. He'd even caused her harm at Shady Stream Orchards.

Kodi alluded to it first.

"Tomorrow morning, I don't want any excuses about how you can't go to the doctor because you've been up half the night."

"No excuses, promise."

"Then breakfast sounds great. Do they have flapjacks?"

"Only about eight different kinds."

"Let's get started."

They drove out of Middletown and up into Portsmouth, reminding them of yesterday.

"Ever been to Prudence Island?" Kodi asked.

"No, no reason to. Not much there but a small community, a Wildlife Management Area, farms, and one big swamp."

"Me either. Guess we'll eventually have to go to complete the work."

Micah said only if they wanted the "flavor" of the place for background. The important information was to be found at the Portsmouth Historical Society, and that was on East Main Road, on which they were now driving. It came up presently; Micah pointed it out.

"I'm not looking forward to it," Kodi said. "I kinda wanted a lot to work out differently."

She was referring to Professor Jordan's historical perspective on the lives of Icobar and Morning Dew and what the journals had revealed. They lapsed into silence, each reflecting on it.

As Icobar and Morning Dew traveled north from Washington by wagon, a lot was happening at the Bureau of Indian Affairs and in Congress.

The Indian Appropriation Act was passed. As of March 1, 1871, all Native Americans were officially designated as wards of the United States. There would be no more recognition of tribes; Indians were Indians, and the Constitution did not apply to them as they were not citizens, but wards.

On hearing the news, Icobar stopped outside of Philadelphia and they camped. He spent a week in research and collecting the necessary materials. Then he set to work. When he was done, Morning Dew, niece of Chief Red Cloud of the Oglala Sioux, ceased to exist. She was now Mary Claussen, third generation removed from an interracial marriage, daughter of Isaiah and Ruth Claussen, Dakota Christian missionaries of Dutch and German descent, intermingled with Oglala. And Mary had the Dakota Territory birth certificate to prove it. Dated, signed, and stamped with the skill of an expert forger. A marriage certificate from a territorial magistrate followed a day later.

It was on to Rhode Island for Mr. and Mrs. Ohlm and the child she carried.

Following Route 77, they came into Little Compton and took the Reservation Road cutoff, which ended at Riverside Farm. Indeed, the Shaws were not poor; there was a pillared archway with the name above the paved drive. To either side were fields already plowed for spring planting.

There was a welcome sign and arrows for directions to barns denoted by letters and one indicating "Homestead." Kodi followed that arrow.

"You're going up to the house?" Micah said.

"It's their contract."

The house had once been simple, you could tell, but added on to by generations of Shaws into an amalgamation of styles from colonial to sprawling ranch to columned southern.

A golden retriever appeared in the lane and blocked their way. Kodi braked to a stop. That satisfied the dog for a moment, because he sat down. Kodi and Micah waited. The dog's patience gave out first; he rose up and barked. The main door of the house opened and out came an elderly lady, drying her hands with a kitchen towel. She called the dog and it loped to her side. She waved at the pickup for them to come closer.

Kodi was out first.

"Mrs. Shaw, my name is Kodi," she said, extending her hand. "I'll be hunting your coyote tonight."

"You're welcome to him," Mrs. Shaw said, gripping the hand. "If he's not killing stock, he's howling the night long." She stuffed the end of the towel in one pocket of her jeans and took out a walkie-talkie from the other. "Bart, the coyote hunter's dropped by. Come on in and meet her." To Kodi she said, "My husband will be by directly. He's at our mill installing a new compressor."

Kodi introduced Micah, no explanation, just his name. Mrs. Shaw asked for no explanation.

"Come in and have some coffee."

"Don't go to any trouble, ma'am," Kodi said.

"If it ain't brewing by the time he gets here . . ." she didn't finish the thought but laughed to herself. "My husband's a man of few faults, but wanting his coffee when he wants it is one of them."

"Got a man like that myself," Kodi said.

Micah wasn't sure if she meant him, or Paka. *No, it's me.*

RANGER FERZOCO was dead-on about the Shaw family. They were decent, practical, hardworking farm folk, no matter how much money they had.

The four of them sat in a kitchen the size of Micah's whole floor plan at Green End Pond. Bart Shaw had to excuse himself regularly to answer questions on his walkie-talkie and give directions to sons, daughters, and farmhands at their chores. He had a pleasant disposition, laughed easily, and usually exchanged a quip or two with whoever was on the other end. Mrs. Shaw offered cake, but each declined.

When coffee was done, Bart Shaw said, "Got a Jeep in the shed. I'll give you two the lay of the land."

It was a full tour. Kodi asked him to point out spots where anyone had seen the coyote and where they'd found fresh field kills. With the size of the farm, it took more than an hour.

Back at the house, Mrs. Shaw come out and they all said their good-byes. As they parted, she presented Kodi with a check.

"Take your pay. I know you'll do fine and finish this. No sense having you make another trip only to get what you've earned. But come back anytime you want. You're always welcome."

Kodi thanked her, and she and Micah left the farm.

Kodi had her flapjacks and Micah an omelet. Back at home, Micah returned to Icobar's journals while Kodi cleaned the Winchester. When she finished, she joined him. The afternoon passed in study. They were too full from their huge breakfast for any lunch or supper and retired for naps after watching the sun set from the spit on Green End Pond.

As Micah lay down, having removed only his shoes, he felt the tightness return to his chest.

Damn doctor tomorrow, and propped an extra pillow behind him. He was starting to doze when he felt her presence and opened his eyes.

"Kodi, what is it?"

"They were nice people, the Shaws. I feel bad taking their money for something maybe I should do as a neighbor. You know what I mean?"

"I do, but I don't think they'd have it any other way. They're proud people, in the good sense. You have a skill you've worked hard to perfect. They respect that and need it to make them feel safe. The Shaws also respect honest labor and know this is what you do for a living, at least for the time being. I'd bet they'd be insulted if you tried to give it back."

Kodi sat on the edge of the bed.

"Pumpok, did I ever tell you you're a wise man?"

"No, and it isn't true anyway."

Then she noticed. "Why the extra pillow?"

"I thought I might read until I fell asleep."

There was no book on the nightstand.

"Your chest hurts again."

"It's like my leg or my hands, comes and goes. It will pass."

"Tomorrow the doctor will know for sure."

"That's why he's got all those degrees on his wall. As for me, I don't care, don't want to know. Everything in the present. What will happen will happen. You know that, only in this instance, you wish you didn't. Can't help you, my dear. So let it happen, it's my life, and I'm fine with it."

Kodi turned and swung her legs up onto the bed. She was barefoot.

"Scoot over," she said.

"What are you doing?"

"I'm taking my nap. Go to sleep."

Micah shifted over on his pillows and Kodi laid her head down, their shoulders touching.

"I'm the wise man," Micah said. "You go to sleep."

Micah woke first. The pressure he felt was not in his chest, nor was it uncomfortable. He gently turned his head. Kodi's head was tilted, resting on his shoulder. Her hair brushed his neck. She was still asleep, and dreaming, he thought, because her lips moved slightly and not in rhythm with her breathing.

What do you dream about? he asked Kodi in his mind. *The war, the hunt, Coco, Paka . . . me? No, I think you dream something else, something only the gifted can conjure up from the darkness. Dream your dreams.*

She was stirring awake.

"Hey, you," Micah said. "You still want to go?"

"No, that's what sucks about being paid in advance."

They sat up.

"How's your chest?" Kodi said.

"Fine, I told you it would go away."

"I'm going to make you some of my tea anyway."

Kodi went to the kitchen, Micah to the study. He checked his weather station; barometer steady, clear forecast. Current temperature outside at forty-six degrees. Might see low sixties later in the day, later, but by then it would be over.

Over on both ends: one dead coyote and a diagnosis. Not a diagnosis, we've already done that part. More like a timeline. And what's a timeline if everything is in the present?

CHAPTER THIRTY-FOUR

The wind was out of the east and there was a stream of fog above the Sakonnet River. They parked to the side of the road near the archway, but did not enter Riverside Farm. On foot, Kodi leading, they swung around in an arc, skirting the farm proper, and ended up in a cove. From there, they went along the river shore until they were on Shaw property. The ground along the riverbank was soft, slow going for Micah, who did the best he could and was not urged to hurry by Kodi.

A greenhouse appeared and Kodi said they'd swing around it for cover and head inland from there.

"This is all tight space," she said in a low voice. "I might have to react for a quick shot. With the wind coming at us, we might even stumble upon Coyote before he knows we're here. When we enter the field, stay about three yards behind me, directly behind me, don't drift to either side."

"I'll walk right in your footsteps."

As they turned at the greenhouse, Micah could see their dark reflections in the glass. Two shapes, one crouched low, one tilted. It was eerie.

Clear of the greenhouse, they entered a field. Slow going again for Micah: recently plowed earth interspersed with clods.

Micah swore to himself the three-yard gap would get no wider and took longer strides, wedging his stick ahead and pulling himself up to it.

A howl came from ahead and to their right. They stopped and turned. Over that way was a hedgerow marking the end of this field.

Micah realized he hadn't been startled by the coyote's howl. It somehow seemed natural, the perfect sound on a night like this, like an old hoot owl in a barn.

It came again. Yawhoool. Yat-yat. Yawhoool.

Kodi beckoned Micah forward. When he got there, she whispered in his ear.

"He's on the other side of that hedge ahead. We've got to cross here to stay downwind. Watch your step in the furrows. I'm counting on there being rabbits or squirrels in that hedge to keep Coyote busy. He sure sounds hungry enough."

Micah only nodded.

Furrow by furrow they crossed the field to the hedgerow. When they reached it, it wasn't as thick and dense as it seemed in the dark from farther away. It also had a bank of mulch, and Micah figured one on the other side as well.

Kodi turned, bent to one knee, and put a finger to her lips. Turned back, and inched forward in a squat to the bank.

There was no way Micah could move like that to follow. His left leg was already trembling from crossing the field. If he was going to follow, he had one option, and did it. Down on both knees, hands to the ground, cane in one, he crawled.

Kodi was at the hedge. Micah saw her release the Winchester's safety. She lay flat on her stomach and slithered into the hedge. Micah reached the bank and also flattened. His face now a foot from the upturned heels of her boots.

Micah could taste the dirt in his mouth. Dung and phosphate. Willed himself not to spit. Inched some more into the hedge. Thought Kodi must be coming out the other side.

Kodi's boots stopped. Her left hand came back and patted her butt with no sound. Then, the index finger: one coyote. Next the okay sign: she was ready. The hand withdrew.

Micah raised his head a little more. Saw Kodi's shoulders flatten out as she positioned the rifle, and her head dip to the sight.

Blaze of light. Micah's reaction: *Skylined.* A scream.

"Don't shoot . . ."

Crack!

". . . murderer."

Kodi was up in an instant, lightning flashed all around. Micah twisting and grasping at the hedge to get to his feet. Kodi standing there, illuminated. Voices in the distance.

Micah finally spit the dirt. "What's happening?"

Kodi reached back to help him with her free hand. "We've been bushwhacked. But they're too late. Coyote's dead."

Micah brushed earth and leaves from his face, blinked, and tried focusing on the light. It was the high-beam headlights of an SUV parked alongside a shed at the end of the field. What he'd thought was lightning was the flash attachments of cameras, at least three, still popping away.

He turned back to Kodi. She released his arm and started walking in the other direction, the way she'd fired. Micah glanced back once, four figures approaching in front of the headlamps. The flashing over. Then he followed Kodi. He gave it all he had, came astride of her, and they walked side by side to the kill.

Kodi knelt to the coyote, murmured something, and gently shut its eyes. "Very old," she said. Pointed to the foreleg. "Look at the swelling in that joint. Arthritis."

Micah knelt too. The coyote did look old in the face. Muzzle fur gray and stretched thin. Same with the gnarly legs. But the flank coat and back fur were a satiny, tawny brown.

"Beautiful creature," he heard himself say aloud.

"They all are. All creatures."

"Except some I could list on two legs."

"Hmm," said Kodi.

They didn't rise, or turn around, but could hear the approaching people.

A woman's voice, Micah sure not the one that screamed, "How could you?" Emphatic, demanding, again, "How could you?"

Directly behind them now. A foot in view as one approached the body. Kodi spun, so did the rifle.

"Back up," Kodi said, not loud, but from the very depth of her.

"You're crazy, bitch. I should have figured that."

There were four of them, two women and two men. Micah could tell despite the hooded sweatshirt tops drawn up on their heads in the dark. Three had held back, and now the impudent one joined them. All had night vision scopes dangling from their necks by lanyards.

Kodi hadn't pointed the Winchester at the first one; it had been cradled across her chest. Micah assumed that wouldn't matter by the time these interlopers told their versions.

The other woman, on the right, let loose a sneering giggle, followed by, "Is it Halloween already? Ooh, you look so fearsome, Micah. It could be sexy, if it wasn't so pathetic."

"Fuck you, Laurie," Micah said evenly. "What are you doing here?"

"What we try to do," Laurie Catlett said. "Save the innocent creatures of this earth one at a time. Alas, we were a split-second too late."

"Now who's pathetic," Micah said.

Catlett ignored that and turned to one of the men. "Get pictures of the carcass. Splay it out a bit for effect. Use your handkerchief and smear some blood."

"No," Kodi shouted. The Winchester no longer cradled, not aimed, but within a hair's breadth of choosing a target. "This animal is the property of Fish and Wildlife. I will protect it if you force me."

All, except Catlett, stepped back.

"Pretty spunky there, Hiawatha," Catlett said. "Yet protecting anything doesn't seem like your business." She nodded at Micah. "Unless it's lame never-will-be-anythings."

"*Wuk-yoc,*" Kodi called her.

"What did she say?" Catlett demanded.

"It's Indian," Micah said. "It means mail her a pamphlet, she'll make a donation."

"Asshole," Catlett said.

"You're right, it does mean that."

Catlett spun away and barked orders at her party.

"Fan out, at least get some wide shots, do something, goddammit."

Kodi lowered the rifle. Took the cell phone from her pocket and tossed it to Micah.

"Speed dial one. Tell Ferzie to get here, ASAP."

While Micah made the call, Catlett's associates backed up farther, but did circle Micah, Kodi, and the coyote, snapping pictures.

As Micah spoke to Ranger Ferzoco, he kept sight of Catlett. She drifted farther away toward the hedgerow, stopped on the mulch bank, lit a cigarette.

Micah finished the call. "She's on her way," he said to Kodi.

Predawn had arrived. The show over, the other three headed back toward their vehicle. Not Catlett—she pulled off her hood and lit another cigarette. Called over to Micah.

"Naked swimming, huh? I slept with you for three months and never saw you naked with the light on. Finally got yourself a prescription, I'll bet."

Kodi put a hand on Micah's shoulder. "Forget the thousand bucks, I'd shoot her for free."

"Don't waste the bullet." It was trite, he knew it, but he felt like saying it anyway. When else would he ever get the chance? He looked back at Catlett.

Catlett jerked violently, the cigarette fell from her lips, and she screamed.

"God, it's got me! Fuck. Help!"

Kodi reacted first. "It wasn't a *cacaw.* Look."

A live coyote, only the head protruding from the hedgerow, had its jaws locked on Catlett's calf.

"The mate," Kodi said.

Catlett screaming. "Fuck. Kill it. Shoot it. Kill this damn thing. It's eating me. Shoot the motherfucker."

Kodi approached her. The coyote wouldn't let go. Probably couldn't. Too old, too stiff. It painfully laid down, Catlett's leg still in its teeth.

"Poor thing," Kodi said working the rifle bolt. She looked at Catlett. "Sure I should?"

"Kill it, damn you," Catlett shrieked.

Kodi put a bullet behind the ear.

Dead, it still didn't let go.

"Get it off me," Catlett shouted at her.

"Not me," Kodi said. "Might be rabid. Best wait for Animal Control. Want us to call them?"

The three had come running back. Catlett yelled at them to do something. The two guys found sticks and tried prying the jaw open, neither wanting to touch it with their bare hands.

"Hurry. I'm in fucking agony."

The woman used her cell phone to call the EMTs.

Kodi walked back to Micah. They sat down in the dirt beside the first coyote.

"Why did the Shaws think it was only one?" Micah asked.

"Most coyotes mate for life. These two have been together a long time. Come to depend on each other, look out for each other, especially since there've been no pups for many seasons. They probably hunted in shifts. One one night, the other the next, sharing the food. Like old folks do, if they still can. Help each other."

"So why'd she attack Wawokak?"

"You already know."

"Yes, I believe I do."

RANGER FERZOCO arrived first. Micah remembered Kodi mentioning Ferzie lived in Little Compton. The female coyote was still locked on Catlett's leg, the efforts of the two men with the sticks proving worthless and causing Catlett more pain than simply lying still. Ferzoco had heavy gloves in her van and used them to pull the jaws apart.

"Not to worry," Ferzoco told Catlett, "she's not rabid. I can tell. Still, you need the wound cleaned and sutured, and antibiotics."

They heard the sirens of the EMTs arriving. Micah, Kodi, and Ferzoco busied themselves loading the two coyotes into Ferzoco's van. The medical personnel saw to Catlett. For their efforts, she bombarded them with vulgarities, to the point where the one in charge said, "If you don't want our help, suit yourself." Catlett apologized and finally let them do their jobs.

Bart and Mrs. Shaw appeared in the farm Jeep. Ferzoco explained about the two coyotes.

"Son of a gun," Bart said. He looked to Kodi. "We owe you another check."

"It was all one hunt," Kodi said. "We're square."

Mrs. Shaw invited Kodi and Micah to the house to clean up. They accepted.

As they boarded the Jeep, a Little Compton police cruiser pulled up in the lane that led to the greenhouse. Ferzoco waved the Jeep on its way, calling, "I got this."

The last Micah saw of Catlett, she was being buckled down to a stretcher. She wasn't yelling and cursing now, and Micah wasn't sure, but he thought she was crying.

CHAPTER THIRTY-FIVE

It was Friday and, despite the dawn commotion, Micah still had a doctor's appointment that afternoon. He didn't feel like keeping it, didn't see the point, but had given Kodi his word.

Back in Middletown, they each showered and dressed.

"It's only over at Newport Hospital," Micah said. "I usually walk."

"Not this time. You've done enough for one day."

"Me, I didn't do anything."

"Like we say in the army, gearing up and showing up is half the mission. The rest plays out however it plays."

It was a thank you and a compliment in one. Micah appreciated it.

When the time came, they got in Kodi's pickup for the five-minute ride to Newport Hospital.

"Maybe we'll run into Wawokak," Kodi said.

"Unless they committed her to the psych ward, more likely they sewed her up and sent her on her way as soon as possible."

"They should stitch her mouth closed."

"I'm sure that occurred to them."

Attached to Newport Hospital is its medical arts center with the offices of Aquidneck Island's finest doctors, including Richard Flood, Chief of Neurology.

"You'll tell me what he says, won't you?"

"Don't expect much," Micah said. "It usually means scheduling more tests. Been there, done that, more than once."

Micah signed in with the receptionist.

"Dr. Flood will be with you shortly."

As they took seats, Micah said to Kodi, "Shortly is a medical term for when Flood's good and ready."

"Don't you like this doctor?"

"He's great. I see him once a year for a progress check. Wouldn't trust anyone else. He's simply not prompt."

Micah didn't expound. His was a progressive, debilitating, incurable disease. Things were to be expected and coped with accordingly. There were no medications. He didn't run to his doctor every time a new tremor appeared. After ten years with Flood, Micah was down to the yearly checkup.

Although the waiting area was empty except for the two of them, it took thirty minutes before Flood came to the room.

He was younger than Kodi expected. A boyish-looking midforties, fit and trim, with rimless spectacles above a white shirt and tie.

"Micah, I looked at my schedule and said to myself: Is it a year already?"

Micah introduced Kodi. There was a reaction, Flood recognized the name, but never brought it up. He ushered Micah out of the room and into the examination suites.

Flood did the preliminary workup and then had Micah tell him about the new symptoms. Flood jotted down the chest tightness, pain, coughing, and phlegm, noting it was intermittent. Then he capped his pen and closed the chart.

"I'm sending you downstairs for some tests. No argument, Micah, today, right now. I'm the boss of Neurology and can schedule whenever I see fit. You're going to be here awhile."

Micah requested a minute, reminding Flood he had someone waiting.

"I'll make the arrangements, you make your apologies."

Micah went to the waiting room and told Kodi he needed some tests, as expected, and since he was there already, Flood could do them now.

"So get out of here, you've got a date tonight. I'll take a cab home."

"No, you won't. I already called Paka and canceled. Tonight, I'd rather be with you."

"You shouldn't have done that. It's nothing but precautions."

"My choice, you're too late. Now go have those tests."

"There's a cafeteria on the main floor, let me give you some money."

"Micah, go."

An orderly appeared with a wheelchair.

"Mr. LaVeck, I'm your ride to Radiology."

"That's not necessary."

"I get that all the time." The guy smiled. "Are you a doctor? I'm not either. Get in the chair, Mr. LaVeck."

Kodi nudged Micah toward the wheelchair. "Do what he says, I like him."

"You would."

THREE HOURS of tests: lie down, stand up, turn that way, now the other, this won't hurt, only a slight pinch. Many pinches. There can be music if you like. Soft jazz, it is, Mr. LaVeck.

Deep breath, another. Hold still, don't move. Blow into this tube.

Afterward it was another orderly and wheelchair. A wave to Kodi in the waiting area; she waved back. Into Flood's private office.

"There're two types of breathing, Micah: subconscious reflex and conscious control. The conscious one is kind of like your legs. You will them, they move. Or, in your case, misinterpret or ignore the message, do nothing, or do something else: spasm, jerk, you know what I'm talking about and have been dealing with it for years."

Yes, Micah thought, *anticipate nothing except to expect the unexpected.* Voilà, *I'm on my ass.*

Flood went on. Breathing is facilitated by the diaphragm, which is stimulated to act by a nerve network called the pulmonary plexuses. Conscious or unconscious, breath is still prompted by the central nervous system responding to the brain. With Micah, the pulmonary plexuses were starting not to listen, same as his legs.

"Here's the upside," Flood said. "You were first diagnosed ten years ago and you're still reasonably ambulatory. The progression has been steady, but slow. Only reached your hands in the last two years. The degeneration, or ataxia, is not looking to win any races against any other natural causes resulting in death, like old age."

"What's the downside?" Micah said.

"You can live without the use of your arms or legs, but not without lungs. If the progression of this phase is faster, I'd be remiss not to tell you to get your affairs in order. We will use the results today as a benchmark, and I want to see you again in two months to measure again. In essence, you're missing breaths. You might not notice it, except as a cough or fatigue, but it's there. That has its own complications, particularly accumulation of fluids."

"Pneumonia."

"Among other things, but the greatest hazard."

Micah asked about supplemental oxygen, like an inhalator.

"In time, probably," Flood said. "It will help keep your blood oxygenated and your brain fed. But only if enough of your lungs still responds. If there is a major shutdown, it does nothing, doesn't breathe for you. Should that occur, you'd need a ventilator or resuscitator and there's no such thing as self-administered resuscitation. You'd need help, and you'd need it in minutes."

"Or suffocate."

Flood nodded.

"Will it be quick?"

"Not quick enough that you won't be in distress. There are two options though, if it comes to that stage. One is round-the-clock in-home nursing personnel. The other is entering a facility."

"Fuck that," Micah said.

"Of course, you can, and probably should, get a second opinion."

"I don't like your opinion, why would I risk getting a worse one?"

Flood laughed. "Be back here in two months. And Micah, don't make my staff have to chase you down. They hate that and they take it out on me."

KODI DIDN'T pester Micah, much appreciated. He knew he would tell her and sensed she knew it too. No need to rush. Even though the episodes were not as intermittent as he'd told Flood.

Besides, Kodi had a surprise.

The nurse had informed her the tests would last several hours.

"I went shopping and got steaks, potatoes on the half-shell, and stuff for salad. After you build a fire, relax and I'll cook the meal. I watched you the last time and know what I have to do."

"No argument from me. That's the best thing I've heard all day."

"Do you like Pinot Noir?"

"Sure, why?"

"I bought three bottles. I feel like wine myself tonight. Don't know what Pinot Noir is, but I've heard of it."

"Perfect choice."

They pulled into 18 Green End Avenue.

"Let's take a walk to the pond," Micah said.

"You go and I'll meet you. Let me put the food in the house."

Micah said okay and walked toward the water, Kodi, with her bundles, to the house.

It was around six o'clock; the sun wouldn't set until after seven. The trees, the pond, the birds were there, and for a moment, he pushed everything else from his mind. It all felt good, felt right.

Even if, maybe, everything wasn't, you could still feel that way.

Put my affairs in order. What affairs?

Micah had the ground he stood on and the house behind him. He had Kodi for as long as she stayed. He had Melvin Sturgis for as long as he could get to the shop. Mary Boyd and Laurie Catlett had betrayed him. Good riddance. He had his work.

I want to finish Icobar's story. Finish it and write it. Not for Roger Ohlm, for Icobar and Morning Dew, for Kodi and Paka, for Nathan Jordan, and for me. There will be time, I swear it.

He turned around and saw Kodi coming from the house.

I wonder if she'd like the house. She, and maybe Paka if it works out, could live here. If he'll ever leave the reservation. He'd better not be a fool. I'd leave heaven itself for that woman. He's no fool. I'm the fool, and finally enjoying the hell out of it.

She came near. "What are you looking at?"

"Everything."

"And what are you thinking about?"

Micah took her hand and turned. Before them on the ground was the *okosu-wacuw* with the blue stone, their blue stone, still on top.

"I'm thinking it's time you changed the stone."

"It's not only mine."

"I know, but it's time."

"A little longer," she said.

"If you like, but soon."

THE FIRE warmed the room, the wine warmed their spirit, the food was perfect. They ate picnic-style on the floor by the hearth, the coffee table between them for dining. Micah asked if she wanted music, Kodi said the fire was music. He clinked her glass.

"Also music," he said.

"It's all music."

TWO BOTTLES of wine were finished.

"Why don't you turn in and I'll clean up."

"We'll both clean up, in the morning. Thank you for your company and a wonderful dinner."

Micah rose from the floor. Wanted to say something else, wasn't sure what it was, said only, "Good night, Kodi."

"Good night, Pumpok."

Micah went to the bathroom to prepare for bed. When he took off his shirt, there were welts across his chest from the devices and monitors he'd been subjected to all afternoon.

You definitely lost that fight.

Laughed at himself, and went to the bedroom. Got his pants off and laid down, still feeling flushed from the wine and being so close to the fire all night. Felt warm and comfortable and peaceful.

Doesn't get better than this.

Dozed.

"Are you still awake?"

Kodi at the bedroom door—the glow from the kitchen light down the hall behind her—naked.

Micah awoke. He asked, "What are you doing?" Then, "You're so beautiful."

She came to the foot of the bed, knelt onto it. Micah felt the bed move. Kodi reached and turned on the lamp.

"What are you doing?"

"Go with me on this, Pumpok," Kodi said, her voice husky, "but let's not make it into something it's not, not yet. It's now, we're here, and that may be all there is."

Micah choked on his words. "All right. Don't . . . I don't know if I can . . . want to . . . don't . . . don't know what I mean."

Kodi grasped his shorts, drew them to his knees, then stripped them off completely, flinging them to the floor, her breasts rising and falling with her deep breaths.

"You don't have to," he said.

"Shh, everything in the present."

His penis lay flaccid against his thigh. Kodi lifted it gently and made a fist about its shaft. There was a slow, almost grudging, response. She licked the cap, then again, and circled it with her tongue. More response. Loosened her grip and lacquered the shaft with saliva, hilt to cap, in long, slow strokes, as her nipples brushed his thighs.

Micah thought he would die. Felt the sudden pressure from within, begrudged its sudden haste. Refused it.

Kodi sensed his resolve and took him into her mouth. With each plunge came more rigidness. Micah tried to will it sturdier, but it didn't work. Relaxed, let her efforts work the magic. Finally felt something necessary. Said, "Turn around. Please, Kodi."

Saw a spark light Kodi's eyes. She slipped her mouth off his penis and smiled up at him.

"You sure?"

"Let me. I want to, I need to."

Kodi sat up. Then on all fours, she turned around on the bed and settled her butt on Micah's stomach as she took hold of his penis again and fed it slowly between her lips.

Micah put his palms beneath the coppery globes of her buttocks and lifted. Kodi went with it, sliding up on his hands as he parted her half-moons, his thumb in the crack.

She lowered back to him until his tongue was in the top of the divide. Quivered as he traced it down.

Micah stopped, beheld the delicately blossoming, valley wild flower. Drew a breath and put his tongue to it. The scent, the taste, hints of cinnamon and cumin: sweet, yet feral. Thought he would swoon. Drew another breath. Pushed his tongue through as Kodi moaned.

"Pumpok, Pumpok." Then filled her mouth again with him in renewed attention.

Micah withdrew his tongue, slid down more, the spices giving way to the smoky, salty depths of the ocean. Parted this place, explored, sought out the pearl and sucked it between his lips, dazzling it with his tongue.

Micah had the earth, the sea, and sky all at once.

Another moan from Kodi's full mouth, a playful hesitation, another plunge.

Neither could hold out another instant.

Micah came, Kodi came, and they collapsed.

CHAPTER THIRTY-SIX

They sat naked on the bed, glasses in hand, the last bottle of Pinot Noir on the nightstand.

Kodi smiled at Micah. "You say you're Alsace-Lorraine, *Monsieur* LaVeck, but I think you're really French. You do certain things like a Frenchman."

"The region was fought over for centuries."

"Well, the French won, at least in the bedroom."

"And you, my dear, are all native, all Indian."

"How so?"

"You taste like the earth and the sea and have opened the heavens."

"Ever done anything like that with Wawokak?"

"Never felt inspired that way. Besides, Wawokak was never pleased with anything she couldn't do herself, or to herself."

That brought a wicked snicker from Kodi.

Micah grew serious. "Was it pity, or the wine, the dinner, and the fire?"

"None of those. I decided at the doctor's office. Sitting in the waiting room, I knew I couldn't bear to lose you. Made up my mind not to lose you. The nurse said it would be hours. I only went shopping so I wouldn't be sitting there letting it drive me crazy."

"Hmm. A fateful decision, with too many consequences to contemplate."

"Be realistic, Pumpok, we were beyond that point already. You can't act like lovers in every other respect and then draw a line and say do not cross. Tonight, a new force between us has been released. The fact that you made it mutual makes it only more precious."

"Be realistic yourself. I'm old enough to be your father."

"I'm experienced enough and wise enough to deal with that."

"I thought I was the wise one."

Kodi drank her wine, eyes shining over the rim of the glass. "You are wise in your ways; I am wise in other ways." Kodi finished the wine in her glass. "Good night, Pumpok."

"You're not staying?"

"I've been sleeping in the next room for weeks; you snore like a chain saw. I need some rest."

"This is going to be weird, isn't it?"

"No, it's going to be what it's going to be."

Micah was up first and showered. Kodi came to the kitchen in a sweat suit and Micah poured cups of coffee.

"What did the doctor say?" Kodi asked.

"It's all related, and somewhat inevitable."

"That doesn't tell me anything."

Micah explained exactly what Dr. Flood had told him. When he finished, Kodi said only one thing.

"Then it's a good thing I'm here."

"You can't take that responsibility. I wouldn't ask you to, and I wouldn't want you to."

"Then don't ask, let it be."

"Pretty much the same thing."

"I told you what I felt in the doctor's office. I can't change that, not even for you, and I would do anything for you."

"What about Paka? You thought you might start over."

"And once I thought I'd marry Coco. Things change. The truth is my only wisdom is to recognize changes when they happen and not pretend otherwise. For one night Paka and I thought we'd come full circle, but when I turned the last corner in the morning, there you were."

"Sorry about that."

"Don't be. We've been circling this campfire for more than a month."

Kodi got up and stretched. "I'm for a shower, and then we have some work to do. Get our notes ready for the Portsmouth Historical Society."

"I wasn't sure you'd want to go."

"I'm over it. I want to see this through, wherever it leads us."

What had she said yesterday? Gearing up and showing up is half the mission.

Icobar and Mary Ohlm bought a parcel of land on Prudence Island with most of their savings. There were only three other farms on the island, the rest was forests, swamps, and beaches. With the last of their money they purchased chickens, pigs, and cows, and planted vegetable crops in the spring. That summer, Icobar Junior was born. He was baptized in a Christian church on Aquidneck Island and his birth recorded by the Portsmouth Town Clerk.

Ding-dong.

What the hell is that?

Micah hadn't heard the sound since the day he moved into Green End Avenue, so it took a minute to realize it was his front doorbell. He grabbed his stick and went to the front door, passing the bathroom where he heard Kodi still in the shower.

"Someone's out front," he called through the closed door.

"Isn't it kind of early?" Kodi called back.

"I'll see who it is."

Micah opened the front door.

"Still an early riser. You never really do change."

"What are you doing here, Laurie?"

"Didn't you once remind me about manners? Coffee would be nice."

"There's a Dunkin' Donuts on West Main. It opens early too."

"All right, jeez, skip the fucking coffee."

"What do you want?"

"I'm leaving today and I won't be back. I thought we owed it to each other to set the record straight. If nothing else, for old time's sake."

"We don't owe each other anything. Good luck with animal rights."

Catlett tilted her head and pursed her lips. "Yeah, well, that's become a problem. That bitch that was with us captured the whole damn thing on her cell phone. Me calling the coyote a motherfucker and demanding Kodi kill it went viral. The people that were backing me weren't too pleased."

"So try the NRA."

"Don't think I'm not considering it."

"You would."

"Why not? They've got even more money than the coyote lovers." Catlett looked around, shifted from one foot to the other. "Can I at least use your bathroom; I've got a long drive ahead of me."

"It's in use right now."

"Really, so I'll wait."

Micah took a step back and Catlett immediately stepped in.

"That's the gentleman I remember," Catlett said. "You know, Micah, there was a time I had a plan for you and me. Crazy, huh?"

"Completely."

"I always thought of you as that quaint country inn you discover by accident after a long drive and stay there because you've traveled enough. Quaint, and expectations are not high."

"Who's at the door?" Kodi called from the hallway.

"Wawokak," Micah called back.

"What the hell does that mean?" Catlett said.

"It doesn't matter. The bathroom's free, you know the way."

Catlett walked past Micah to the kitchen and down the hall to the bathroom. Micah closed the front door and followed as far as the kitchen. Kodi was in her bedroom, dressing, Micah assumed. He did not feel hospitable in the least. Wanted Catlett gone.

Catlett appeared first.

"As I was saying . . ."

"I wasn't listening," Micah said.

"Ooh, you interrupted me. You never did that before."

Micah didn't rise to the bait. Catlett cocked an eyebrow.

"For me, the perfect husband is a silent partner. I do the work I have to do, and he's there for comfort, recreation, and security. I once thought you were that man. With a little training, of course."

Catlett saw the two coffee mugs in the sink, and when none was offered, poured herself a glass of tap water.

"I do have one question, Laurie. How did you know about the Shaw hunt?"

Catlett smiled. "I would have thought you'd at least learned not to underestimate me and what I'm capable of accomplishing."

"That's not an answer."

"All right, if you must know, you and the princess told us yourselves."

"That's bullshit."

"Hardly. You and she had breakfast in Little Compton the morning before the hunt. Sizing up the terrain at the Shaws' place, I imagine. What does Kodi call it? Ah yes, recon. Everybody knows there's barely anything in that town but farmland. Farmland, coyotes, you think? And you couldn't resist a little tryst at a local pancake house. One of my people was there having breakfast as well. Kodi's cover was blown, all the animal rights people would recognize her. He did, and called me."

"That still wouldn't pinpoint us for the hunt."

"Did I mention what my associate was doing in Little Compton?"

"No, you didn't."

"Electronically tagging wild turkeys with a dart gun for another study. When he called me, I told him to stick a dart in the back of Kodi's truck and turn it on. The rest can be done with a laptop. We may be owl- and tree-huggers, but we've got great equipment."

"So you tracked us."

"Ironic, isn't it? Track the tracker. What else would you be doing in Little Compton at three the next morning?"

"It's not ironic, it's pathetic."

Kodi came traipsing, barefoot, into the kitchen. The sight of her astounded Micah. She wore a white, sheer tee shirt, no bra, and a skimpy pair of panties.

"Sorry, babe," Kodi said to Micah, "I didn't know your company stayed," in mock surprise.

Catlett turned scarlet and almost dropped her glass.

"She needed to use our bathroom," Micah said, "and now she's leaving."

Catlett regained what composure she had left and flung the water glass into the sink.

"What is this, a fucking college dorm?" Catlett said. "Go to hell, both of you," and she stormed out of the house.

"What was that about?" Kodi said.

"Having the last word. It belonged to you."

Kodi laughed.

"You don't expect us to get any work done with you dressed like that," Micah said.

She laughed again and went to change.

THERE WERE only two journals left. Farming is hard work, especially for a man crippled in the war; there started, again, to be gaps in the entries. Like any grower would, Icobar took particular notice of the weather and recorded it. The Ohlms stayed very much to themselves, only crossing to Portsmouth proper for needed provisions on market day. Money was an issue, but not so that it strained the relationship. Icobar sold a pocket watch he'd been presented by the BMI. One of the other families on Prudence Island was elderly, without children, private and simple, but comfortably situated. Mary Ohlm did their washing and sewing for a few cents a week.

Icobar had an idea. On a trip to Portsmouth, he stopped in the local print shop. He wasn't interested in resuming that profession, but did offer his services as a calligrapher, and provided samples. Soon he was writing birth and death notices along with wedding invitations for the more prosperous

Portsmouth families. He also got a commission to produce diplomas for the local school and official proclamations of the town council for public display. The money was needed; there were three meager harvests in a row. But the people of Portsmouth were decent folk, by and large, in the tradition of Roger Williams. Mary's ancestry, apparent in her features, was never discussed, and they received fair prices for their produce: not charity, fair. The product of a missionary education, Mary homeschooled the young Icobar. Icobar Senior liked domestic life, loved his wife and son, and had optimism they would eventually prevail.

Then, in their fourth year, typhoid fever came to Portsmouth and out to Prudence Island.

"I HAVE to stop," Kodi said.

Micah saw tears in her eyes, the first real ones he'd ever seen from her. They'd had their emotional moments, the welling up, the caught breath. But this was deeper, fuller, and started down her cheeks.

"It can't be all bad," he tried to say. "Paka bears the family name. Maybe Icobar's talking about his neighbors. That old couple that Mary works for."

"Please, Pumpok, call her Morning Dew. It is her birth name. Mary is something they had to do. We should honor their true memory."

"So we shall."

They left the journals and the study and walked out in the yard. Almost noon, the sun was high over Green End Pond.

"They're good people and deserve a chance," Kodi said.

Micah had a sudden reflection of guilt, remembered how he'd regarded Icobar in the beginning. Recalcitrant, petty, and all the other words. Suddenly tested in battle and measured up. Then found himself: first in work, then in a woman. Developed principles and compassion. Decided his world was not the world he wanted. Chose boldly, and was living up to it. Facing an unknown future with commitment. Using every resource he could muster to provide for his family.

"It will be all right," Micah said.

"No, it won't. But we have to finish this."

Kodi started back to the house.

ICOBAR'S FINAL journal bore out Kodi's apprehension. It was Morning Dew who contracted the fever. She was dead in two weeks.

According to the custom of her people, the Oglala Sioux, Icobar buried her in an unmarked grave on the farm near a brook, with only wild flowers and a white oak sapling for a memorial. A preacher came from the mainland to make it official, bringing the necessary documents to sign for the town record. A man wiser than his ministry, he knew there was nothing fitting to say or do, so didn't. He simply blessed the site, then the father and the son, murmured "Morning Dew" into the breeze and went on his way.

CHAPTER THIRTY-SEVEN

Micah called Nathan Jordan to share what the journal had revealed.

"I recall reading somewhere about the typhus," Jordan said. "Not epidemic level that year, but cause for concern. Most likely birds in select water sources, not wells, but surface water."

Micah asked him to explain.

"Say Morning Dew was hanging up wash to dry outside. It's hot. She dips her hand in the brook for a cool sip of fresh water. Unknown to her, it's been contaminated with infected bird feces. It's not the home's supply, which comes from a well. But a natural thing for a Plains Indian to do on reflex. She gets typhus, Icobar and the boy don't. Such was life in the 1800s."

"He grieved, severely," Micah said.

"No doubt."

"Writes that he walked out every morning to feel the fresh dew on his hands and rub it on his face."

"Poetic, he truly loved her."

Micah heard Kodi sniffle at the table.

"That's all so far," Micah said to Jordan. "We'll finish the last journal this afternoon and visit the historical society tomorrow. It's open on Sunday, twelve to four."

"Use my name," Jordan said, "they know me."

"Thanks."

"No, thank you. It's an important story and is in good hands, yours and Kodi's."

"I'd like you to edit it when it's done."

"I should live so long."

"That makes two of us."

Silence. "I didn't know."

Micah regretted it. "A writer's expression about tempting the fates."

"Well, then, carry on, my friend."

"Good-bye." Micah hung up.

"He's a nice man," Kodi said.

"Yes, he is. Are you up for this, or have you had enough for today?"

Before Kodi could reply, the house phone rang and Micah answered. Handed the phone to Kodi. "It's Ferzie."

Kodi took the phone and spoke with the ranger. Listened a long time, then said, "I don't want to walk into another animal rights ambush. What kind of security will they provide?" Listened more and agreed. "Monday night, Ferzie. Set it up." Hung up.

"Seems you're in demand," Micah said.

"Wish I weren't."

"Then why take it?"

"There're two *wuk-yocs* advertising themselves all over the state. Private property contracts only. Not locals, a guy from New Mexico and the other from Alabama. They think this is a growing market and want to get in on it."

"Professionals?"

"So they claim."

"Why not let them have it?"

"Remember High Street? I only agreed to do this in the first place so it would be done right. It's not like I want an open season on every coyote in the state."

"Where's this one?"

"Prudence Island."

Kodi was brave and committed, Micah had to admit. They spent that afternoon finishing the last Icobar Ohlm journal, hard as it was for both of them.

After a year of grief, Icobar had to focus on reality. Reality was a farm to maintain, a cottage industry in calligraphy for extra money, and a four-year-old son to raise who needed a mother. As was practical and customary for that era, he needed a new wife.

In Portsmouth, and the rest of Aquidneck Island, opportunities for a spouse were slim. Young men home from the war had plucked up the flowers of Rhode Island maidenhood in short order, ready to start new lives without muskets and carnage. The wilting petals that were left, for the most part, were war widows. These ladies, also, had to bury their grief and move on, more often than not, with children.

Through his calligraphy contacts, Icobar met Haddy, a year older than himself, with an eleven-year-old son and nine-year-old daughter. Icobar thought the sibling aspect would be good for his island-isolated son. Subsequent events proved otherwise.

After an amiable and superficial courtship, Haddy and Icobar were married. The amiability and superficiality ended. Haddy was used to having her own way. Her husband had been away for the war and died shortly afterward. For eight years she was a single mother and sole provider. She was domineering and demanding. Took charge of everything. Everything, except for young Icobar, whom she treated as though she couldn't stand the sight of him; and with his Indian features, that was probably true.

Icobars, father and son, endured it for four years. That last year, Icobar Senior developed consumption, which, Micah explained to Kodi, in those days meant either cancer or tuberculosis. The end came swiftly, but not before the father made a fateful decision on his true son's behalf.

Unbeknownst to Haddy, since the deed to the farm was in his and Mary's name, Icobar sold some acreage to the neighboring farm during the fallow winter. He tucked this money aside until spring, when it appeared his end was near. There was one last thing he wanted to do: get his son away from Haddy. She was always rude and hurtful to him. It would surely get worse when Icobar died.

Slipping away before dawn, he rowed young Icobar to Aquidneck Island, and then over to the mainland. He hoped the Pocasset tribe would adopt and raise him. The boy's Indian features were very pronounced. The money from the land sale was his offering. Back at home, he would tell Haddy that Icobar Junior fell from the boat and was swept away with the river's current before his sick and weak father could save him from drowning. He doubted she would mourn very much.

Icobar's last entry:

"Watuppa Pocasset Indian Reservation. This is where my son belongs. He has the blood of a great chief in his veins. He has his mother's heart and spirit. When I go to her, together we will smile down on him and his children for all the seasons to come."

The journal ended.

They poured some wine and shared another tear or two. Toasted Icobar and Morning Dew. Toasted each other. Toasted the end of a journey.

"When will you tell Paka?" Micah said.

Kodi considered that a moment. "Told you once before; you should tell him. I also think it's how you should end the book you write from it."

"I'm not sure Roger Ohlm would agree."

"Then he's more Haddy than Icobar."

Micah realized something. "I get it now. Paka and Roger don't share a bloodline. Icobar and Haddy didn't have a child between them. Haddy and her kids got the Ohlm name by marriage. For the record, there is no real Ohlm gene in Roger Ohlm, only in Paka. He's descended from Icobar Junior, raised on the Pocasset reservation."

Kodi took it another step. "Then by rights, the journals should belong to White Oak Brother, it's Paka's lineage."

"I'm going to get sued over this."

"Doubt it. Once Roger hears the truth, he won't want the journals anymore. It's not the story he was hoping for but you did your job."

"Not completely," Micah said. "I owe him a transcription, it's in the contract."

"Then do it and you're free and clear. Come on, Pumpok, you know you want to, and not for Roger."

Micah did want to, as he had sworn to himself out by the pond.

Back in the study, they made their plan for the Portsmouth visit and composed a list of research questions.

Knocking on the front door.

"We know it's not Wawokak," Kodi said.

Micah went to answer.

"Sorry I didn't call first," Chief Harry Reismann said. He was in plain clothes, jeans and flannel shirt, work boots. "I stopped by the station and an alert was waiting for me from an old friend at the State Police."

"Come in, Chief."

"Kodi here?"

"Yes, she is."

Reismann followed Micah to the kitchen as Kodi came down the hall from the study.

"Evening," Reismann said to her.

"You're off-duty, I presume," Micah said. "We've got beer or wine."

Reismann chose beer and they sat around the table. He looked at Kodi. "You and me been upfront from the start, I appreciate that, so felt I owed you a heads-up. I know Ranger Ferzoco has been moving some work your way, out of Middletown. All legal, I got no beef, but a buddy in command in Providence put me wise to something you oughta know."

Kodi nodded, Reismann continued.

Since the coyote hunt became news, and was successful, as far as it went with Kodi, the state licensing department had become flooded with out-of-state hunters requesting their weapons be registered in Rhode Island.

"This state has decent hunting," Reismann said, "wild turkey, duck, and deer, but only of local interest. The department might get two or three requests a year from out of state. Nobody makes a trip to Rhode Island for a prize buck. Not with Vermont or New Hampshire another half-day's drive."

"How many requests?" Kodi asked.

"About 300."

Kodi and Micah were shocked. Kodi told Reismann about the two fellows advertising, one from New Mexico, the other Alabama.

"I know about them," Reismann said. "They slipped through before the deluge, had clean records, paid the fee, and were approved. The only deterrents are they still need a permit for specific town land, like the Kempenaar Valley, or written permission from the owner of private property. With all the hubbub, neither is gonna happen.

"Anyways, the state police superintendent, who is also by statute the Commissioner of Public Safety, got a call, then called the governor, who called the attorney general. Short of the long, the AG is filing Monday morning for a statewide injunction against any and all coyote hunting, even private land, as a matter of public safety. If the AG personally files for an injunction, he gets it. Come the gavel drop on Monday morning, there'll be no coyote hunting in Rhode Island. Wanted you to know, so you didn't get caught in the middle of something."

"Caught again, you mean," Kodi said.

Reismann laughed, raised his beer.

"It's finally, really over," Micah said.

"That's my take," Reismann said. "Our AG is gonna be the next governor. That injunction will be enforced for as long as he pleases, meaning till all this dies down and is not a campaign issue, and not a day sooner."

"It's the right call," Kodi said.

"Thought you'd see it that way."

Reismann drank off some beer. Put the can down and sat back, keeping eye contact with Kodi.

"While we're off the record, young lady, a couple of my guys are facing retirement. Be some open slots in my department next year. If you're thinking of staying sorta permanently, I wouldn't mind seeing your application cross my desk. Might even nudge it in the right direction."

"Chief, you offering me a job?"

"Whoa. I made a suggestion. You'd still have to pass every test and complete the state academy on your own." Reismann winked at her. "An army vet like you, how tough is that gonna be?"

"I'll give it a lot of thought, thanks."

"Elmer will drop off the paperwork when he's in the neighborhood."

Micah was wide-eyed. "This calls for another round."

"Don't mind if I do," said Reismann.

Perhaps it was the discovery, or the excitement, or the sudden unexpected relief; Micah's cough came back. He hacked until he was out of breath and physically drained. When he was able, Kodi guided him to the bedroom and lay down beside him.

"Tonight you decide to stay," he said weakly.

"Shh, until you fall asleep. Then I'll be right next door, quite content you snore from that distance. At least I'll know you're breathing. Don't worry, I won't sneak back naked."

"Good, I haven't had sex two nights in a row in a decade. Now there's something that might kill me."

"Shh."

Whether he snored or not, Micah didn't know, but when he woke early Sunday, Kodi was still beside him, still dressed, dreaming dreams that made her lips move so slightly.

I thought it would be weird. So why do I feel so good?

He lay still until she stirred.

"Good morning."

"Hmm. It is, isn't it?"

"A very, very good morning."

Micah left her to fully wake up, checked the weather station in the study. Still an hour until dawn and already forty-eight degrees. Forecast clear.

When he returned to dress, Kodi was already in her own room changing out of the clothes she'd slept in beside him. They met back in the kitchen.

"I've been thinking about Paka," Micah said. "From what you've told me, I like the guy. Now we're gonna clobber him twice over. One, with his ancestry of abandonment, followed by you and me and whatever we've got. Makes me feel sad and guilty."

"Sad's okay," Kodi said, "but not the guilt. Neither is your fault. He's strong and, in the Indian way, wise for his age. He'll accept both for what they are."

"If you say so. I had a vision of him beating the crap out of me with the hornbeam."

"No, you didn't."

"All right, call it a thought in the back of my head."

"Then get your mind on today. Hopefully, the last pieces to pull it all together."

The curator and the archivist at the Portsmouth Historical Society, a husband and wife team, were pleasant enough, but when Micah mentioned Professor Nathan Jordan, they fell over each other to be helpful. Kodi presented them with the prepared list. They consulted it, and then scurried in different directions. Not being tourist season, Kodi and Micah were the only visitors and Micah thought they were also grateful for the diversion.

When the records were assembled on a large table in a conference room, white cotton gloves were distributed for handling documents a century and a half old. The wife, the archivist, set up a laptop computer with which, by special permission, she could access Town Clerk records at Town Hall.

The work lasted beyond closing time. The husband locked the door and they stayed at it until nearly seven P.M.

"I think that's everything on your list," the archivist said.

"And much more," Micah said. "It confirms the journals to the letter. I don't know how to thank you properly."

The husband-curator thought of a way. "You could become Society patrons. Fifty bucks a year, seventy-five for both of you."

"Done, and a pleasure," Micah said.

"Before you go," the wife said, "I think we should do a quick review, so nothing was skipped over."

"We don't want to impose," Kodi said. "You've both done so much."

The wife pointed at her husband. "Look at his face. He lives for days like this."

There was no reference to any Morning Dew. Icobar's forgeries had succeeded. Mary and Icobar Ohlm had bought farmland on Prudence Island, Township of Portsmouth. The same year, they had a son, registered and baptized, Icobar Ohlm Jr. There was a comparatively small typhus scare that claimed seven lives in Portsmouth three years later.

Icobar married Haddy and adopted her two children, Roger and Abigail, to ensure their security. Icobar died four years later, Haddy, seven years after that, of heart failure. Roger inherited the farm, which he sold, and moved to the mainland where he purchased, of all things, the printing business for which his stepfather had done calligraphy, and married a sea captain's daughter. Abigail Ohlm married a lawyer and moved to Boston.

Other than his birth and baptism, there was not a single official record of Icobar Ohlm Jr. thereafter. There were, however, some personal diaries of the period in the Society's archives, by unrelated Portsmouth residents, that mentioned a boy of approximately eight years drowning in the Narragansett River dividing Prudence Island from Aquidneck Island. It was believed he was from Prudence Island, but not confirmed, the body never found. After all, who could impinge on such family grief? A father rowing his son home, only to lose him forever.

Icobar's lie to Haddy had worked. As the only blood descendent of Morning Dew and Icobar Ohlm, young Icobar's secret was safe and his future was with the Pocasset.

CHAPTER THIRTY-EIGHT

Roger Ohlm didn't sue, didn't want the transcription, didn't even want the journals back. For authenticity in the book he was writing, Micah asked for the full provenance of the journals. He knew Icobar would have protected them from Haddy. Otherwise, the fateful decision for his son's future would have been compromised. How did Roger's great-grandmother get the journals? The answer did not surprise Micah.

"My great-grandfather bought a printing shop in Portsmouth after Icobar and Haddy died. Icobar was the previous owner's calligrapher. The journals were in a trunk in a supply room under bolts of cloth used to clean the presses. At least that's the way the story came down to me. If there's nothing else, Mr. LaVeck, I think our business is concluded."

White Oak Brother, Paka, didn't beat the crap out of Micah; they became friends and remained so until the end of Micah's life. When not at work on his book, Micah could sometimes be found at Paka's shop on the reservation working on a walking stick.

When the transcription of the Icobar journals was completed, Kodi and Micah presented them to Paka. He didn't want them either. Presently they are a featured exhibit at the Portsmouth Historical Society.

To Chief Harry Reismann's dismay, Kodi decided not to join the Middletown Police Department. In fact, after that spring, Kodi never held a gun again. That, Reismann could understand.

Spring became summer. The blue stone remained on the *okosu-wacuw*. Sometimes they heard Coyote at night, held each other close, and whispered secrets. In the fall, a fierce nor'easter did in the chicken coop. After the winter, the debris was hauled away, Kodi pleading for her bonfire, but finally granting that the trees were too close.

Another year passed. Though he didn't hear an owl three times, Micah knew when it was coming. Got around to putting his affairs in order. Felt good about providing for Kodi, felt bad putting her through it.

They sat often on the spit that summer. Sometimes talking or reading. Sometimes only listening and watching in their rare concept of contentment.

Only once, Micah said, "It would be easier on me, if you go now."

"Shh, no it won't. Love yesterday, love today, love tomorrow."

It was all in the present. Micah knew it, felt it, believed it, happily—even though *Icobar and Morning Dew* was published posthumously, to much acclaim.